Praise for Jessica
The Summer of Na...

"If books could be trains, *The Summer of Naked Swim Parties* would be a high-speed zephyr, traveling at great speed from California to Baltimore, providing great scenery and good company. To carry the metaphor further, this novel has energy and power and will be a great ride for everyone who reads it. Ms. Blau is a writer of wit, intelligence, deep feeling, humor, and imagination, and she gets into the head of a young person like almost nobody since J. D. Salinger. All aboard!"

–Stephen Dixon

"You're fourteen years old in 1976 and your parents throw naked swim parties. How the hell are you supposed to have your own private sexual awakening? Jessica Anya Blau creates a charming protagonist, her charismatic Santa Barbara family and a summer of love, lust, and confusion. You won't want summer–and this wonderful book–to end."

–Ellen Sussman, author of *Dirty Words: A Literary Encyclopedia of Sex*; *Bad Girls: 25 Writers Misbehave*; and *On a Night Like This*

"This book will make you laugh and cry in public. Jessica Anya Blau has written a soaring teenage lament, perfectly pitched, containing the single saddest and funniest line of seduction ever uttered."

–Larry Doyle, author of *I Love You, Beth Cooper*

"Funny and charming, moving and sweet–Jessica Anya Blau beautifully captures the awkwardness and the wonder of coming of age. *The Summer of Naked Swim Parties* is a remarkable debut novel."

–Michael Kimball, author of *Dear Everybody*

"Once you dive into this sweet, sparkling coming-of-age story, dripping with heart and heartbreak, you won't want to come up–even for air."

–Hillary Carlip, author of *Queen of the Oddballs: And Other True Stories from a Life Unaccording to Plan*

"Among the many truths in this intelligent, funny novel about family, sex, and coming of age in the 1970s is this: no one can embarrass us more than our parents."

–Geoffrey Becker, author of *Dangerous Men* and *Bluestown*

"Having grown up in 1970s Southern California, I can personally attest to this novel's utterly uncanny evocation of the era. It's also really, really fucking funny."

–Jonathan Selwood, author of *The Pinball Theory of Apocalypse*

"Jessica Anya Blau's *Summer of Naked Swim Parties* is a time capsule of 1970s details, from pot parties to the backseat of a VW bus. But, reader, hold your breath: This novel is moreover a plunge into that stage of life they call "coming of age," and for Blau's protagonist, Jamie, that plunge is risky and deep. At fourteen, Jamie is a precociously wise observer of human behavior; she's also a chronic worrier. Hippie parents, an unavailable older sister, traitorous girlfriends, and a sex-charged boyfriend–one sees them all through Jamie's smart, engaging point of view. But behind the scenes one also senses the implied author herself. It's in her tenderness for young Jamie, as though she too were holding her breath." –Madeleine Mysko, author of *Bringing Vincent Home*

"Jessica Anya Blau is a warm and funny storyteller. *The Summer of Naked Swim Parties* conjures the thrills and anxieties of 1970s California adolescence in a world awash in sex."

–Gabriel Brownstein, author of *The Man from Beyond*

"A nervous child of the 1970s takes on the excesses of the '60s in the form of her nude-swimming, dope-smoking parents. A funny, slightly chilling account through the sharp, unforgiving eyes of a fourteen-year-old girl."

–Jean McGarry, author of the novella *A Bad and Stupid Girl*

The Summer of Naked Swim Parties

HARPER ● PERENNIAL

NEW YORK • LONDON • TORONTO • SYDNEY • NEW DELHI • AUCKLAND

The Summer of Naked Swim Parties

A Novel

JESSICA ANYA BLAU

HARPER ● PERENNIAL

P.S.™ is a trademark of HarperCollins Publishers.

HarperCollins books may be purchased for educational, business, or sales promotional use. For information please write: Special Markets Department, HarperCollins Publishers, 10 East 53rd Street, New York, NY 10022.

FIRST EDITION

Designed by Jessica Shatan Heslin/Studio Shatan, Inc.

Library of Congress Cataloging-in-Publication Data
Blau, Jessica Anya.
The summer of naked swim parties : a novel / Jessica Anya Blau.—1st Harper Perennial ed.
p. cm.
ISBN 978-0-06-145202-4
1. Teenage girls—Fiction. 2. California, southern—Fiction. I. Title.
PS3602.L397S86 2008
813'.6–dc22   2007038064

08 09 10 11 12 ID/RRD 10 9 8 7 6 5 4 3 2 1

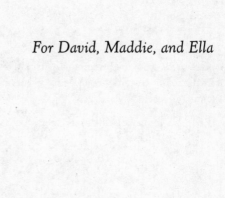

For David, Maddie, and Ella

The Summer of Naked Swim Parties

After all, it was the seventies, so Allen and Betty thought nothing of leaving their younger daughter, Jamie, home alone for three nights while they went camping in Death Valley. And although most girls who had just turned fourteen would love a rambling Spanish-style house (with a rock formation pool, of course) to themselves for four days, Jamie, who erupted with bouts of fear with the here-now/gone-now pattern of a recurring nightmare, found the idea of her parents spending three nights in Death Valley terrifying. Jamie was not afraid for Allen and Betty—she did not fear their death by heat stroke, or scorpion sting, or dehydration (although each of these occurred to her in the days preceding their departure). She feared her own death—being murdered by one of the homeless men who slept between the roots of the giant fig tree near the train station or being trapped on the first floor of the house, the second floor sitting on her like a fat giant, after having fallen in an earthquake.

Jamie's older sister, Renee, was also away that weekend, at a lake with the family of her best and only friend. But even if she had been home, Renee would have provided little comfort for Jamie, as her tolerance for the whims of her younger sister seemed to have vanished around the time Jamie began menstruating while Renee still hadn't grown hips.

"I invited Debbie and Tammy to stay with me while you're gone," Jamie told her mother.

They were in the kitchen. Betty wore only cutoff shorts and an apron (no shoes, no shirt, no bra); it was her standard uniform while cooking. Betty's large, buoyant breasts sat on either side of the bib–her long, gummy nipples matched the polka dots on the apron.

"I know," Betty said. "Their mothers called."

Jamie's stomach thumped. Of course their mothers called. They each had a mother who considered her daughter the central showpiece of her life. "So what'd you say?" Jamie prayed that her mother had said nothing that would cause Tammy's and Debbie's mothers to keep them home.

"I told them that I had left about a hundred dollars' worth of TV dinners in the freezer, that there was spending money in the cookie jar, and that there was nothing to worry about."

"What'd they say?"

"Tammy's mother wanted to know what the house rules were."

"What'd you say?"

"I told her there were no rules. We trust you."

Jamie knew her parents trusted her, and she knew they were right to do so–she couldn't imagine herself doing something they would disapprove of. The problem, as she saw it, was that she didn't trust *them* not to do something that *she* disapproved of. She had already prepared herself for the possibility that her parents would not return at the time they had promised, for anything–an artichoke festival, a nudists' rights parade–could detain them for hours or even days. There was nothing internal in either of her parents, no alarms or bells or buzzing, that alerted them to the panic their younger daughter felt periodically, like she was an astronaut untethered from the mother ship—floating without any boundaries against which she could bounce back to home.

Allen walked into the kitchen. He'd been going in and out of the house, loading the Volvo with sleeping bags, a tent, lanterns, flashlights, food.

"You know Debbie and Tammy are staying here with Jamie," Betty said, and she flipped an omelet over—it was a perfect half-moon, and she, for a second, was like a perfect mother.

"Why do all your friend's names end in *y*?" Allen asked.

"Tammy," Jamie recited, "Debbie . . . Debbie's *i e*."

"But it sounds like a *y*."

"So does my name."

"You're *i e*," Betty said, "You've been *i e* since you were born."

"Yeah, but Jamie sounds like Jamey with a *y*."

"There's no such thing as Jamie with a *y*," Allen said. "But there is Debby with a *y*."

"Well Mom's a *y*—Betty!"

"I'm a different generation," Betty said, "I don't count."

"And she's not your friend, she's your mother," Allen said.

"Oh, there's also Kathy and Suzy and Pammy," Betty said.

"No one calls her Pammy except you," Jamie said.

"Too many *y*'s," Allen said. "You need friends with more solid names. Carol or Ann."

"No way I'm hanging out with Carol or Ann."

"They've got good names." Allen sat on a stool at the counter, picked up his fork and knife, and held each in a fist on either side of his plate.

"They're dorks," Jamie said.

Betty slid the omelet off the pan and onto Allen's plate just as their neighbor, Leon, walked in.

"Betty," he said, and he kissed Jamie's mother on the cheek. His right hand grazed one breast as they pulled away from the kiss.

"Allen," Leon stuck out the hand that had just touched Betty's breast toward Allen, who was hovered over his omelet, oblivious.

"Did you find some?" Allen asked.

"I stuck it in your trunk," Leon said.

"What?" Jamie asked.

"Nothing," Allen said, although he must have known that Jamie knew they were talking about marijuana. They rolled it in front of their daughters, they smoked it in front of them, they left abalone ashtrays full of Chiclet-sized butts all over the house. Yet the actual purchasing of it was treated like a secret—as if the girls were supposed to think that although their parents would smoke an illegal substance, they'd never be so profligate as to buy one.

"So what are you going to do in Death Valley?" Leon asked.

Allen lifted his left hand and made an O. He stuck the extended middle finger of his right hand in and out of the O. The three of them laughed. Jamie turned her head so she could pretend to not have seen. Unlike her sister, Jamie was successfully able to block herself from her parents' overwhelming sexuality, which often filled the room they were in, in the same way that air fills whatever space contains it.

"And what are you doing home alone?" Leon winked at Jamie.

"Debbie and Tammy are staying with me," she said. "I guess we'll watch TV and eat TV dinners."

"You want an omelet?" Betty asked Leon, and her voice was so cheerful, her cheeks so rouged and smooth, that it just didn't seem right that she should walk around half-naked all the time.

"Sure," Leon said, and he slid onto the stool next to Allen as Betty prepared another omelet.

Jamie looked back at the three of them as she left the kitchen. Allen and Leon were dressed in jeans and T-shirts, being served food by chatty, cheerful Betty. Wide bands of light shafted into the room and highlighted them as if they were on a stage. It was a scene from a sitcom gone wrong. There was the friendly neighbor guy, the slightly grumpy father, the mother with perfectly coiffed short brown hair that sat on her head like a wig. But when the mother bent down to pick up an eggshell that had dropped, the friendly neighbor leaned forward on his stool so he could catch a glimpse of the smooth orbs of his friend's wife's ass peeking out from the fringe of her too-short shorts.

Jamie wished her life were as simple as playing Color-forms; she would love to stick a plastic dress over her shiny cardboard mother. If it didn't stick, she'd lick the dress and hold it down with her thumb until it stayed.

Debbie and Tammy were dropped off together by Tammy's father, who got out of the car and walked into the house with them.

"Did your parents leave already?" he asked.

"Yes, Mr. Hopkins," Jamie said.

Mr. Hopkins looked around the kitchen, toward the dining room, then out the French doors toward the pool, which had an open-air thatched bar in the shape of a squat

British telephone booth, and boulders like stone club chairs embedded in the surrounding tile.

"What are the pool rules?" he asked, his belly pointing in the direction of his gaze as if it, too, were scrutinizing the situation.

"No one is allowed to swim alone." Jamie recited the rules from Debbie's house: "No glass or other breakable items by the pool, no food by the pool, no running by the pool, no skinny-dipping, no friends over unless my parents are informed ahead of time . . . Uh . . ."

"No swimming after dark," Debbie said.

"Right. No swimming after dark."

"What are the house rules?" Mr. Hopkins asked.

Jamie was stumped. She had heard house rules at other people's houses during sleepovers but couldn't recall a single one.

"Um." She yawned once, and then yawned again. "We have to behave like ladies." She had little faith that that would go over, but it did. Mr. Hopkins nodded and smiled, the corners of his mouth folding into his cheeks like cake batter.

"Well then," he said, "you girls have fun. And call us if you need anything."

When his car had pulled out of the driveway, the girls tumbled into one another, laughing.

"House rules?!" Debbie said. "He's got the wrong house!"

Tammy burrowed into her pressed-leather purse and pulled out a pack of Marlboro Light 100's. "He's got the wrong century," she said, lighting her cigarette, and then Debbie's, with a yellow Bic.

Tammy was wiry and small with bony knees and elbows,

big floppy feet, knobby breasts, and shiny dangerous-looking braces on her upper teeth. Somehow, the cigarette made her look more pointed than she already was. Even her hair appeared sharp, hanging down her back in white clumpy daggers.

Debbie was round and smooth. She had black, shiny hair, thick black eyebrows, and lashes that made it look as if her eyes had been painted with liquid velvet. Her skin was white in the winter, golden in the summer, and always a contrast to her deep eyes and red mouth, which at that moment was smacking against a Marlboro.

Tammy offered Jamie a cigarette because Jamie had smoked one with her once and Tammy couldn't believe that she didn't plan on smoking another in her lifetime. The problem with smoking, Jamie had decided, was that it didn't look right on her. She had straight, matter-of-fact brown hair that hung to just past her shoulders. There were freckles running across her nose and cheeks. Her eyes were round, brown dots. Her nose was a third dot on her face. If you were to draw a caricature of her, she would be mostly mouth: soft pink lips, straight wide teeth; she smiled when she talked, a broad smile that glinted on her face. In her most self-flattering moments she thought of herself as Mary Ann on *Gilligan's Island*; she knew she could never be Ginger.

By seven o'clock, the thrill of having the house to themselves had dampened. Tammy played *Frampton Comes Alive!* so loudly that the windows vibrated; they ate ice cream out of the carton using their bent first two fingers as a spoon; they perused the deeply unsexy drawings in *The Joy of Sex*, which sat beside the toilet in Allen and Betty's bathroom;

and they squeezed into and modeled sixteen-year-old Renee's child-sized clothes. Eventually the three girls ended up back in the kitchen, where Tammy and Jamie leaned their flat bellies across the stools while Debbie stood at the open freezer door looking for dinner.

"Didn't your mother buy any frozen pizza?"

"I dunno. She bought whatever's in there," Jamie said.

"I don't even know what this stuff is." Debbie pulled out a box, rotated it and examined it. "*What* is kasha and bowties?"

"Just order pizza," Jamie said. "My mom left me money in the cookie jar."

Debbie, who knew her way around the kitchen, left the freezer and went to a cupboard drawer, where she pulled out the phone book. She picked up the receiver on the white wall phone and dialed. Tammy and Jamie pulled themselves up and sat properly on the stools.

"Can you deliver a pizza?" Debbie said.

"Get pepperoni!" Tammy said.

"He said they don't deliver," Debbie said.

"Let me talk." Tammy went to Debbie and took the phone. "Hey, what's your name?"

This question alone caused Debbie and Jamie to hunch up in silent laughter. Although this was the first summer where boys and men had paid attention to them, they understood the rules of fourteen years old, one of which was to not take the initiative with someone older than you, especially if you wanted that someone to be interested in you.

"I'm Tammy," Tammy said, and she twirled a blond rope of hair with one finger, as if the voice on the phone could see her. "Uh huh . . . uh huh . . . uh huh." Tammy's chin tapped down each time she responded to whatever the pizza guy had said. She smiled. With words alone, Tammy seemed to have reeled in someone old enough to work in a pizza parlor.

"We're at my friend's house. Her parents are camping in Death Valley and so it's just us three girls alone."

Jamie's mouth gaped wide as she mimed a silent scream. What if this guy was a pervert, like the man two doors down who watered his front garden in his bathrobe, which always seemed to accidentally flap open when Jamie and her sister rode by on their bikes? What if he was a serial killer?

"Uh huh . . . Me, Jamie, and Debbie. We're sixteen, but we don't have a car."

Debbie and Jamie gave each other open-mouthed stares. The girls often exaggerated their expressions, as if they were actresses on a daytime soap opera; they thrilled in experiencing everything beyond routine with self-aware hyperbole. But this, their names and false ages being given to the anonymous pizza guy, was even more huge than their usual excitement.

"2703 Garden Street," Tammy said.

Debbie and Jamie jumped off the stools, went to the phone, and leaned their heads into the earpiece so they could hear.

"So, someone will be there in about twenty minutes." Tammy's boy had a surfer's drawl: low, slow, mellow.

"Great," Tammy said.

"Cool," he said.

"Cool," Tammy said.

"Later," he said.

"Later." Tammy rushed the phone into its cradle before bending over and screaming the way girls scream when they win things at school: first cut for cheerleading tryouts, last cut for drill team, a solo in *My Fair Lady*.

"Oh my god." Debbie was breathless.

"He's sending a friend over to pick us up," Tammy said. "His friend is going to bring us back to Pizza Rhea so we can have a pizza."

"How will we get home?" Jamie asked, imagining the three of them standing on the windy freeway entrance, thumbs out as an invitation to rapists. Imagination, at the time, was Jamie's greatest problem—her parents had taken to hiding the *Los Angeles Times* so as not to feed her the fuel on which her neurosis ran. The local paper, the *Santa Barbara News-Press*, however, with its front-page articles on the shifting sand at the breakwater, the drought, seagulls with tar glued to their greasy feathers, was never off-limits. The in-town news, Allen and Betty knew, did not carry the same perceived threats as the dramas that played throughout the frayed web of L.A.

"He'll drive us home when he gets off work at eleven."

"Are you sure?" Jamie asked.

"Yeah, of course! He is *such* a nice guy, a total sweetheart!" Tammy spoke as if he were an intimate friend. Her absolute confidence was all Jamie needed to reformulate logic, like when her mother insisted that there wasn't a building high enough in Santa Barbara to topple in an earthquake; Jamie was always happy to give up her fears to a voice of authority.

The girls rushed up to Jamie's bedroom to change their clothes. Each outfit they tried on was neither better nor worse than the one they had previously been wearing; the act of changing was simply an act of momentum. (Although the girls did believe that clothes had more influence on the events to which they were worn than did the person who wore them.)

Tammy put on a cap-sleeved, striped T-shirt. Her arms hung out the sleeve holes like straight, hollow plumbing. She pressed her white hair with a curling iron, framing her face with perfect, toilet-paper-roll-sized cylinders. With a blue makeup pencil she underlined each eye: facial italics. Debbie combed her hair down, a thick black waterfall that tumbled over her shoulders. Then she leaned over the sink, mouth hanging open as if she were getting her teeth checked, and brushed black mascara onto her thick lashes, which looked like tarantula legs stuck to her face. She held the mascara wand out toward Jamie, who waved it away. To Jamie, there was an edge to mascara, like smoking, that didn't match her good-girl persona—as if suddenly wearing it would put her into a level of maturity for which she wasn't prepared, the way losing one's virginity pushes you around a bend from which you just can't return. She did, however, slather her lips with bubble-gum lip gloss, which was oily and tacky and caused her hair to stick to her mouth when she shook her head. She combed her thin hair flat against her head, then changed her shirt several times so that her hair was tangled again and the lip gloss had rubbed off, finally settling on a red T-shirt that belonged to Debbie and said MAIDEN FRANCE across the breast line. Debbie's maternal grandmother was from France, so she considered herself more French then American. Before Jamie could recomb her hair and regloss her lips there was a knock at the front door. The girls froze, looking toward the bedroom door, like dogs pointing, then collapsed over their knees in silent, restrained laughter.

Duckishly, they descended the stairs in a row. Jamie opened the front door and immediately started laughing, although there was nothing funny before her. Standing on the porch were two beach-haired, college-aged boys. These were the kind of boys who grow only in Southern California. Girls in Minnesota dream of boys like this. Certain men in New York and San Francisco dream of boys like this, too.

"Hey," the taller of the two said. His eyes were sea green. He was swinging a single key on a dirty string around his finger.

"Hey," Jamie said, and then uncontrollable laughter overcame the three girls. They hunched over their knees, holding their stomachs, until finally—after clasping hands and taking deep, stuttering breaths—the laughing stopped. The guys stood there, both of them open-mouthed breathers, staring with dazed, patient smiles.

"You're the girls who wanted the pizza, right?" the other guy said. His hair was dark brown at the center part and yellow-blond on the ends. His skin and eyes were identical in color: the brown of a buckskin shoe. He wore a Mr. Zogs Sex Wax T-shirt, which was practically a uniform for surfers that year. Jamie couldn't speak when she looked at him; it was as if she were suddenly asthmatic and couldn't get enough air.

"Well," Sea-Eyes said, "let's go."

The boys sat in the front and the girls sat in the back of the gasoline-smelling Dodge Dart. Debbie, Tammy, and Jamie smiled the entire ride, their shoulders pressed together, digging their nails into one another's knees and giggling at anything the boys said. The driver, sea-eyed Mike, was going to be a junior at the university, studying marine biology. The other guy, Joseph, had graduated over a year ago. He was hanging out in town, he told the girls, working at the pizza parlor at night, surfing in the day, and waiting for his friends to graduate so they'd have more time to hang out with him.

"College must be fun," Jamie said. Debbie widened her eyes and nudged Jamie with her elbow as if to say, Good one!

"Yeah," Joseph said, "it's a fuck of a lot better than junior high."

This, of course, sent fingers flying into nervous, clandestine pinches as the girls wondered if the boys had somehow figured their true age not to be sixteen.

Bill, the pizza boy Tammy had spoken with on the phone, was cute, too. He had bunny-white hair, white eyebrows, and a golden-pink tan. His T-shirt had a saucer-sized hole under the breast pocket, revealing taut, smooth skin. When the girls walked in, he gave a coolheaded jut of his chin as a greeting. Then, like a gymnast on a pommel horse, he pressed his hands onto the bar counter and propelled his body up and over to the other side. The girls stood motionless, watching and waiting, as the pizza boy walked to the door, flipped over the "open" sign, and turned the key in the lock.

"Beer?" Joseph asked. He had poured one for himself and was carrying the mug with him as he cleared tables with his free hand.

"No-o," the girls sang.

"Coke?" he asked.

"I made you pepperoni," Bill said.

"Beer?" Mike asked. He stood at the tap, pouring one for himself.

"They want Coke." Joseph winked at Jamie and she stiffened up as if they were playing freeze tag.

Mike poured three Cokes into bumpy, opaque plastic cups, then carried them to a booth where Bill had set down a large pepperoni pizza. The girls rushed to the booth; Tammy and Jamie began eating immediately. Debbie removed her retainer and gingerly placed it underneath a napkin.

"Don't let me forget that," she said. "My mom will kill me."

Somebody turned up the stereo and a Hall & Oates song reverberated out of hidden speakers. The boys went about their business, closing out the cash register, wiping down the tables with a scrunched-up grayed rag, and covering giant silver tubs of grated cheese and sliced pepperoni with Saran Wrap. They drank beer as they worked, and shouted a conversation that had something to do with the size of the waves at various beaches that day. Occasionally one or the other of them looked over at the girls and smiled; in response, the girls giggled and dropped their heads, reached for a new piece of pizza, or took a sip of Coke.

They ate more than three quarters of the large pizza. Debbie's chin was slick and shiny and Tammy had a piece of pepperoni caught in a square of her braces. Debbie picked the food from Tammy's braces, then dipped a corner of a paper napkin into her Coke and worked a smear of tomato sauce off Jamie's face. Jamie sat still and quiet as Debbie groomed her. She remembered when her sister used to make her ponytail in the morning and how good it felt to have her sister's tiny hands running against her neck as she picked up the scrawny clods of Jamie's hair.

Mike tossed the leftover pizza into the trash, then flung the silver platter, Frisbee-style, over the counter and into the sink, where it made a hollow, clanking ruckus.

"You girls ready to get outta here?" Mike said, dangling the stringed key from his index finger.

Mike drove, Bill sat up front, Jamie sat on Debbie's lap in the backseat, and Joseph sat in between Debbie and Tammy.

"You're not really sixteen, are you?" Bill asked.

"No-o." They giggled.

"They turned fourteen last month and I turned fourteen in February," Tammy said. "Two Geminis and a Pisces."

"That's cool," Bill said.

"They're as cute as any sixteen-year-olds I've ever seen," Joseph said, looking at Jamie. She met his stare for a moment, then dropped her head, terrified.

"So your parents are at Joshua Tree?" Mike pulled the car into the driveway.

"Death Valley," Jamie barely whispered.

"Oh yeah, Death Valley," Mike said. He turned off the ignition.

They all climbed out and stood in a circle with the boys on one side and the girls on the other. Joseph looked at Jamie and she looked away at his friends. Bill was eyeing the house up and down, the way men in movies ogle pretty women.

"Rich girls," he said.

"Her dad hardly works," Tammy said, and she pulled out two cigarettes and passed one to Debbie. "My dad's always saying he must be a spy or something, 'cause they have this gnarly house and her dad never even wears a tie."

"Whose house is it?" Bill asked.

"Mine." Jamie flushed as she spoke. "And my dad's not a spy, even though everyone thinks he is!"

"Well, what does he do?" Bill asked.

"What difference does it make?" Joseph said. "She's the one who's interesting."

Jamie looked toward the house because she could not bring herself to look at this college-aged boy who had just said she was interesting.

"He, like, tells businesses how to make money, right?" Smoke puffed out of Debbie's mouth as she spoke.

"Her dad's home all the time," Tammy said. "My mom said if my dad was home that much she'd have to divorce him."

"Maybe I should tell businesses how to make money," Bill said.

"Oh my god," Debbie said. "That would be so cool if you did exactly what Jamie's dad does!"

"So, can we come in?" Bill asked. He stood in the center of the group. All faces were turned toward Jamie, who felt like a helium balloon bobbing above everyone—remote and out of reach.

"Uh . . . sure," she said, and she rushed to the front door and waited for everyone to catch up.

Once inside, the girls headed for the kitchen.

"Let's make brownies," Debbie said.

The boys filed into the kitchen behind them. Bill went to the French doors, opened them, and spread his arms as if he were presenting the backyard to the group.

"Pool," he said.

"Pool." Mike stood behind Bill and looked out.

"We need music," Joseph said. "Do you have any music?"

"They have speakers all over the house, and you can turn a knob and the music comes out by the pool!" Tammy said.

Jamie had always felt that her life and her friends' lives were equal—they all had nice houses, pools, parents who weren't troubled with money. But Tammy's enthusiasm for the things Jamie barely noticed—a father who is home, speakers by the pool—startled her and she saw, not uncomfortably, how padded her life was.

"Who's making brownies with me?" Debbie asked.

"Got any weed for them?" Bill said, and the boys laughed.

"I'll make brownies," Mike said. He walked behind the counter and stood beside Debbie. Jamie looked over at them and could barely breathe. Mike was holding up the box of brownie mix and reading the directions. Debbie was *baking brownies* with a sea-eyed college boy.

Tammy stepped just outside the French doors; Bill followed, while pulling his ripped T-shirt off over his head.

"Awesome boulders," he said. "Do I have to wear a suit?"

"No way," Tammy said. "This is a party house. Jamie's parents don't even own swimsuits!"

Jamie was relieved that Bill seemed impressed by this fact.

"Where are your records?" Joseph asked. He stood so close to Jamie that his voice was like a whisper.

"I don't have any records."

"You don't have any records?"

"No. My parents have records."

"What do they have? Burt Bacharach? Barry Manilow?"

"They have Barry Manilow!"

"I was kidding." Joseph smiled. His eyes alit on her the

same way her parents did when she said something they found adorable. She hoped he couldn't see how deeply she blushed.

"Show me their records," Joseph said, and he put his man-sized hand on Jamie's twiggish, near-hairless forearm.

Jamie took Joseph to the tiny, internal room off the living room, which was a walk-in closet when her parents bought the house but had been converted into the record room. There was a multilayered black stereo system on one shelf. The other shelves held records, perhaps a thousand, filed by category and then alphabetically. On the far wall was a panel with white circular knobs that sent music from the record player into various rooms, or the backyard. The single over-head dome light was dim and Joseph had shut the door. Jamie had the feeling she was in a taped-up cardboard box.

"This is so, way, totally, cool," Joseph said.

He squinted and read the room names, which had been meticulously typed out on Allen's plastic label maker and stuck below the corresponding knob.

"Rock and roll is over here." Jamie waved her hand up and down a wall of records, then suddenly shoved it in her jeans pocket. It had looked floppy and strange to her—like someone else's hand.

"Help me choose something," Joseph said. He put his palm on the small of Jamie's back and lead her over one step so that they were standing together in front of the floor-to-ceiling shelves of rock and roll.

"What do you like?" His voice was slow and hushed.

"I dunno," she said. And she really didn't know. Jamie's parents chose the music; they chose what to play and when to play it. She had never thought to choose music for her-self—as if she had no right to fill the air with something she in particular wanted to hear. And when Jamie's friends were over, *they* chose the music.

"Tammy loves *Frampton Comes Alive!*," Jamie said.

"Nah," Joseph said, "you can't understand a word he's saying."

"Debbie always puts on Jethro Tull, but I think it's kinda boring."

"How about Wild Cherry." Joseph pulled the record off the shelf and smiled at the cover.

"Cool photo," he said, and he looked at Jamie so she'd look down at the picture of glassy red lips holding a dripping cherry. The stem came out the corner of the mouth and made a line that ran off the edge of the album. Jamie felt a jolt of panic. She was reminded of the time a year ago when Tammy's older brother had been packing to leave for college. He had called Jamie into his room as she was walking by to use the bathroom. Once she was standing near him at his desk, he had opened a drawer, pulled out a *Playboy* magazine, and unfurled the centerfold while staring intently at Jamie.

"What do you think?" Tammy's brother had said, and Jamie had just shrugged her shoulders and hurried out of the room. She didn't know what she thought, all she knew was that Tammy's brother's intentions were beyond her understanding–they took place in a world where she didn't know how things operated or what the rules were. And now, Jamie was standing on the border of that world again, this time with Joseph, who was the cutest boy she'd ever seen in person, but who scared her nonetheless.

"I like maraschino cherries," Jamie said, trying to rein the focus into her world, "but my mom won't let me eat them because she says they cause cancer."

"One won't kill you." Joseph slipped the record out of its jacket and held it perpendicular to his flat palms.

"That's how my dad holds the records," Jamie said.

"You don't want to get grease or fingerprints on it," Joseph said. "Oh, get that House of Honey record, too."

Jamie pulled House of Honey out of the jacket and handed it to Joseph, who sandwiched it between his hands with Wild Cherry. He slowly lowered the records, piercing the tiny eyeholes with the silver prong that stood up from the center of the turntable. When he turned on the power, House of Honey dropped down, leaving Wild Cherry hovering above like a spaceship. The music started and in her head Jamie heard her mother singing along as she always did.

She was a sweet, sweet lady with big blue eyes . . .

"Now, who should we let listen?" Joseph asked, and he turned to face the panel of knobs.

"Pool," Jamie said.

"Pool," Joseph said, turning the knob.

"Kitchen," Jamie said.

"Kitchen."

"Living room?"

"Okay, living room."

"Uh . . . I guess that's it."

"What about the bedrooms?"

"No one's in the bedrooms."

"Let's put the music on in your room." Joseph turned the knob that rested above the piece of red plastic tape with JAMIE BED popping out in white.

"Jamie bed," Joseph said. The word *bed* seemed pornographic when Joseph said it. Jamie felt as if he were talking about her sexual anatomy rather than simply the place where she slept.

"It's my bedroom," Jamie said. "Not my bed. I think Dad just got tired of turning that dial and punching."

"Take me to your bedroom," Joseph said. "I want to see if this system really works."

"Uh, okay." Obedience had always been a problem for Jamie. She didn't know how to not do what she'd been told. And with Joseph, whose very presence dulled her intellect into a warm ball of Play-Doh, Jamie didn't even think to not do what he had asked.

Upon entering the bedroom, Joseph walked straight to Jamie's bed and flung himself across it, facedown. Jamie couldn't see him at first, as all she could focus on was the white bra and rejected T-shirts that lay in a heap on her floor.

"Where are the speakers?" Joseph asked.

Jamie kicked the pile of clothes under her bed.

"Up there and there," she said, pointing to the black boot-box-sized cubes hanging from the corners of the ceiling.

Joseph rolled onto his back and patted the bed beside him.

"Come here," he said. "Let's lie together and listen."

Jamie stared at her unmade bed, the pink, chenille bedspread bunched in a corner at Joseph's feet. He was wearing flip-flops that had a layer of hardened beach tar on the soles. His feet were bony-cadaverous looking-anachronistic on his solid body. Jamie moved to the edge of the bed, put her hands on the brass foot rail, and looked at Joseph. There was a clicking in her brain, like a playing card clicking in a bike tire. This clicking told her what hadn't yet occurred to her: Joseph might try something. What he'd try, she wasn't sure, but she knew it would be something she'd never done before, as thus far Jamie had kissed only three boys and had yet to be touched anywhere on her body by any boy.

Jamie exhaled and laughed because she didn't know what to do or say.

"Come on the bed with me," Joseph said again. "I won't hurt you. I swear."

It was a promise Jamie didn't doubt, and so she did as she had been asked. So, for the first time in her life, Jamie was on her bed listening to House of Honey with a boy. A post-college boy. A post-college boy who had the dazzling looks of a *Tiger Beat* cover.

"Do you have a boyfriend?" Joseph asked.

"No." Jamie snorted and laughed and didn't even think to ask him if he had a girlfriend.

Joseph rolled to his side, head propped on the triangle of his right arm. With his left hand he traced his fingers up and down Jamie's out-turned forearm.

"You have beautiful, soft skin," he whispered.

She didn't answer. The song ended. For a second all was silent and still.

Jamie looked at the ceiling, afraid to turn toward Joseph, whose face was inches from hers, and whom she sensed was staring at her.

"You know," Joseph said, continuing to stroke her arm, "when a man touches a woman it's a beautiful thing. A beautiful, wonderful thing."

"Oh yeah?" Jamie looked at him quickly, then turned away.

Joseph shifted Jamie's T-shirt up toward her rib cage. She tensed up momentarily, and then tensed up in a different, less fearful way as he stroked her belly. A tingling began to run through Jamie–an internal telephone line, calling up all her bits and parts. Somewhere in her mind was the unfocused idea of pressing her body against Joseph's.

"You're very beautiful," Joseph said, and he swirled his long, dark finger into the whorl of Jamie's belly button. The telephone ringing echoed in a hollow Jamie never knew she had–she found the sensation captivating and disturbing.

"Have you ever kissed a boy?" Joseph leaned in so close to Jamie's face that she could feel his hot breath on her cheek.

"Yes," she said.

"With tongues or without?"

"With."

"Did he touch your breasts?"

The word *breasts* three inches from Jamie's ear caused her to shudder.

"No."

"Did he touch you between your legs?" Joseph's hand paused just below her navel. Jamie felt a ghost sensation of him touching her lower, but she glanced down and saw that it wasn't true.

"No," she said.

"He didn't touch you right there?" And then Joseph delicately placed his hand over the fly of Jamie's jeans. A shooting heat ran up and down her body.

"No," she whispered.

"You see, I love to make girls happy," Joseph said. "And there's nothing that makes a girl happier than when you touch her . . . right there."

Jamie's right leg kicked in a spasm as he pulsed his fingers against her. She looked at him, her mouth half open–hypnotized by this good, scary feeling. She was being fed something that, prior to that instant, she had never hungered for. And now that the feeling was there, now that desire for a body other than her own had been pressed into her, she couldn't remember not feeling it.

There was a clomping of fast feet coming up the steps. Joseph pulled his hand away just as the bedroom door swung open and Debbie appeared, a giant red oven mitt on one hand.

"Brownies will be ready soon," she said. "I'm borrowing one of your suits–Tammy's swimming in her underwear!"

Debbie flung open the top drawer of the white, painted dresser and pulled out a black crocheted bikini Betty had bought Jamie at Sabado y Domingo, the local arts and crafts show. She rushed into Jamie's bathroom and pushed the door shut but not hard enough for it to fully close. Jamie hopped off the bed and stumbled toward the door. She turned and looked back at Joseph.

"Do you want brownies?" Her voice was paced with Debbie's staccato.

Joseph rotated his legs off the bed and sat up slowly; he reminded Jamie of her father trying to rise on Sunday mornings.

"Okay!" Jamie chirped. "So I'll see you down at the pool!"

Tammy sat on the shallow-end steps in her padded white nylon bra and blue cotton underwear, holding a fistful of gooey barely baked brownie. Her braces were spackled a tarry brown.

"Oh my god," she said. "These are so, so good! Can you believe that Debbie could make such good brownies? I mean, they're, like, *raw!*"

Bill was in his boxer shorts jumping on the diving board. He jumped higher and higher, his arms whirling like rotors. Finally he threw himself off the board, screaming a war cry that was silenced by the water. When he popped up for air there was a new explosion of sound as he belted along with the song that had just started. Bill swam to Tammy on the steps and took a bite of brownie straight from her fist.

Mike sauntered out from the kitchen wearing an oven mitt that matched the one Debbie had on. The pan of brownies was in his hand. He was picking at it with his finger, feeding himself frosting-soft balls.

"Want some?" he asked.

Jamie reached into the pan and pulled out a wad just as Joseph emerged from the house. As she was eating, standing beside Mike, Joseph quietly slipped off his jeans and T-shirt to reveal a pair of loose-hanging, faded yellow boxers.

"Pool heated?" he asked.

"Um," Jamie had a wad of brownie in her mouth that stuck her teeth together, clogged her throat. "Uh huh," she hummed.

Joseph looked back at Jamie with one long, cinematic gaze and she regretted that her finger was in her mouth loosening splotches of brownie from her gum line. He dove into the water and swam two fast laps: back and forth, back and forth. No one watched except Jamie, who felt like her body was operating on its own—she had no choice but to look at what every cell beneath her skin insisted she look at, pointing her to the place her body wanted her to be.

Debbie appeared in the black crocheted suit.

"Oh my god," she said. "Do you love those brownies? Mike and I made them! Can you believe how good they are?!"

"They're great," Jamie said, although she was still trying to swallow. The mass of brownie was stuck like peanut butter; she could feel the forces of her body squeezing and undulating the lump down her throat.

Tammy's favorite song, "Pick It Up," came on. She screamed like she was at a concert, then climbed out of the pool to dance. Debbie clapped her hands and danced beside her, then Mike jumped in and did the bump between them. Bill raised his fist in the air, bouncing in the pool, singing along so loudly that they could hardly hear House of Honey.

Jamie looked over at Joseph, floating on his back, his head cocked in her direction. She wished she could break the spell and crawl out from beneath his gaze so she could do the bump and sing loudly and put on a swimsuit and eat more wet brownies off her fingers. And not worry about swallowing them down.

At two in the morning the boys loaded into the Dodge Dart and drove away. Tammy, Debbie, and Jamie each threw on oversized T-shirts and climbed into Allen and Betty's king-sized bed, Jamie in the middle. Tammy and Debbie fell asleep instantly, as if each had an Off switch in her head that had just been flicked down. Jamie lay still between them, careful not to breathe too loudly or shift and jostle them. Her heart fluttered as she feared she'd never fall asleep, that she'd be struck with a years-long case of insomnia, a world-record-worthy feat, like the man in the Guinness book who had been hiccupping since 1922. Tammy rolled to her side and tossed a bony leg over

Jamie's knee. Her friend's flesh against her own made Jamie tingle, made her forget about interminable insomnia. She shut her eyes and she could feel it all over again: the buzzing down deep, the stirring of newly discovered pockets of sensation.

2

The encounter with the pizza boys came at a time before Jamie, Debbie, or Tammy had developed the sense of entitlement that usually accompanies lust (or love) and always gives way to demands. And so the girls neither expected to hear, nor heard, from the boys again. It didn't even occur to them to feel slighted or disappointed. Yet something inside Jamie changed after that encounter.

The pool didn't look the same after the pizza boys had swum in it. It wasn't that it was bigger or smaller; the embedded boulders still looked like dead, limbless elephants; the thatched-roof bar still had a strange stage-set feel to it; and the red phone hidden under the weightless, fake rock still seemed funny to Jamie, as if Maxwell Smart would show up any minute and use the phone to call Agent 99. What was different was the water and air. Before it had just been water and air. But now it was imbued with something slippery, something pungent, something that snaked up and down her legs like an invisible finger. The pool was now, Jamie finally decided, sexy.

So when Allen and Betty threw a party in the end of June

to celebrate the opening of the bicentennial summer (the only bicentennial summer they'd all be alive for, Allen pointed out to his daughters), Jamie couldn't witness it with same detached obliviousness as she had witnessed her parents' past parties.

Jamie sat on the steps of the pool. Her sister, Renee, sat beside her. Jamie was staring up, her flat hand making an awning over her eyes, watching Leon, their neighbor, naked on the diving board. His hairy grown-up body looked slightly melted as he jumped: up and down, up and down. His penis and balls flew in the air in unison like a long bird attached to its eggs. Was this what Joseph's penis would look like? Jamie studied the flying penis, wondered how it happened that people actually wanted to touch penises, put them in their mouths, put them in their bodies.

Renee elbowed Jamie to look away. Jamie elbowed her back and continued to stare at Leon's penis.

There were twelve adults and eight kids at the party. The children clumped together in an approximation of their parents' friendship; theirs was an intimacy borne of the shared experience of witnessing the grown-ups' revelries.

All of the adults were naked. All of the kids were in swimsuits, even the one-year-old girl, Lacey, who wore a bandana-print suit.

Lacey waddled to the edge of the pool. Jamie turned toward her, pleased to have the distraction. Lacey's father, Rod, sat on one of the boulders. On his lap, covering his penis, was a paper plate piled with garbanzo bean salad, which Betty had made.

Jamie pushed off from the steps and swam to the baby at the edge of the pool.

"What are you doing?" Renee was always bossy, sharp. She followed Jamie.

"I'm just making sure the baby won't drown," Jamie said.

Renee rolled her eyes. This was the difference between Renee and Jamie: Everywhere Jamie went, she imagined death first and humiliation second. Everywhere Renee went, she imagined humiliation first and greater humiliation second.

"If her parents weren't so stoned," Renee whispered, "you wouldn't have to be watching her."

"Do you think *we're* getting lung cancer from all the smoke in the air?" Jamie flicked her eyes back and forth, tennis-match style, between the precariously perched baby and her black-eyed sister.

"We're probably just getting stoned," Renee said. "I'm going inside. If the police come I don't wanna be here." Renee hoisted herself out of the pool. She was as lean and shapeless as a twelve-year-old, a body without the necessary fat pad, the doctor had explained, to induce a regular period.

Lacey dipped a curled white hand into the water. She teetered forward, then back, and landed on her fat, diapered bottom. Jamie was about to reach up and collect her into her arms when Rod approached and stood right behind her. Foot level is a bad place to be when viewing a naked, grown man. His cactus-pear-looking testicles sagged toward Jamie's face; she could see pimples on the inside of his upper thighs. She wondered, Do boys who have pimples on their faces have them on their thighs, too?

"They say if you throw a baby into water it will just know how to swim," Rod said.

"Oh yeah?" Jamie squinted as she aimed her gaze toward his pointed face. She wondered who *they* were.

"How 'bout I toss her in and you just stay there to get her if she needs help."

"You haven't tried it before?" Jamie asked.

"We don't have a pool," Rod said. "And the ocean's too cold for a little kid."

"Okay," Jamie said.

Rod lifted his doughy child and in one swift motion swung her out over the pool and dropped her. His face was blank, bored almost, like a man tossing a bag of dog food into the corner of the garage. Lacey plunged down then surged up, but not all the way to air. The top of her head skimmed the surface of the water, her silky hair floated in a little swirling pile, a sea anemone in a tide pool. Jamie reached down, wrapped an arm around her belly, and heaved her up, head above the water. Lacey's fat legs clamped around Jamie's waist as Jamie held onto the edge of the pool with one hand. The baby gasped in a burping sort of way, a croak really. Then she let out a scream that instantly dappled her face with pink. Her fists were in the air: angry white, flower buds.

"You should have given her another couple seconds." Rod was unmoved by the crying; he pulled the baby from Jamie's arms and returned to his rock. Jamie wanted to take Lacey back from him, kiss her and press her against her chest until the baby was sure that the ground below her was solid.

Jamie turned away from Rod and joined the kids who were drifting in the shallow end, an amorphous circle of heads and half bodies. There was Paul, a year older than Renee, stocky and built like a miniature man; his younger brother, Mitch, who was almost Jamie's age; and the furry white-haired, preteen Olsen boy. The Layman twins were there, too; they were a year younger than Jamie but seemed far more sophisticated in their stringy, spare bikinis. The Layman girls were dark and looked like they smelled of spice; they flirted with the boys so extensively that Jamie often felt jealous for their attention.

Paul was organizing a game of wink-murder, but before they could get started someone turned the music up so loud that Jamie thought she could see sound waves bouncing from the tiles to the rocks to the trees. Everyone watched as naked Betty stepped onto the diving board, dancing to "Fifty-Two-Card Pick Up." There was hooting and applause as naked Leon got on the board with her. Betty was singing along, almost shouting the words to the song, her eyes shut, head swinging from side to side:

. . . *and then she said pick me up, take me home, tell me how you like it then fetch me a bone.* . . .

Leon lifted Betty's hand and they did a partner dance but as if on a gangplank since they could only move up and down the board. With his hand extended toward Betty's, Jamie thought Leon looked a bit like Captain Hook forc-ing Peter Pan into the ocean with his rapier. Allen was dancing, too, but from behind the bar. Jamie was glad that if the police walked in, they wouldn't be able to see her father's penis. And then all the adults were dancing, even Lois, Leon's bony blond wife, who reminded Jamie of reedy sun-bleached grass. Even Rod, who had left his perch on the rock. He was holding sleeping Lacey in his arms. After a couple of stiff pointed steps, he took the towel-bundled child and laid her under a spiky bush that grew where the grass met the tile.

Here's the thing adults should know when they choose to dance naked, Jamie thought: Everything bounces. And the bouncing isn't necessarily on beat with the music. So watching a naked adult dance is like watching a 3-D movie without the glasses; a shadow image moves beside the real one. Women's butts shift up and down, a cover sliding over a pillow. Penises flip-flop in all directions, testicles tagging along. Breasts move more or less, not depending on size, but depending on a certain amount of stringiness of the skin. And men's breasts bounce too. Chubby Frank's pubescent fat-girl wedges shook and the aged Daniel had a bounce in his chest where a sheet of skin shifted over the muscle beneath it.

At the end of the song, Betty and Leon held hands and leaped off the board together. Betty was laughing, a long, honking, donkey bray that always made her easy to find in crowds. When they hit the water, the splash was so big it sprayed all the way to the shallow end. Jamie turned her back to the adults, shut her eyes, and let herself sink into the hollow echo underwater. When she popped her eyes open, she was startled to see the magnified legs of the boys in front of her, their loose-legged bathing suits flapping like the wings of a stingray.

3

Everyone in the family knew that Renee was angry for the following reasons: (1) Renee's breasts had just started to develop whereas Jamie was pushing out of a B-cup bra. (2) Jamie's period came with the certainty of a full moon while Renee's periods showed up with the spotty irregularity of a distant (usually alcoholic) relative. And, (3) Jamie would not join Renee in her crusade against nakedness and marijuana smoking.

Renee, if she could have chosen, would have preferred to have belonged to the family of her best and only friend, Lori Nambine. The Nambines had professional family portraits hanging on their walls–portraits taken with the dog, under an oak tree, with each blond, ovine-faced Nambine wearing a red pullover sweater. The Nambines stored presliced cheeses and lunch meats in actual Tupperware-brand containers. The Nambines went to the Smorgasborg Restaurant for all-you-can-eat dinner every Sunday, and they drove their mobile home to their cabin at Lake Nacimiento on long weekends. Whenever Renee could accompany them, she did, for time with the Nambines was real time, real life, Renee once said.

Renee let the family know that when she was home she was simply tolerating them, biding time before her scheduled six-week trek in Colorado with Outward Bound.

Sometime after the last pool party, Renee had stopped using Jamie's proper name and now referred to her only as Farrah, as Jamie had begun to curl the front of her hair into wings, which she flipped down the sides of her face, Farrah Fawcett style. The new name, always said with a thorny lilt, led Jamie to erroneously believe that she had succeeded into shaping her flat, thin hair into a mane that resembled Farrah's. Jamie noticed that the happier she was with her hair, the more infuriated Renee became.

It was not Jamie's intention to anger her sister; in truth, she would have liked nothing more than to have her sister by her side again, to feel the soft coziness of when they were the same size and strangers asked if they were twins. They had often said yes, and when they played Barbies together (eleven-year-old Jamie solemnly swearing to her thirteen-year-old sister that she would reveal to no one that Renee still played Barbies) they would make blond Barbie and brunette Barbie twins who would date only identical twin Ken dolls. But at twelve, when Jamie had placed Renee's hand on her, Jamie's, chest and asked her about the achy garbanzo-sized lumps under her skin, the twinship pulled apart like a seam with loose and broken threads. By the time Jamie was thirteen Renee had begun hating her for reasons Jamie could no more control than change. Instead of hating her sister back, Jamie grew indifferent, detached, as if this phase in their sisterhood were just something she'd have to endure in the same way she endured the hour-long wait for the State Street bus, or the theater arts teacher who insisted that Jamie's stage fright was a form of stupidity.

By the summer of 1976, Renee's anger seemed to have swirled into a solid mass, a throwing stone with a single target: Jamie herself, the inexorable fact that she existed.

So, when seventeen-year-old Flip Jenkins called to ask Jamie on a date (Flip Jenkins, who was in high school with Renee; Flip Jenkins, whose yearbook picture Renee circled with a red ink heart; Flip Jenkins, who was voted Luscious Lester the previous year; Flip Jenkins, who drove a red VW bus with at least two surfboards in the back at all times; Flip Jenkins, who even the boys thought was the coolest guy around), Jamie didn't dare tell Renee about it. In the matter of boys they were fairly even at that point, as neither Jamie nor Renee had ever been on a real date, the kind in which a boy picks you up at the house, takes you somewhere, and pays for it the way one's father might. Jamie knew that once she went out with Flip she would be miles beyond Renee—it would be a chasm that could never be closed, for even if Renee went on a date that very same night, Jamie would still have dated two years before her sister in age.

Jamie told Flip that she couldn't go out with him until Wednesday, the day after Renee was to leave for Outward Bound. Betty praised her daughter for sparing Renee the indignity of witnessing her younger sister go on a date, but, really, Jamie was sparing herself the torment that would have been inflicted upon her by Renee, and, additionally, she wanted access to Renee's undulating rubber-heeled Famolare shoes.

On Tuesday morning, Betty, Allen, and Jamie sat on Renee's bed and watched her assemble her last-minute things.

"Farrah," Renee snapped, "don't come in my room while I'm gone. Ever. No matter what."

"She has her own room, honey," Betty said. "Why are you worried about your room?"

"Why do you call her Farrah?" Allen asked.

"After Farrah Fawcett," Jamie said, "because of my hair."

"Because of her wish-hair," Renee said.

"Farrah Fawcett? That blond girl?" Allen said.

"She has awfully big nipples," Betty said. "Did you see that poster?"

"Mom!" Renee said. "How can you talk about someone's nipples?!"

"Well, honey, it's impossible not to notice them."

"I still don't understand why you call your sister Farrah," Allen said. "She doesn't have big nipples."

"Dad!" Renee was almost screaming. "You are inappropriate!"

Jamie slouched over and glanced down at her chest. She had never really thought about her nipples. Lately she'd been spending extensive time examining her face in the bathroom mirror (looking at smiles, profiles, up and down angles), trying to see herself the way Joseph may have, or the way Flip Jenkins might. But she had yet to scrutinize her body with the same thoroughness. Jamie's flesh was still new to her, she was just starting to understand how it felt. But now that the idea had been put forth, Jamie knew that later that day she would be in the mirror looking at her nipples and wondering how they compared to other people's, or what Joseph would have thought had he seen them, or what, if the day ever came, Flip Jenkins would think.

Betty continued laughing at Allen's nipple comment.

"And don't wear my clothes," Renee said.

"They don't fit me," Jamie said. "You're like a kid's size twelve."

"Mom! Do you see how she torments me?" Renee asked.

"I wasn't tormenting her, I was stating a fact!"

"Well, you are a kid's twelve, aren't you, dear?"

"I can fit into some size fourteens, okay? Now can we change the subject?"

"I'm a size five in juniors," Jamie said.

"Mom! Do you hear her?!"

"So she's a size five," Allen said. "What do you care?"

"I can't wait to be away from here," Renee huffed.

On the drive home from the airport Jamie reminded her parents about her date the following night.

"Are we supposed to know who Flip Jenkins is?" Allen asked.

"I guess not," Jamie said.

"Is he cute?" Betty asked.

"He's a total fox," Jamie said.

"Cool," Betty said.

"Do I have a curfew?" Jamie asked. "I mean, is there like some time I should tell him he has to have me home?"

"Why would you want a curfew?" Allen asked.

"I don't want one, I just thought you'd want one."

"Why would we want one if you don't want one?" Betty said.

"I just thought you'd want to keep track of me since I'm going to be with a boy, like, on a real date and all."

"Jesus, Jamie," Allen said, "you're fourteen years old now. You can keep track of yourself."

"Well, how about if I wake you up when I get home, so you know I got in okay?"

"Honey, you woke us enough when you were a baby,"

Betty said. "Just let us sleep, you can tell us you got in okay in the morning."

"All right, whatever."

"When did you say this date was?" Betty asked.

"Tomorrow night," Jamie said.

"Dad and I won't even be home," Betty said. "We're going grunion hunting with Leon and Lois."

"Well, what time will you be home?"

"I dunno, three, four in the morning."

"Mom! Please be home by midnight. I don't want to come home to an empty house!"

"So stay out past three."

"Mom!"

"The door will be unlocked," Allen said.

"That's the problem," Jamie said. "Anyone could go in the house while we're all gone, and then I'd be the first one home and so I'd be the one who'd get murdered by the intruder."

"For crissakes," Allen sighed, "have you ever even heard of an intruder in this town?"

"Honey, why don't you just sleep at a friend's house? That way someone will be there when you get home."

"But Tammy and Debbie have eleven o'clock curfews. I don't want to tell Flip Jenkins that I have to be back at eleven o'clock."

"Sleep at Flip's house then," Allen said, and he and Betty laughed.

"Dad! I'm not going to have a sleepover for a first date!"

"So take a key and lock the door," Allen said.

"But you'll probably be leaving after I leave on my date so you'll have to remember to lock it," Jamie said.

"Fine," Allen said, "we'll lock the house. You unlock it when you get home from your date."

"But what if I forget the key and then I'm locked out till four in the morning when you get home?"

Betty turned around in her seat and looked at her daughter. Allen was shaking his head.

"There are no intruders," Betty said with finality. "You'll come home when the date is over and your father and I may or may not be home already."

Debbie and Tammy were on Jamie's bed waiting with her for the arrival of Flip Jenkins. Jamie wore a red-and-white-striped sailor shirt that belonged to Debbie, Renee's size-fourteen white pants, which were so small Jamie had to lie on her back and let Debbie and Tammy work the zipper in the same way one would close an overstuffed suitcase, and Renee's Famolare shoes.

"You look perfect," Debbie said.

"You look the best you could possibly look," Tammy said.

Jamie jumped off her bed and went to the full-length mirror on the bathroom door. If this was her best, she thought, what exactly did it look like? Her face appeared as a blur in the mirror: a smudge of freckles, a smear of white teeth.

"Are you sure this is okay?" Jamie asked. "I mean, like, is my best any good at all or is my best, like, you know, like if you told a retarded kid he did the best he could on a spelling test but the test was all three letter words?"

"What are you talking about?" Tammy asked, and at that moment the doorbell rang.

"Stay here!" Jamie commanded, before running downstairs to answer the door.

Flip Jenkins was in jeans and a white T-shirt. His skin

was brown, like a deer, his hair was white and frothy, like ocean foam, and his eyes were blue polished stones.

"Hey," he said.

"Hey," Jamie said, and she stood in the doorway staring at Flip Jenkins. She had no idea what happened on a date after you said hey.

"Should I come in and meet your parents before we go?"

"Uh . . . " Jamie rewound a film in her head, trying to remember if her mother was dressed or not.

Allen walked out of his study and wandered toward the kitchen.

"Dad!"

Allen looked up as if Jamie had interrupted his thoughts.

"This is Flip."

"Are you collecting for the newspaper?"

"No, Dad, he's my . . ." Jamie couldn't bring herself to say "date" as it suddenly occurred to her that maybe she'd been mistaken and it wasn't a date, maybe it was a get-together, maybe he was just giving her a ride to a party.

"Don't you have a date tonight?" Allen asked.

"Dad, I'm going to be hanging out with Flip tonight."

Flip stepped into the house and took three loping steps with his hand out toward Allen. Jamie was afraid Allen wouldn't respond correctly, wouldn't shake his hand, or—worse—would hug him, instead.

"Pleased to meet you, sir," Flip said.

"Call me Allen." Allen shook his hand but pulled his head back away from Flip. Jamie knew he didn't believe in that kind of formality—he found it insincere; Flip was actually losing points with a method that had likely been a clear winner thus far in his dating experience.

"So, like, what time should I have Jamie home, Allen?"

"I guess you should have her home when you think your date is over."

"Oh . . . uh." Flip was smiling, flitting his eyes back and forth between Jamie and Allen. Jamie imagined him sorting through the mental Rolodex in his head, trying to find the best response to this situation.

"My parents are going grunion hunting," Jamie said, "so they won't be here to check on me."

"Cool," Flip said. "I love grunion hunting."

"Well, you should meet us at the beach, then," Allen said. "The grunion will probably come out sometime after midnight. We've got buckets and everything."

"Where are you doing the hunting?" Flip asked, and there was an audible gasp from someplace behind the up-stairs banister.

"East Beach," Allen said. "We'll be there till three or four in the morning."

Allen smiled and wandered toward the kitchen.

"Bye, Dad!" Jamie cringed at the cheerfulness in her voice. She hoped Flip hadn't noticed how forced her words were, how she was, at that moment, trying to act like she was the normal daughter of a normal father. People her sister would love to be related to.

"Have fun," Allen said, and he walked out of sight.

"See you at East Beach, Allen," Flip called after him.

Flip and Jamie sat in the battered Volkswagen bus, parked in the back row of the drive-in theater. There was a case of Heineken on the floor of the backseat and a picnic dinner in a wicker basket on the floor between them. In all her imaginings of dating, Jamie had never even fathomed that a boy might bring a picnic to a movie. Jamie wanted the date to be over only so she could tell Tammy and Debbie about it—how Flip had pulled out two blue-and-white-checked napkins and laid one on each of their laps. How he had set up her plate of food first: chicken breast, corn on the cob, and a dinner roll, before setting up his own plate. How he had opened Jamie's beer, then snapped the metal top with his thumb and middle finger so it went sailing across the bus, hitting the back window.

Mother, Jugs & Speed played on the giant screen. Bill Cosby was in the movie so they both expected to laugh, but never did. Jamie sat up straight and tried to arrange her face so it looked like she was watching the film, but really all she could think about was if she had cheesy-looking corn bits mashed into her teeth, if she should finish everything on her plate to flatter Flip (even though she had no appetite), or if the button on her pants was going to pop off if she took just one more sip of beer. Flip was hunched over his plate, eyes turned up toward the screen, holding his roll with his left hand while he lifted chicken or corn with his right hand. Every now and then he turned to Jamie and said something short and quick, like "Did you ever see Bill Cosby's TV show?" To which she answered, "Uh huh. He's funny." Every time Raquel Welch came on the screen Jamie felt small and bland, like a boiled Idaho potato. She worried that Flip would look up at Raquel, look back at Jamie, and wonder why she was sitting in his VW bus when someone more like Raquel would fit in much better. But he didn't seem interested in Raquel, he seemed interested in Jamie, as she silently gnawed at her meal.

"Did you make this food?" Jamie asked, after finally finishing everything on her plate.

"My mother made it," Flip said. "She's, like, totally into doing anything to make me happy."

"Cool," Jamie said.

"Your dad seems cool," Flip said.

"Yeah, I guess he is."

"Should we meet them grunion hunting?"

"Uh, if you want to." Jamie wondered if the addition of her parents made her an attractive package.

Flip opened his third beer while Jamie worked on her first. She had tasted beer before, but had never drunk a whole bottle. When her Heineken was three quarters gone Jamie felt so bloated that she imagined untying her belly button and deflating her stomach with one long, slow hiss.

"Another brew-ha-ha?" Flip asked.

Jamie was shaking her head no when Flip leaned over and kissed her: deliberately, intently. She was unsure of what to do with the beer bottle in her hand, if she should put her arms around him while still holding it or if she should try to put it down somewhere. She could feel Flip's beer cold against her back.

"Come on," Flip said, and he took Jamie's hand and led her to the bench seat in the back. She left her beer on the floor by the front seat as she climbed into the back and settled into a body-engaged kiss. Flip's bus smelled like tar and surf wax, his breath smelled like chicken and beer, his body smelled warm and musky, like the sun. Jamie felt like she was melting—oozing into the seat, into his chest, into his lap. There was a sound track to this extended kiss: the blaring, hollow, horn whines from *Mother, Jugs & Speed*, Bill Cosby's stilted drawl, and Raquel Welch's airy whisper. This kiss was like the Matterhorn ride at Disneyland: a scary thrill.

When it felt like seconds had passed, or perhaps hours
(Jamie's sense of time as well as her senses of smell and
touch seemed new to her, as if she were just figuring out
how to use them), Flip sat up and centered the top button
of his jeans at his waist.

"Should we go grunion hunting?"

"Uh . . . uh . . . okay." Jamie felt she would go anywhere
and do anything with Flip; asking what she wanted seemed
pointless.

"You ever been before?"

"No," Jamie said. "My parents go with a couple of their
friends every year but I've always been home sleeping while
they do it."

"It's so cool. You'll flip out . . . " and then Flip laughed.
"Get it? Flip out?"

"Oh yeah," Jamie panted, "your name." And she realized
just then that she was already flipped out–she was both
herself and someone totally new to herself, someone who
was frothing with a happiness she had never before felt.

"The grunion," Flip said, "they just, like, come streaking
out of the water, like these silver flashes . . . you know,
and you just, like, you just snatch them and put them in a
bucket and then you take them home, fry them up in a pan
with some butter, and they taste, like, so good."

"I hate fish," Jamie said, but what she was really thinking
is how strange it was that her body was fizzing, carbon-
ated somehow, simply by listening to Flip Jenkins talk about
frying grunion.

Jamie took off her sister's shoes and rolled up the bottoms
of her pants before getting out of Flip's car. It occurred to

her, as they walked from the parking lot onto the beach, that Renee would be shocked to know that her shoes were sitting in Flip Jenkins's VW bus. The previous year, when Betty and Allen were briefly looking to buy a different house, they discovered that one of the houses they were considering belonged to Bo and John Derek. Renee was so thrilled with this fact that she stole a pencil from John Derek's study. She kept the pencil in a shoe box under her bed with the ballet slipper she was given from a principal dancer in the New York City Ballet (they danced in Santa Barbara every summer) and the autographed picture of David Cassidy that she got when she wrote to his fan club. Jamie imagined that if the Famolares in Flip's car had had nothing to do with her, Renee might have simply retired them to the celebrity box.

It was a full moon; from a distance the water looked like slick, black glass. As they edged closer to the shore, Jamie could see small waves breaking, each one bringing with it a vibrating flash of silver. Bands of people with buckets ran along the foaming water, scooping up grunion with their fists. Everyone seemed to be whispering, as if they were sneaking up on the helpless fish.

"The grunion look cool," Jamie said.

"They're, like, totally beautiful." The word *beautiful* sounded different when Flip said it; to Jamie it sounded more . . . beautiful.

"Yeah, they're beautiful," she said.

"Think we can find your parents?" The grunion schedule was printed in the daily paper—a fact the true grunion hunters resented, as the midnight beaches were often overrun with people who simply liked the party atmosphere of the Hunt.

"Uh . . . my Mom has a big laugh," Jamie said. "It's sort of like what the Lost Boys sound like in the movie *Peter Pan* . . . you know, when they turn into asses."

"Never saw it," Flip said.

"Oh." Jamie instantly regretted the Disney film reference and decided that if Flip never asked her out again, *that* would be the reason.

"Someone's smokin' some doobage," Flip said. "Do you smell it?"

"Yeah."

"Do you get high?"

"I haven't yet," Jamie said.

"That's cool," he said. "You're only fourteen, there's plenty of time to try that stuff out."

"Do you get high?"

"Not too much," Flip said. "Don't want to be a burnout."

"Yeah, that's gross," Jamie said, hoping that Flip wouldn't think her parents were burnouts.

"Well, let's go catch some grunion," Flip said, and he led Jamie closer to the water, where their toes felt muddy and slick.

Jamie stood with Flip, her hand tucked into his, and watched as each wave deposited hundreds of silvery grunion. Many of them wormed into the sand, digging shallow holes; others flailed their long, arced bodies atop the hole diggers.

"The females are laying eggs in the sand," Flip said, "and the males are, like, jumping on the females and fertilizing the eggs." He sounded so smart that Jamie was swooning.

"But if their eggs are in the sand," she said, "how come they're jumping on the females?"

"Just for fun probably," Flip laughed, and Jamie laughed,

too. "No, really, I think the girls aren't strong enough to get out of those, like, pits they dig, so they're, like, totally stuck, you know."

"Yeah."

"Then the boys totally don't care. They just spew it out all over the place."

The word *spew* made Jamie blush; it seemed too intimate.

And then the honk of Betty's laugh sounded out like a fog horn. It was growing, moving toward Jamie and Flip like an ambulance in traffic. Jamie looked up and saw her mother tumbling down the beach. Betty puffed in and out on a joint that was wedged in her mouth as she swooped down on a grunion and tossed it into the green plastic bucket dangling in her hand. Leon was right beside her. He mumbled something into Betty's ear that made her laugh so hard she had to pull the joint from her mouth and bend over her knees as if she were vomiting.

Jamie considered turning away before they saw her, but then, with the wishful thought that Flip might become her boyfriend, she figured it was better to introduce him then, lest he meet Betty at the house later, remember seeing her, and wonder why Jamie never said anything.

"Mom!" Jamie said.

Betty looked up, startled, still smiling.

"What are you doing here?"

"Didn't Dad tell you I might come?"

"No."

"This is Flip."

"I thought you had a date tonight with that high school boy Renee has a crush on."

Jamie felt like she was hanging upside down, blood rushing from her feet to her head.

"Nice to meet you Mrs. . . . . eh." Flip took a step forward, his hand jutting out to be shaken, when Betty passed him the joint.

"What happened to your date?" Betty asked.

Flip took a hit off the joint, then turned to Jamie and lifted his eyebrows to see if she wanted some. She waved the joint away as casually as her shaking hand would allow. As much as her parents had smoked pot in front of her, Jamie had never imagined that she would smoke pot in front of them. That would be like kissing in front of them, an act a child is naturally inclined to not do with her parents present. Flip extended his arm across Jamie and passed the joint to Leon.

"Betty," Leon said, "I think this is Jamie's date."

"Really?!" Betty laugh-honked. "So how was it?"

Jamie was on the verge of tearing up with embarrassment when Flip started laughing.

"Totally awesome!" he said. "We went to the movies and had a picnic dinner."

Allen and Lois caught up to the group. They each had a bucketful of fish compared to the single fish slouching limply in Betty's bucket and Leon's hollow empty bucket.

"Sweetheart!" Allen said. "How was your date?"

Flip laughed again and said, "I think she's still on it."

"Fred, right?" Allen asked.

"Flip," Jamie said. Flip couldn't talk because the joint had been passed to him again and he was sucking another slow, deep inhale.

Lois was alternately watching Jamie and Flip. Her mouth was zippered shut, almost puckering. She and Leon didn't have kids and Jamie always suspected it was because they didn't like kids, as neither one had ever paid particular attention to her or Renee. But just then, as Jamie stood next to Flip, she thought that maybe Lois, who had to go home with balding, loose-skinned Leon, might, instead, be jealous.

"Come see our sunken living room!" Betty blurted while Lois rolled her eyes.

The sunken living room was a giant pit that Allen and Leon had dug into the sand. They carved it out so that there was a built-in sand bench—a cold, damp circular seat. There was also a carved stairway with three steps, so one didn't have to jump straight into the pit. Jamie jumped anyway, and so did Flip. Betty jumped, too, and for a second Jamie feared she was going to tumble onto Flip's lap, but she caught herself.

"Why do we bother with the steps when no one uses them?" Allen said, stepping down into the pit. "What kind of schmucks are we?"

"I like the steps," Lois said, and she gingerly stepped down with Leon following.

Flip sat next to Jamie on the bench, their bodies touching from the shoulder down. Jamie wondered if her parents noticed or cared that a seventeen-year-old boy's thigh was ironed against her own. Betty lit up another joint and she, Allen, Leon, and Lois immediately launched into a conversation that sounded to Jamie like all their conversations, talking emphatically about things that didn't interest her: politics, the economy, books she hadn't yet read, movies she had yet to see. It was as if Flip and Jamie weren't even there, yet there was a sense that, unlike the past when Jamie might have been shooed away or told to scram, she was now *allowed* to be there. Somehow, because of her one date with Flip Jenkins, Jamie's parents had decided that she was grown up enough to sit in their circle and smoke their pot, which Leon kept handing her and which she continually passed off to Flip.

At three in the morning, Flip drove Jamie home with his left hand on the steering wheel and his right hand on her knee. Betty and Allen were driving in front them, going well below the speed limit on the empty, slick road.

"You can always tell who the high drivers are 'cause they go so, so slow."

"Oh yeah?" Jamie leaned forward in her seat and watched the red brake lights of her parents' Volvo beam on as Allen glided into a stop at a light. A flash of worry lit up her brain as Jamie imagined the slow-moving car as a perfect target for a speeding drunk—a tin can through which a bullet would effortlessly fly.

"Your parents are totally cool," Flip said. "That was, like, the best date I've been on in a long, long time."

"Really?" Jamie's worry vanished as she turned to Flip.

"Yeah, totally."

"What's the worst date you've ever been on?"

"Uh . . ." Flip lifted his hand from Jamie's knee and scratched his nose. "I guess this girl from San Marcos High. She, like, told me she loved me and started crying, like, from *love*, you know?"

"That's intense."

"Yeah, it was totally intense. And the weird thing is, I thought I was in love with her until the moment that happened."

"Yeah, I can see that," Jamie said, but what she could really see was that she herself was falling so hard for Flip

Jenkins that she could imagine crying over it. The urge to be with him was suddenly stronger than any urge she had ever had before: sleep, or food, or a need to use a bathroom.

"So, beach tomorrow?" Flip asked. They were parked in the driveway behind Allen and Betty, who had already gone into the house.

"I'll be there with Tammy and Debbie."

"How do you get there?"

"One of our moms drops us off, usually."

"I'll pick you guys up."

"Really?" This, more than anything, seemed like proof that the date had gone well. Flip must not have been comparing her to Rachel Welch, Jamie thought; he couldn't have minded the Disney reference, and her parents must not have seemed like burnouts.

"I'll call you in the morning as soon as I wake up. We could, like, go before lunch."

"Cool." Jamie tried to contain her smile. Everyone at the beach would see her climbing out of the front seat of Flip Jenkin's VW bus. It was a scene she had never dared to imagine–and before she could conjure up the infinite ways it could go wrong (Flip forgetting to pick her up, Flip changing his mind about her, Jamie suddenly struck with car sickness on the ride to the beach, etc.) Jamie boldly kissed Flip flat on the mouth until it felt as if she had suckled from him a blissful mindlessness.

4

Flip came with friends. He came to the beach with friends, he came to the movies with friends, he came to Jamie's house with friends. He was only one beer in a six-pack that was permanently bound by a rubber neck cuff. All his friends were cute, surfers, almost interchangeable in their cool-dude drawl, tawny skin, and disregard for hair-combing, shirts, shoes, glasses, jewelry, and anything that didn't hang on them like skin.

Betty liked seeing Flip's friends in the kitchen. She cooked for them, talked to them, laughed at their jokes. By the second week of Jamie's dating Flip, Betty had yet to walk into the kitchen without a shirt, although she had come fairly close: once wearing a sheer tank top with no bra, and once wearing a loose, diaphanous strappy dress with the arms cut down so low one could see half her breast from the side. Jamie was so relieved that there had been no half-nudity that she never dared mention it to her mother for fear that a recognition of this good service would jinx it and bring it to an end. No one ever spoke to Jamie about her mother's breasts, but Flip told her, in private, that every one of his friends had a mad, sexual crush on Betty. Jamie was strangely flattered by this thought and, naturally, repulsed.

With his friends eating Irish oatmeal or quesadillas that Betty cooked up, Flip and Jamie often snuck off to the record room on the pretense of changing the music. Closed up in there, they'd make out or grope for as long as was reasonably possible. Betty was so enthralled with her high school admirers that Jamie and Flip often managed to escape for forty minutes, seemingly without having been missed.

Unlike Betty, Allen was uninterested in Flip and his friends. He walked though the kitchen, or by the pool when they were swimming, and looked them over as if he were surprised to see them, as if they were foreigners whose every motion was odd to him. And he never got anyone's name right, stumbling–Chip, er, uh, Fritz–even when he was talking to Flip.

Tammy and Debbie were mixed into this group, of course. They each dated a couple of Flip's friends and usually developed crushes on anyone who showed an interest in them.

One day, the boys wanted to go surfing at Hollister Ranch, a private beach about forty miles away. Debbie couldn't go because her mother wanted her home for supper, and Tammy couldn't go because they had Family Night at her church. Jamie didn't want to sit on the beach alone while the boys surfed, so she stayed back with Debbie and Tammy. Allen and Betty were at the nude beach and Renee was still at Outward Bound, so the girls met up at Jamie's house.

Lying on towels beside the pool, they dribbled baby oil on one another's bodies to increase the intensity of their tans, drank warm Tab that Tammy brought over, read *Seventeen* magazine, and ate carob almonds out of the glass canister Betty used to store what she considered snack food.

Tammy slipped onto a raft and floated off in the pool.

"Hand me the carob," she said, and Jamie placed the open glass container on Tammy's brown belly.

Debbie was facedown on her towel, reading, her suit untied in the back to prevent a tan line. Jamie shook out her towel to get rid of carob crumbs, then lay on her belly and looked out at the pool, at the magenta flower beds tucked here and there around the pool, at the sky that was so blue and flat and solid-looking that it resembled an endless taut balloon.

"Isn't everything perfect?" Jamie said.

"Huh?" Tammy tossed some carob almonds in her mouth. Debbie turned the page of her magazine.

"Everything's perfect," Jamie said. "I mean, we're young, there's nothing wrong with any of us—you know, no deformities or anything, no acne, we're smart enough—no one's failing school—we're super-tan, I mean, we're like as tan as you can be without passing into a different race—"

"I'm darker than Lupe," Tammy said.

"She is," Debbie said. "Lupe was, like, scrubbing the top of the stove yesterday and Tammy came in and was standing beside her and their arms were side by side and I swear, Tammy was darker than Lupe."

"And I'm blond," Tammy said. "How many people are as dark as a Mexican but are blond?"

"Mexicans who dye their hair," Jamie said.

"Mexicans don't dye their hair," Debbie said.

"Wait, let me say why our lives are so perfect."

"Okay, so we're tan," Debbie said.

"And we don't really have to do anything, I mean, we're not like those kids who have to work in factories sewing on buttons, or like Lupe's daughter who helps Lupe out at Tammy's house all the time. . . . I mean, really, we just have to show up for dinner every now and then."

"I have to go to church," Tammy said. She paddled the raft, with her one free hand, toward the edge of the pool where Jamie and Debbie lay.

"But you love church," Debbie said.

"It's not that I love it," Tammy said, "it's just that I think it's good to go. I think my parents are right in making us go. I mean, God wants me there, so how can I say no?"

"And then there's Flip," Jamie went on as if Tammy hadn't spoken, "I mean, like, I love him. He's so dang cute and he said he loves me and that's like the best feeling in the world, like better than thinking that God loves you or your parents love you or your sister loves you. . . . It's just better than everything."

"I need a boyfriend," Tammy said.

"Me too," Debbie said.

"And I need darker lips," Tammy said, rubbing her bottom lip with her index finger. "I hate how pale my lips are."

"Put on lip gloss," Debbie said.

"Yeah, but it, like, comes off when I go swimming. I want to come out of the ocean, and, like, walk toward everyone on the beach and have my lips perfectly rose-colored. You know, like yours." Tammy turned her head toward Debbie.

"My coloring is French," Debbie said. "All French women have these really dark lips."

"Get waterproof lipstick," Jamie said.

"Lipstick is for old ladies," Tammy said. "And they don't make waterproof gloss. You know, it really upsets me sometimes. I, like, come up from a wave and my hair might be scooped back just so and I'll have on the best suit, like that white one with ties on the sides, but then I know that I look all washed-out because my lips are so pale!"

"Okay, so with the exception of pale lips, your life is perfect," Jamie said.

"No," Tammy said, "I need a boyfriend."

"Go for Brett," Jamie said. "Flip said he's so in love with you that he's intimidated. If you wanted him, he could be your boyfriend tomorrow."

"When did Flip say that? Why didn't you tell me?"

"I did, I told you last night."

"I don't remember you telling me anything last night."

"Maybe I just meant to tell you but forgot."

"Go for it," Debbie said.

"Brett's hot," Tammy said. "I thought he didn't like me."

"He loves you," Jamie said. "You just have to let him know you're interested."

"I think I love Jimmy," Debbie said. She had gone on three dates with him and it seemed to be developing into something.

"You should love Jimmy, he's, like, the nicest guy I've ever met," Jamie said. And she meant it. Jimmy asked questions when you talked to him; he didn't just make jokes or quips. Jimmy opened doors. Jimmy helped Betty clear the counter. Jimmy actually went to La Cumbre Plaza with his mother and retarded twenty-eight-year-old brother (who drooled and held Jimmy's hand) and wasn't embarrassed to run into friends. Jimmy's eyes were so huge and brown you'd think you could dip a finger into them and taste them.

"I bet Jimmy's a Christian," Tammy said. "He reminds me

of the boys at church except he's got white sun streaks in his hair and he doesn't have acne and he surfs."

"Jimmy Golden?" Debbie said. "Isn't Golden Jewish or something?"

They both looked at Jamie.

"I don't know," she said. "My dad's the only Jewish person I know."

Tammy put the glass canister on the tile, then dove off the raft and swam underwater. Debbie stood, tied her suit in the back, and dove in. Jamie was too sun-drunk to stand, so she rolled, as if she were rolling down a grass hill, across the tile until she tumbled into the pool. When she came up, Tammy and Debbie were laughing.

It didn't take long for Debbie and Jimmy to become an official couple. And once Tammy turned her full attention to Brett, they were a couple, too (a consortium that allowed Tammy the guiltless freedom to pause and then quickly advance from each of the stations of sexual exploit). And so Flip's gang of many became a gang of three as Flip, Brett, and Jimmy passed the summer days with Jamie, Tammy, and Debbie.

Jamie had a romantic fantasy that had persisted since she was eight years old and had watched a teenage couple make out on the Pinocchio boat ride at Disneyland. She wanted to go to Disneyland with a boyfriend; she wanted to sit cozy, pressed against his lap on the Jungle Cruise, hold his hand, and maybe even sing along on Small World, or kiss in the darkness of the General Electric Theater. When Jamie learned that Debbie had a similar fantasy, they were both astounded. When she heard that Flip, Brett, and Jimmy were enthusiastic about the idea of a day at Disneyland, Jamie felt that her already lovely life was becoming so painfully good that guilt for her sister's chaste life slipped under her skin like splinters you'd need a magnifying glass to find.

Brett's father gave him the mobile home for the trip to Disneyland—he even filled it with gas. Brett went to the driver's cushy, loungelike seat. Tammy sat right beside him in her cushy, loungelike seat. Jamie looked at them and imagined Tammy thirty five years old, the mother of two clean, towheaded kids, wife of someone less like Brett and more like Brett's big-bellied, Ken-doll-haired father. Flip slouched into the booth seat at the table, picked up the brick-sized, beige remote control, and clicked on the TV.

"Reception's no good here," Brett's dad said, leaning into the doorway. "Wait till you get on the San Diego Freeway and you'll be able to pick up channel eleven in L.A."

"Met-ro, me-dia, television," Jamie and Debbie sang the theme song for channel 11, "eleven, eleven, eleven . . ." The girls fell into each other, giggling, then Debbie broke away and went to examine the kitchen cupboards.

Brett's mother was leaning in the doorway, her head tucked under Brett's father's arm. Her eyes looked wild and mousy as she watched Debbie.

"The stove's not hooked up, dear," Brett's mother said. "But the fridge is working."

"Darn!" Debbie said. "I brought brownie mix and everything."

"You know the Electric Parade isn't running," Brett's dad said. "They've got some special parade instead."

No one seemed interested except Jamie.

"But I love the Electric Parade!" she said.

"They've got America Parade, or something like that," Brett's dad said. "You know people wearing those giant head costumes, playing out scenes from United States history."

"Yeah, yeah, Dad," Brett said, "the whole bicentennial thing–I saw the ads for it on TV."

"God, I'm so bummed there's no Electric Parade," Jamie said.

When they pulled onto the freeway, Tammy picked up the CB radio, held it like a microphone against her mouth, and said, "This is Pink Panties, anyone else out there headed to Disneyland?"

A grumbling voice broke in over the CB, "Where you at now Pink Panties? Let's convoy to Disneyland!"

They each bought the Adult Magic Kingdom Pass for $5.75. The pass gave you entrance to the park and eleven tickets that could be used on any ride–even the E ticket rides, which, really, were the only ones Jamie and her friends were interested in going on.

As they hustled from one ride to the next, Jamie began to feel like they were simply checking events off a list. From the Jungle Cruise they ran to get in line for the Pirates of the Caribbean. When the pirate ride was over they hauled off the boats and dashed around the flocks of families to get in line for the Haunted Mansion. In the capsule-shaped car of the Haunted Mansion Flip talked into Jamie's ear, pointing out what looked fake, what seemed lame, and what just bored him. And then he didn't want to go on the Pinocchio ride, the ride that was, to Jamie, the purpose of their trip. How could they make out on the Pinocchio ride if Flip refused to ride?

"It's a C ride," Flip said. "We can't waste our pass on a C."

"But we have seven tickets left," Jamie said. "There's no way we're going to go on seven more E rides."

"We should use our time wisely," Flip said, "like, on E rides, get it?"

The bantering continued for a while, a fact that made Jamie feel proudly mature—as if she were a wife who had to mollify her cranky, overworked husband.

Eventually Jamie agreed that instead of going on a C or E ride they could sneak off to the mobile home for a couple hours alone. Making out in the parking lot of Disneyland seemed like a reasonable compromise to her fantasy. She'd probably be disappointed, Jamie thought, if they made out on a ride and it wasn't exactly as she had imagined it would be after having witnessed the kissing teens so many years earlier.

There were two beds in the back of the mobile home. One was a double bed and the other was a single bunk bed perched above it. Flip turned down the covers of the double bed, peeled off his shirt and shorts so that he was naked, and got in without pulling the covers up. It was the first time Jamie had witnessed his nakedness in open daylight.

"C'mon," he said, patting the mattress.

Jamie stared at his penis—the neat packaging of his balls, the even color throughout.

"Well?" Flip asked.

Jamie took off her flip-flops, shorts, and T-shirt and lay beside Flip in her white cotton bra and panties. She was awkward, self-contained with her knees up and arms by her side as she stared down at Flip's genitals.

"I totally think it's time we move on," Flip said, "move ahead, you know."

Jamie's stomach lurched. She had been so drunk with love for Flip that the idea that he'd ever break up with her, that they'd ever move on and not be together, had never even flitted into her mind.

"Why?" Jamie shut her eyes and prayed that he wasn't trying to break up with her.

"I don't know. I just think that sex is an amazing thing, and . . . well, we've been making out, you've felt my dick a little, I've been feeling your . . . bosoms–"

"Bosoms?" Jamie laughed, relieved.

"I thought it was a respectful word," Flip said. "I was gonna say tits."

"But isn't it just bosom, without the s?"

"Well if you're looking at one it's a bosom. But when you've got two in front of you, they're bosoms."

"Bosoms."

"Yeah, so I was thinking we need to do some exploring. Like, I'd like to introduce my dick to your mouth."

"Pleased to meet you," Jamie said, looking down at Flip's dick, which was now pointing up at her, punching out of its skin.

"And I'd like to meet your Virginia."

"Virginia? Like the state?"

"That's what I called it when I was a little kid 'cause I thought vagina and Virginia were the same thing."

"So you thought one of the fifty states was Vagina?" Jamie laughed.

"Yeah, I guess I did." Flip grinned. "So anyway, can everyone meet now?"

And with that, Flip bent down and slipped off Jamie's underpants. Jamie started laughing, although she wasn't sure why. There was something absurd about this naked moment, like when she and her sister, when they still felt they were twins, would jump naked on their parents' bed after a bath.

"What?" Flip said.

"Nothing." Jamie remembered her mother laughing like this—a hiccupping twitter instead of her usual bray—at the funeral of the old woman from the corner of their street. It was a laugh that didn't feel right, like getting tickled by someone you don't trust.

Flip stared at Jamie until her laugh petered out like a car running out of gas.

"So what are we doing first?" Jamie asked.

"I guess I should finger bang you," Flip said, and he hunched over Jamie and stuck his index finger in her vagina.

"Huh." Jamie looked down at Flip's finger moving in and out. She remembered the first time they kissed and how it felt scary and thrilling, like the Matterhorn ride. And now, here they were at Disneyland with the Matterhorn just a short walk away and their sex was, well, less exciting than an A ticket ride, less thrilling then the Great Moments with Mr. Lincoln ride where you sat in a small velvety theater and watched a robot Abe Lincoln deliver a speech.

"Does it feel good?"

"I guess. It doesn't really feel like anything."

"Well, why don't you try me." Flip pulled his finger out.

"Should I give you a hand job?"

"You've done that," Flip said. "I think we need to have oral sex."

"Uh, okay." Jamie looked down at his penis and decided

it wasn't anything like Leon's penis or her father's penis or any other penis she had seen wagging around her backyard. This one looked pinker, newer. The thought of putting it in her mouth seemed strange but not repugnant. Jamie scooted down on her hands and knees and placed her face near Flip's crotch.

"Just pretend you're licking a Popsicle." Flip laid his palm on her head and nudged it toward his penis. Jamie licked.

"Now pretend the Popsicle's melted down a little," he said, "and so you stick the whole thing in your mouth, you know, sucking it down to the stick so it doesn't drip on you."

Jamie followed his instructions while thinking about Taffy Longue, who had a reputation for being someone who loved to suck dicks. All the boys flirted with her, hoping she would suck them; all the girls snubbed her, claiming she was so slutty she'd suck Mr. Vandekamp, the pockmarked, potato-nosed eighth grade math teacher, if he'd let her.

After several seconds Jamie rested with her mouth open. Then Flip put his hands on the back of her head and thumped up into her face until he released a shocking burst of semen that Jamie swallowed without thinking. Was this what Taffy had been doing? Jamie wondered. Holding her jaw slack while boys blasted semen into her mouth? Jamie's throat spasmed as she wondered what the difference was now between herself and Taffy Longue. Was it simply the number they had each taken in?

"That was totally great." Flip pulled up Jamie and kissed her, his tongue flitting in and out of her mouth. "Now flip back."

"Huh?" Jamie was feeling nauseous and dreamy, as if she were floating away from the current reality.

"Flip back," he giggled. "Get it, *flip* back."

"Oh, yeah, like you, Flip."

"Yeah! You're going to *flip* back for Flip!"

Jamie lay back and put her knees up, grasshopper style. Flip planted his shoulders at her feet.

"Relax," he said, before ducking into her crotch. Flip lapped at Jamie like a poodle at sweaty toes, with ineffectual little licks.

Jamie stared at the beige, vinyl swirl-patterned wallpaper. She wondered if Brett's mother had chosen the wallpaper or if it just came with the mobile home. She wondered if Brett's parents had ever had oral sex in the mobile home. She wondered if Taffy Longue let the boys do this to her or if she just "ate and ran." Then she worried about what she would say to Flip—surely he would want to know if she was enjoying this. Could she tell him that taking a shower with a strong nozzle felt better than this? Could she tell him she would rather be sitting in the Abe Lincoln theater on Main Street in Disneyland? Could she tell him that just because she now did the things that Taffy Longue did she really wasn't anything like Taffy? Jamie would never wear a tube top to school, for example, or a terry-cloth shorts jumpsuit with the shorts no bigger than a pair of underpants. And Jamie would never write on the third stall of the C quad bathroom, "My Mother is a fucking Bitch and my father is a fucking Prick and they're fucking each other because they fucking deserve each other. Fuck them, Taffy." Jamie thought that graffiti was as destructive to a society as littering and all her friends could vouch for the fact that Jamie *never* littered!

"Feel good?" Flip mumbled into Jamie's crotch.

"Yup." Jamie looked at the door to the bathroom—it was so narrow! She wondered how obese people who owned mobile homes managed the doorway. Did they make special doors? Or did they just take the door off and squeeze into the bathroom bare butt first? And what about oral sex? Would an obese man's stomach obscure his penis so as to make oral sex impossible? Would a man performing oral sex an obese woman just lift her stomach, rest it on his head, and carry on?

"Think you're gonna come yet?" Flip asked. "'Cause my jaw's getting, like, totally tired."

"Yeah, any second." Tammy and Debbie had talked about coming. They talked about orgasms that made their toes shiver. Jamie shut her eyes and internally focused on her toes. Nothing was happening. And then she felt a stirring near Flip's mouth and she wondered if it was an orgasm peering out from deep inside somewhere, or if it was just that she had to pee. The urge became stronger and Jamie was convinced that if Flip went on much longer she might begin urinating right then, on his face, an act that would surely end their relationship and put her in the oral history books with the likes of Kenny Marino, who was caught masturbating against a tree in his backyard when a group of kids were cutting through his yard to a lemon orchard.

"I'm done!" Jamie put her hands on Flip's ears and lifted him like an urn.

Flip pushed up to Jamie's face and kissed her. He smelled chalky and slightly sour and Jamie couldn't help but think how odd it was that their genitals were now meeting through their mouths, each imbued with the other's juice.

"I gotta pee," Jamie said, and she went to the narrow door of the bathroom, opened it, and entered. Once inside she sat on the toilet and stared at her face in the mirror mounted over the sink. The urge to pee vanished.

"Don't be disappointed," she whispered to herself in the mirror. Then she looked at the stripes on the wallpaper and began to count them as if she were trying to lull herself to sleep, right there, on the toilet.

When Jamie returned to Flip he was sleeping, body spread limply across the sheets, one arm bent up by his head, the other sticking out as if he were pointing to the bathroom. Jamie put on her clothes, went to the kitchen, sat at the table, and turned on the TV. *The Munsters* was on channel 11. She watched, silent and still, wishing her head was as hollow and clanking as Herman Munster's so she could stop thinking about the ways in which her body would never be the same.

5

Jamie hoped Flip wouldn't be able to come to her parents' aura-reading party as there was a good chance it would eventually turn into a swim party. Lately, Jamie had come to realize that every moment with Flip was not perfect. The boredom of an isolated surfing beach with no friends wasn't perfect; the discomfort of Flip licking her in search of her orgasm, until she was as raw and swollen as a diaper-rashed baby, wasn't perfect; the idea of being with Flip while her parents frolicked naked wasn't perfect. But Flip called on the night of the event and said he could come, of course, as he had no more obligations that summer than Jamie did. Betty had slipped him the invitation one after-noon while Jamie was in the bathroom. Jamie said nothing to her mother about her discomfort with Flip's attending as Betty's and Allen's usual reaction to anything that caused their daughters embarrassment or shame was to boldly continue the embarrassing or shameful act in the hope that their daughters would become desensitized to it.

"There's really nothing to do," Betty told Flip, who showed up an hour early, offering to help out. Betty was standing in the kitchen wearing bell-bottom jeans and a maroon silk blouse, untucked, flowing.

"Mom hired caterers," Jamie said.

"Chumash," Betty said.

"Chumash?" Flip said. "That is totally gnarly. I didn't know Chumash catered."

"Chumash are beautiful people," Betty said.

"Chumash believe in four celestial gods," Jamie said.

Allen walked in. "Chumash are ripping me off," he said.

"No way," Flip said. "Chumash wouldn't rip anyone off."

"It costs a fortune to have Chumash. I don't know why your mother wants Chumash." Allen looked at Jamie as if she could explain. "Since when are Chumash known for their culinary skills?"

"Allen," Flip said, "it's way cool to hire Chumash. I mean, man, we *owe* them."

Allen looked over at Flip and contorted his mouth as if he'd just bitten into an orange seed.

"Thank god Renee's not here," Jamie said.

"Why don't you want your sister here?" Allen asked. "Your sister's a wonderful person."

"She thinks aura readings are fake," Jamie said. "Remember when you went to that aura reading at the Gants' house?"

"How could you fake an aura reading?" Betty said. "It's right there. You can see it."

"Does your sister have blond hair?" Flip asked. "I think I maybe remember seeing her at school."

"Black hair," Jamie said. Unlike her friends' homes, where framed photos of the family covered grand pianos and corner tables whose only apparent purpose was to hold frames, there were no pictures of Jamie and Renee displayed in the house. Jamie often felt that photos of her-self and Renee might be a good thing—something to remind her parents that they had two people in their charge, two people to keep track of, to come home for, to lock and unlock doors for.

"You know how you fake an aura reading?!" Allen said. "The same way you fake being a Chumash. If you say it, everyone believes it."

"I believe in the Chumash celestial gods," Jamie said, al-though she had never really thought about whether she be-lieved in them or not.

A knock sounded from the kitchen door. Betty gave hush-up eyes to everyone and went to let the caterers in.

Betty was overly friendly, as if she were making up for some past wrongdoing, as she showed the sturdy, thick woman and toreador-looking man around the kitchen. Allen, Flip, and Jamie watched.

"Well," Betty said, "let's let them do their stuff."

The lights were off and the living room was lit with can-dles perched on every flat surface: the grand piano, the windowsills, the coffee table, the hearth. Jamie had always found the living room a little ominous with its worn Persian rugs, black leather chairs, and massive unframed paintings. That night, lit only by candlelight, she thought it could have been a room in a haunted house. There were fifteen people, including Jamie and Flip, gathered in the room. The aura reader was blond, thin, German; she looked college-age but spoke with the authority of an old woman.

"I hope everyone remembered to wear a bathing suit—the only way to truly see the aura, is to see it reflected off bare skin." The aura reader slowly enunciated each word as if she were translating from German.

Lois went first. She stood in the center of the room wearing a baggy yellow bikini. Jamie thought she looked like a woman waiting for the doctor in an exam room. She was followed by a fat woman in a leotard, whose skin folded out at the arm and leg holes and looked as soft as underbaked dough. Then it was Betty's turn. She stood and removed her clothes until she was completely naked.

Jamie listened to Flip's breathing beside her; she felt his body growing tense. The aura reader walked slowly around Betty, bouncing her hands Marcel Marceau—style against an invisible contour.

"Beautiful," she said. "You have a beautiful deep orange aura."

Betty opened her mouth and smiled. She looked peaceful, so relaxed that one could almost forget she was naked. And Jamie did forget she was naked, until Flip took her hand and pushed it onto his crotch so she could feel his solid erection. Jamie jerked her hand away and fled into the kitchen.

Five minutes later, Flip joined Jamie in the kitchen.

"Hey," he said.

"Hey." Jamie was at the counter, eating a bowl of pineneedle soup the Chumash man had given her.

"Something wrong?"

She leaned into his ear and whispered, "You're grossing me out with the boner for my mom."

"That was for you!" Flip said.

"Pardon?" the Chumash lady said.

"So you're Chumash, huh?" Flip sat on the stool beside Jamie and smiled at the woman.

"I'm from Mexico," she said. "He's Chumash." She pointed at the man with her thumb.

"Cool," Flip said.

"You like Chumash?" the man asked.

"Chumash are cool," Flip said.

"Chumash used to own Santa Barbara," Jamie said.

"Mexico owned it once, too," the woman said.

"Now look who owns it!" the Chumash man said, and he laughed as a keg-bellied man, wearing only white cotton briefs, walked in with an empty wine glass.

When Jamie finished her soup, Flip insisted that they skip the rest of the aura reading and go out in the backyard to look at the stars. They settled in a patch of soft grass; Jamie folded her arms behind her head and sighed. She was baffled by moments when she didn't see absolute perfection in Flip. Before their first date Jamie couldn't imagine that anything Flip Jenkins did or said could be wrong or unappealing. But now, here in her backyard, he didn't seem like *Flip Jenkins*, he seemed like a Labrador who could think only about food, who would snap your half-eaten burger off your plate while you sneezed, who assumed everyone wanted him on their couch, or their bed, where he'd leave behind blankets of hair without once thinking about the person who had to clean that hair up.

Flip rolled over and mounted Jamie.

"I am so horny," he said. "I swear, I'm about to explode."

"Gross." Jamie pushed him off. "You're horny from seeing my naked mother!"

"No way," Flip said. "I swear, I was just sitting there and thinking about you standing in that room naked and thinking that maybe someday your bosoms would be as big as your mom's, and I swear, it was all thoughts of you and then I–" Flip began to grind against Jamie, reminding her uncomfortably of Tammy's black Lab, Tigger, who always tried to hump Jamie when she was on her period.

"Flip! You had an erection from my mom!"

Flip rolled back.

"Okay," he said. "So what? So what if I had an erection? Your mom has, like, totally awesome tits. How could I not have an erection?"

"She's my mom!"

"It's, like, so what? I mean, if you stuck a picture of some *Playboy* model in front me I'd probably get an erection, too. You don't understand dicks. Dicks think for themselves, okay? You see big juicy tits and your dick gets hard even if those tits belong to your girlfriend's mom, okay? I mean, fuck. I couldn't help it."

"Okay, that's fine. But I just can't fool around knowing that your boner started with my mother."

"Whoa," Flip said, and he sat up as he noticed Allen, wearing only his underpants, pacing around the pool.

Allen paused at the deep end, slipped off his briefs, and dove in.

"Please don't say anything about my dad's dick."

"I could barely see it from here, although it did look kinda bouncy."

"Please, Flip, please think about me for a second. I don't want to hear about my dad's dick." Jamie imagined Labrador Flip ripping open a Hefty bag, spewing wet, smoldering garbage on the floor as he searched for a stringy chicken bone while Jamie stood beside him scolding, No!

"Man, you don't have to worry about my boner anymore." Flip laughed.

Allen had pulled himself out of the pool and was staring over at Jamie and Flip, water skimming down his body. Flip waved.

"Allen!" Flip motioned for Allen to join them.

"Oh my god." Jamie turned her head.

Allen picked up a towel that was draped over a boulder and wrapped it around his waist.

"Your mother!" he said, as he loped toward them with his lopsided gait.

"Mom okay?" Jamie asked. Now that he was no longer naked, Jamie was relieved by her father's presence—it created a padding between herself and Flip.

Allen sat down and crossed his legs. Jamie and Flip sat up. They were in a circle, facing each other, like the kids who sat way out on the field at Jamie's school and smoked pot. The stoners.

"That Nazi in there said I had a selfish, yellow aura . . . anti-Semitic bitch!"

"Whoa, is she a Nazi?" Flip asked.

Allen looked over at him, then back at Jamie.

"Now your mother thinks I'm fooling around. She believes the *fräulein*."

"What's *fräulein*?" Jamie asked.

"Wait, is she a Nazi aura reader?" Flip asked.

"A *fräulein* is a young woman, in German."

"Is she a Nazi or not?" Flip said.

"No, she's too young to be a real Nazi," Allen said. "But she might be anti-Semitic."

"What's that?" Jamie asked.

"Jesus Christ . . ." Allen slapped his hand on his forehead. "How can you be my child? How can you have grown up in this house and not know what an anti-Semite is? Where did we go wrong?"

"Sorry, Dad." Jamie wondered if her father sometimes felt about her the way she currently felt about Flip: a startling disappointment.

"Have you ever heard me say those words before? Have

you ever heard the term? What about history class? Don't you get history class at school?"

"Last year we studied the California missions. And the Chumash."

"We studied the gold rush," Flip said.

"An anti-Semite is someone who hates Jews," Allen said.

"Are there Jews in there?" Flip asked.

"I'm a Jew!" Allen said. "Jamie's a Jew!"

"Whoa, is that why you guys have bagels in your house?" Bagels were so foreign to Flip that he pronounced the word with a soft *a*.

"We have bagels because I bring them back from Los Angeles, where you can actually buy bagels. I mean, can you believe a town like this, all these fancy people, all this money, and you can't even buy a bagel here?"

"Dad, I'm only a half Jew. Mom's an atheist."

"If the Nazis started exterminating again, you'd be dead. That's all you need to know."

"So you think the German gave you a bad aura reading because you're a Jew?" Flip asked.

"Eh . . ." Allen didn't seem angry anymore. "She probably just thought she had to pick someone from the crowd to have a bad aura and she randomly picked me."

"You think she's making it up?" Jamie asked.

"Sweetheart," Allen said, "your mother's probably the only person in that room who thinks the German can really see auras."

"I bet Leon and Lois believe it."

"I believe it," Flip said.

"Yeah, you'd believe it until she told you that you had a selfish penis and that your selfish penis was carrying shadows from the auras of many other people, from all the people your penis had encountered."

"Whoa," Flip said, "you mean she could see all the women you'd been with?"

"But I haven't been with anyone but Betty!" Allen was angry again.

"You mean she was your first?" Flip asked.

"Flip! Dad! I don't want to hear this!"

"Why are you acting like your sister?"

"Dad, please, I really don't want to know how many people you've been with."

"But it isn't that many. It's nothing to be embarrassed about." Allen reached out and gently patted Jamie's knee.

"Dad, I just–"

"I could see being embarrassed if I were someone like Leon. I mean he's been with hundreds of women, women from all over the world!"

"Has he ever been with a *lady of the night*?" Flip asked, and he leaned forward, resting his elbows on his knees.

"Oh, yeah." Allen shook his head and smiled.

"How does that work?" Flip asked. "Like, do you pay ahead of time? And where do you find someone like that here, in Santa Barbara?"

"I'm going inside." Jamie stood and walked toward the house. She couldn't believe she was actually walking away from Flip Jenkins, walking away from the boy every girl she knew would be happy to lose her virginity to, even Lisa Blair, the most devout member of the Christian Fellowship Club, who told Jamie at the beach one day that she would give up her love of Christ if she could be as lucky as Jamie and have the love of Flip Jenkins. Jamie looked back over her shoulder and watched her father and Flip together. Flip was nodding, seemingly interested in whatever her dad was saying. The moon lit the top of Flip's head so that he appeared to be glowing. He smiled and his teeth flashed like lightning in a dark sky. Jamie imagined Lisa Blair, with her thick hair that hung like a groomed horse tail, tossing her Bible and a bikini into the ocean so she could press her naked body against Flip. Jamie changed the channel in her head, put her own naked body in Flip's arms, and then, just like that, her love was back. She ran into the house before it had time to wane again, before she could let herself imagine Flip in the arms of whoever might be next in line.

Late that night, after Flip and Allen went skinny-dipping together, after Jamie ate two more bowls of pine-needle soup with hard flat bread in the kitchen while talking to the Chumash and his Mexican girlfriend, after Flip gave Jamie a tender, chaste kiss good night, she went to bed and fell asleep to the melodic sounds of the few remaining people at the party. Sometime later, in the middle of a dream, Betty floated into Jamie's room. She stood naked beside the bed, peering down at her daughter.

"Hey Mom," Jamie said.

"Scoot in," Betty said.

Jamie scooted toward the wall. Betty slipped under the covers.

"Your dad and I had a fight," she said.

"You sleeping with me?" Jamie asked. As a young girl, Jamie had loved to sleep with her parents. From around the age of twelve, however, she had begun to dread the uninvited physical intimacy.

"Uh-huh." Betty rolled to her side, pushed her rump out toward her daughter, and yanked the covers over her shoulder. Jamie yanked the covers back and crossed her arms over her chest as if she were cold.

"Why don't you sleep in the guest room, or in Renee's bed?"

"You know I hate to sleep alone. It's unnatural. We're animals, we need to sleep in packs, in litters."

Jamie sighed and shifted closer to the wall. "So how was your aura reading?"

"Great. My aura is loving and generous, all deep oranges and whites—good energy." Betty flipped onto her back and pushed her leg out until her foot rested on Jamie's.

"Dad's wasn't so good, right?"

"He's got some things to work out."

"What exactly did she say?" Jamie pulled her foot out from under her mother's foot and crossed her ankles. She wished there were such thing as a bed divider: a metal plank that would cut the bed in two, creating a small wall through which her mother's naked body could not pass.

"Your father has a selfish penis, dear." Betty scooted closer to Jamie so their thighs were aligned, touching. Thin snakes of nausea ran from Jamie's legs to her gut.

"You mean separate from him? So, it's not like he's selfish, it's just that his penis is selfish?"

"Yes."

"So it *does* think on its own!" Jamie started giggling.

"It's not funny. He listens to his penis. The penis wants certain things and he listens to it."

"Mom, can you please scoot over? I'm getting claustrophobia."

"Are you naked?" Betty turned her head and looked at Jamie without scooting away.

"No! I'm in a T-shirt and underwear."

"You should sleep naked. Or at least without underwear. You know, give your vagina some air every now and then."

Jamie didn't want her mother to be the person Renee wanted her to be, but she often wished that Betty wasn't so comfortable discussing Jamie's anatomy. A couple years back, when Jamie had first indicated that she was ready to try a tampon, Betty burst into Jamie's bathroom one day, holding an open Tampax that she, herself, wanted to insert into her daughter to free her from the bonds of the belted pad. Jamie had snatched the tampon from her mother and violently shoved it in herself, lest her mother get there first. She quickly pulled up her underpants and refused to let Betty look to make sure it was in properly. It wasn't. Five minutes later Jamie snuck into Renee's bathroom, where she removed the dangling, dry tampon and put on her elastic bra strap–like waist belt that held up the brick-shaped pad.

"Mom, back to what you were saying before–are you thinking that Dad's having an affair?" Although the subject matter was, Jamie thought, overly intimate, she preferred talk of her father's selfish penis to matters of her own body.

"I don't really know. Maybe he is. Or maybe it's just that he might have an affair in the future. Or maybe it's the fact that he could have an affair. He has a penis that would lead him to an affair."

"I don't see it."

"Why not?"

"Who would want to sleep with him? He's so skinny and white."

"Your father is a very handsome man!"

"To you, maybe. But Mom, face it, it's not like girls are lining up to be with Dad."

"You've got it all wrong. Women my age think your father is very attractive."

"Dad is not attractive. Flip is attractive." Jamie pulled her leg away from her mother's and bent it at the knee, making a small triangular barrier between herself and her mother.

"Flip's okay," Betty said.

"Okay? He was Luscious Lester, Mom. He was voted the most luscious guy in school."

"I think his friend Jimmy is cuter."

"You think Jimmy's cuter than Flip?"

"Jimmy's sexy. He's sensuous. Jimmy's . . . ah, god, to be in high school again."

The idea that her mother might actually fantasize about Flip's friends made Jamie's stomach lurch. She was glad she couldn't read minds—she didn't want to know what images were pooling in the nooks and recesses of her mother's brain. It seemed much better just to skim across the surface of Betty's thoughts, move quickly enough not to pick up too much of the stuff that was seeping out from her inner life.

"Mom, please. Please don't talk about Flip's friends like you really want to be with them."

"I'm human, Jamie. I'm alive."

"You know, Dad, who has the allegedly selfish penis, would never say something like that. Maybe the aura reader got it all wrong."

"She was trained at a prestigious school in Vienna. She sees things you and I can't see."

"Just like you see things in Flip's friends."

"Jamie, everyone can see how sexy Jimmy is."

"Mom. You're married. And you're old." Why was her mother still even thinking about sex? Jamie wondered. Didn't the urge die down after a couple of kids, wither up the way lips and breasts eventually did? Or were her mother's plump, unwithered parts proof that Betty had years to go before she dried up?

"I'm not old, for godsakes. And I'm married to a man with a selfish penis."

"Okay. Whatever."

"Are you having sex?"

"Me? Mom!" Jamie rushed her hands to her cheeks as if to protect herself.

"I just want to check. You don't have to be ashamed."

"NO! There's nothing to check!" Jamie prayed that by "check" her mother did not mean that she intended to examine her hymen. "God! I'm going to sleep. Good night."

"I don't see why you're upset, sweetheart. Listen, there's something I've been meaning to tell you since puberty."

"I know how babies are made, I've already got my period, and I know how to use a tampon." Jamie squeezed her eyes shut as if that would convince her mother that she was sleeping.

"Of course you know how to use a tampon, I was the one who taught you!"

Jamie shook herself in a deliberate shudder as she tried to repel the memory.

"So I know all, Mom," Jamie said.

"Sweetheart." Betty turned to her side, facing Jamie. With her left hand, she pulled Jamie's arm so it was straight and stroked the inside, up and down, just the way Joseph from the pizza parlor had done. Jamie yanked her arm away and crossed it over her chest.

"What do you want to tell me?" She hoped that directly asking her mother would get the conversation over quickly.

"I just want to say that I hope you know, I mean really know and understand, that's it's okay to please yourself."

"Please myself? Mom, I'm happy. I'm plenty pleased."

"No, I mean *please* yourself sensuously. Sexually."

Jamie could feel her body contracting, everything pulling in toward her core, like a sea anemone shutting itself closed to intruders. "Okay Mom, I don't want to talk about this. Let's go to sleep."

"Jamie, it's important to me that you feel free to masturbate."

"Gotcha. Good night." Jamie wondered if her mother would ever lose interest in the discreet workings of Jamie's body. Would Betty be there at the birth of Jamie's first child, shoving her mothering hands into Jamie's vaginal canal and yanking out her grandchild? And would that grandchild be another body to probe and examine as if it were a curious mole on Betty's own flesh?

"It's an important part of developing your sexuality, figuring out who you are, what you like. I mean, it would be a shame if you didn't do it."

"Mom, I do not want to tell you whether I do it or not. I'm glad you want me to be happy, but I really don't want to talk about this. And I want to go to sleep." Jamie considered climbing out of bed and moving into the guest bedroom but she figured her mother would follow her.

"Jesus. You sound like your sister."

"Maybe when my sister's not around to say these things, I have to say them." Jamie really was starting to sound like her sister and she didn't like it. But there seemed to be no other way out of the conversation.

"Oh for chrissakes. I'm trying to help you out here and you start acting like Renee. Good night."

Betty rolled to her side again and pushed her butt up against Jamie's thigh. Jamie rolled over while trying to pull in her behind so that it wouldn't touch her mother's. Betty scooted back more, almost pinning her daughter against the wall. Jamie gave up and lay there, wide awake, listening to the soft ocean sounds of Betty sleeping. She had recently given up her fear of becoming Taffy Longue, the Blowjob Queen, and now she had masturbation to fret about instead. She wondered if she were downright prudish, like Tammy's mother or the women who served coffee at Tammy's church, for not wanting to try it. But how could she? How could she ever do it without hearing her mother's voice or feeling her mother's warm damp rump stuck against her own?

6

On the third of July, the day before a planned camping trip at El Capitán Beach, Debbie organized a bus trip to Planned Parenthood, where the three girls watched a movie about pregnancy and venereal diseases before being fitted with diaphragms. Tammy had been convinced that the diaphragm wasn't forbidden by the Bible when Debbie informed her that Lisa Blair, who lately had been trying to recruit Tammy and Debbie for the Christian Fellowship Club, used a diaphragm. Debbie knew this from Jimmy, who had had sex with Lisa several times the previous summer. Tammy begged Debbie and Jamie to choose the diaphragm, too, as she didn't want to feel like she was the only teenager in Santa Barbara (besides Lisa Blair) who was using one, and they obliged.

The nurse at Planned Parenthood had seemed surprised when Jamie admitted to her that, unlike her friends, she had yet to have intercourse. She instructed Jamie that just because she had the diaphragm didn't mean she had to start having sex.

"Maybe I'll put it off until school starts," Jamie had

said confidently. "My boyfriend said he'd wait until I was ready."

What Jamie didn't tell the nurse was that her two best friends put far more pressure on her than her boyfriend ever did. Debbie and Tammy agreed that if Jamie didn't have sex with Flip soon, he would go looking for it else-where. There were too many girls in town who were ripe and willing, they claimed, so how long, really, would he wait? (Jamie wondered if Flip had a selfish penis. And then she wondered how she could possibly have sex with some-one whose penis aura was similar to, or the same as, her father's.) Additionally, Tammy and Debbie insisted that by not having sex Jamie was missing out on something as elec-trifying and intense as love itself.

Flip's VW bus raised and lowered like a camel as they cruised over speed bumps leading into the beach park. It was while they were going over a bump like that when Jamie said it.

"I'm ready to go all the way."

"Really?" Flip smiled.

"Definitely. I think." Yes, yes, yes, Jamie repeated in her head. She was trying to convince herself that if she were to have sex it would be like doubling up the love—folding over the emotion so that it was sandwiched into a more pure and tangy passion.

"On our nation's two hundredth birthday."

"Yeah, how cool is that?" Jamie smiled because she read once that if you smile even when you don't feel it, the feel-ing will come. And it wasn't that she was particularly un-happy just then. She was just uncomfortable and afraid of the finality of the act. Once her virginity was gone, it would be gone forever. A death of a sort.

"So tonight's the night." Flip put his hand on Jamie's leg and clamped down. "And I'm glad we're going to do it before I leave for Hawaii. I mean, you totally wouldn't want me wandering around the big island all horny and shit."

"No," Jamie said, and then she felt as though it had been confirmed: Flip, too, had a selfish penis. "And I think it's better to get it over with before my sister gets home. I don't want to do it for the first time when she's around." This occurred to Jamie only as she said it.

"God, I just wish I could remember your sister. It would make it so much easier when I first see her at the house and all."

"I've shown you pictures." Jamie focused on the photo album she had shown Flip in an effort to distract herself from her worries. She tried to remember the pictures in the order they appeared, the captions Betty had written beneath them in slanted block print.

"Yeah, but I don't remember ever seeing her at school. I mean, like, I only know her from those pictures and I can't even remember them now. She has blond hair, right?"

"Black," Jamie said.

"Right, that's what I meant. Black."

"So what should we do about birth control?" Jamie had left the diaphragm at home in a fit of anxious indecision.

"I'll pull out," Flip said.

"Okay, but don't forget." Jamie imagined herself pregnant, then blinked hard and tried to refocus on the photo album.

"This is so totally cool." Flip reached up and squeezed Jamie's left breast as if he were pumping a turkey baster. "A cherry-popping on the Fourth of July!"

"Yeah, sounds cool." *April is the cruellest month,* Jamie saw in her head, under a photo of herself and Renee standing in the rain with mud splattered up their bare legs.

Flip smiled, moved his hand to her thigh, and said, "You'll love it, I swear."

Tammy, Debbie, and Jamie lay close together on the crowded beach. There were more than three times the usual number of people there, as everyone was waiting for the Fourth of July fireworks. The girls were eating with their hands from a carton of melted butter pecan ice cream. Jamie had taken the carton from her house along with a rectangle of Cheddar cheese, a box of Wheat Thins, and two bananas her mother handed her as she walked out the door. Debbie's and Tammy's mothers had been told their daughters were sleeping at Jamie's house. Jamie had to reassure Betty that she wouldn't have to lie on their behalf by pointing out that Tammy's and Debbie's mothers had each called the house only once all summer, even though they both spent hours on the phone each day.

Jamie passed the ice cream carton to Tammy and said, "I'm going to go all the way tonight."

Tammy gasped with her fingers in her mouth.

"Really?" Debbie asked.

"Yeah. I mean, you both have been saying that it's time for me catch up, grow up a little, right?"

"Well, you've got to keep up with Flip," Tammy said, and she patted Jamie's hand like a mother, which, in fact, made Jamie feel like a child.

"It was kinda scary at first but, I swear, it's totally fun now," Debbie said.

"I'm worried that it's going to ruin something," Jamie said. "I don't want anything to change. I don't want to change."

"You won't change," Tammy said. "I mean, like, do we seem any different to you?"

"Not really," Jamie said, although they both had seemed different to her since they started having sex. Cooler. Slower, in a way.

Tammy leaned in and hugged Jamie. "I'm so happy I'm going to be with you on this important night!"

Jamie walked out to the water to rinse the ice cream off her hands, wrists, and chest. Flip was out past the breaking waves, sitting up on his surfboard, bobbing like a duck. How odd, she thought, that within hours, his penis is going to be in my vagina. And then she thought, What's the big deal with that?

The beach grew even more crowded as the sun went down. Families gathered with blankets, pillows, children in pyjamas, and picnic dinners, everyone preparing to watch the bigger-than-ever *bicentennial* fireworks. Many people brought shovels to dig sitting holes in the sand, just as they did during grunion hunting. Jamie and her pals were too cool for fireworks on the beach. They decided they'd watch them from the campsite, a club of six with enough beer for a club of sixty. The girls collected the towels, magazines, and empty ice cream carton and walked up to the campsite, which was buried in the trees on the cliff that met the water. They had sleeping bags but no tents. Brett's truck and Flip's bus were backed into the dirt parking spot beside the campsite. The surfboards were piled into the back of the truck and the food was on the backseat of the bus, making the cars home base. There were many other people camping out that night; they were hidden behind the brushy tree barriers, making themselves known by their portable radios and the smell of their fires burning in the cement block grills that marked each site like a giant tombstone.

The boys built a fire and the girls prepared dinner. Debbie handled the steaks while Jamie broke Cheddar cheese into golf-ball-sized hunks that she stuck on American flag paper plates (Tammy had stolen the plates from the cupboard where her mother hoarded her holiday party supplies) with a stack of Wheat Thins. Tammy opened beers and passed out flag napkins (also stolen from her mother) all the while balancing a burning cigarette in her right hand.

"No fork?" Flip asked, staring at his plate with the slab of meat Debbie had just slapped down on it.

"We didn't bring any," Jamie said.

"I'm cooking these with my hands!" Debbie said. "Have you ever turned a steak over with your hands?!"

"If she can cook it with her hands, you can eat it with your hands," Jimmy said, and he lifted up his wedge of steak, dangled it over his mouth, and gnawed off a bite.

By the time the fireworks erupted, Jamie had consumed so much meat, cheese, and beer that the falling explosions made her dizzy. Debbie unzipped her sleeping bag and laid it on the ground so they could lie down and look up at the brilliant sky. In spite of her vertigo, Jamie thought the fireworks were more brilliant than any she'd seen before—bigger, louder; they filled the sky like a million colored beads being dropped from a star.

The boys didn't lie down. They threw rocks at empty beer bottles they had lined up on the edge of the grill—moving farther and farther back to make the game more complicated until they were obscured behind the bushes that separated their campsite from the one beside them.

All the girls could see of them were the colorless stones that whizzed over their heads and plinked against the green Heineken bottles.

When the fireworks were long over and the boys had settled onto the quilt of sleeping bags with the girls, Jamie decided that it was time.

"I'm ready," she said to Flip, stifling a burp. He stood so quickly he almost stumbled backward. Then he grabbed a blanket from the back of the bus, took Jamie's hand, and they walked down to the beach.

There were small piles of people hanging around here and there, but most of the sand pits were empty, making the beach look like the pock-marked moon.

"I don't want anyone to see us," Jamie said. "I mean, what if some pervert starts watching us?"

They walked to where the rocks jutted out from the cliff, almost, but not quite, meeting the pounding waves. There was no one there, and the closest people were so far away that they could barely make out their murky forms in the dark.

Flip led Jamie into a niche between two giant rocks. Jamie held on to the back of Flip's shirt as she followed behind; she felt as if she were walking into a crack in the earth that was sure to swallow her up. Flip flapped the blanket in the air, like he was airing it out, then gently laid it on the sand. It didn't seem to come out straight, so he picked up the blanket and flapped it again, and again, until three corners lay flat. He pushed the forth down with his foot.

It had been scorching hot all day, with the bright sun bleaching everything so that the whole world appeared to be a washed blue; but by sunset it had grown cool, as if the thick ocean fog had swallowed the heat. Flip lay down on the blanket and waited. Jamie stood over him, surveying the scene as her eyes adjusted. In uncontrollable exaggeration, Jamie's teeth clattered and she shivered.

"There were so many people partying tonight, there's probably broken glass down here," she said.

"Don't worry, we're on the blanket," Flip said. "Just don't roll off the blanket."

"What if you put the blanket down on a jagged piece of glass and it breaks through while we're doing it and stabs me in the back and kills me, and you don't even realize it because you're so caught up in the moment?"

"Then I guess I'd be a necrophiliac," Flip said, and then he started to sing a little song that Jamie had been hearing boys sing since around sixth grade. *My name is Jack, Jack, Jack. I'm a necrophiliac, ac, ac. I love them dead, dead, dead. . . .*

Jamie stood there, each of her hands holding the opposite arm. She looked around and studied the crumbling sides of the rocks and the bumpy sand, littered with leafy orange strands of kelp that reminded her of hair off a giant mermaid.

"What if there's an earthquake? What if there's an earthquake and the whole side of this cliff collapses on top of us and we're smashed under these rocks, but we don't die. We just lie there stranded and stuck, unable to wedge ourselves out while sand crabs creep into our butt cracks and we bleed to death from our dented, ravaged heads."

"There won't be an earthquake." Flip grunted in a voice of impatience. "There hasn't been an earthquake in, like, months."

"All the more reason there'd be one now," Jamie said,

and she turned to run out from the rocks when Flip stood, grabbed her arms, and kissed her hard, like he was drilling for oil with his tongue.

They lay on the blanket and took off their clothes. Jamie gave herself a pep talk as she tried to think thoughts like, *I'm on a beautiful beach on the bicentennial Fourth of July with a gorgeous, popular guy who loves me, and this is the most beautiful night of my life.* She could barely complete a single thought, however, without her focus switching to her stomach, which suddenly felt like an overinflated tire. Jamie wished Flip would leave long enough for her to burp. Then she realized she would rather have left herself, as she still wasn't convinced that there weren't deadly shards of glass under the blanket or that the cliff wasn't waiting to unglue itself in order to crush them.

Flip positioned himself on top of Jamie and said, "Okay, I'm totally going to do it now, I love you."

Jamie said, "I love you too."

Flip pushed, and he pushed, and he banged himself against her. It was like trying to pop a balloon with a spoon. And then his penis was a little ways in, not halfway, maybe a third, or a quarter even. As he pushed Jamie could tell it wasn't working; it felt as if his penis were bending back and forth while Flip went up and down.

Flip's mouth was on Jamie's, pretending to kiss, in what Jamie guessed was an obligatory way to let a girl know that you don't like her just for the sex. Her gums became sore from the pressure; she felt like he was pinning her down with his mouth. Flip was grunting, sweating, and squinting as if he were trying to read an eye chart. Jamie worried about the burp in her stomach; she wondered if Flip's penis hurt when it bent like that; she wondered how old her mother was the first time she had sex. She also wondered about the building discomfort in her stomach—was it from the weight of Flip, or was she truly getting nauseous?

And then she knew that it was nausea, so she wedged her head out from under Flip's and said, "Flip, I think I'm gonna be sick."

"Huh?" Flip pumped at the barrier in Jamie's vagina.

"I'm gonna be sick." Jamie pushed him off and ran toward the water.

A wave rolled up and covered her feet; the chill was startling. Jamie lurched forward and vomited in one foaming stream the color of beer, the consistency of Chunky Soup, the smell of unaired garbage. Jamie coughed and sputtered a bit, then cleared her throat the way her father did during allergy season. At first she hoped that Flip couldn't hear her, but then she felt so deflated and thin, like an empty sock hanging on a clotheline, that she just didn't care.

Jamie wiped the vomit from her lips with the back of her hand and then quickly dipped her hand into the lapping water, rubbing her forearm against the gritty sand. A couple was strolling down the beach. Jamie gathered herself up and ran to Flip before the couple could reach her.

Back at the blanket, Flip directed Jamie down so she was on her back again. He wedged his tongue into her mouth and resumed the pummeling.

Jamie's eyes were running and a chunk of vomit dangled in the back of her throat. She wondered if Flip could taste her barf. She wondered how long this would take. She wondered if Tammy and Debbie had been lying to her about how good this was supposed to feel. And she wondered, most of all, why instead of things getting better as she progressed in sex (kissing, fondling, finger banging, oral sex, sex), they seemed to get worse.

Flip groaned and released a thick stream of sticky liquid onto Jamie's belly. Jamie ignored the puddle, sat up, and rushed to get her clothes on.

"It'll get better," Flip said. "It'll be easier next time, you'll see." He leaned over and kissed her again just as she was swallowing down that wayward chunk of barf.

"Let's go back to the others." Jamie stood and waited for Flip at the edge of the rock.

Flip wrapped his arm around Jamie as they walked back to the campground. Their steps were out of sync and they bumped into each other, Jamie's hand hopelessly bouncing around Flip's waist, as they staggered silently down the beach.

Back at the campsite, Flip drank so much beer that he tripped on a rock and fell onto the fire pit of the barbeque. Everyone jumped up in a panic and Flip rolled in the dirt even though the flames had failed to catch him. The near-burning gave the group a sense of elation and joy, the euphoria that usually follows survival of near-death experiences. They became louder, more active, like animals infused with a whiff of prey. Debbie opened a new bag of potato chips and began breaking handfuls in her palm before shoveling them into her mouth. Tammy held a mouthful of beer in her open mouth, then added potato chips so she could taste the full salt-fizz. And the boys took turns jumping onto the edge of the barbeque and standing, legs splayed, over the licking flames so they could feel a surge of manhood as they risked burning their balls.

Jamie sat alone on a sleeping bag, watching. She felt as if she were trapped behind a panel of one-way glass: she could see through to her friends, but when they looked toward her, all they saw was themselves.

Tammy and Debbie eventually staggered over to Jamie and sat on either side of her.

"I'm so wasted," Tammy said, "that I forgot you just lost your virginity!"

Debbie laughed as she crumbled more chips to put in her mouth.

"Well?" Tammy said. "Did you have an orgasm?"

"Did he make noises?" Debbie asked. "Jimmy always sounds like a puppy, you know, like he's whining to come in the house or something."

"Did it hurt?" Tammy asked.

"I didn't really feel anything." Jamie lowered her voice, even though the boys weren't listening and were too far away to hear.

"Are you sure he was in?" Debbie asked.

"I think so," Jamie said. "But it just felt like, I dunno, like a too big tampon that I couldn't quite get in."

"So he wasn't in?" Tammy said.

"Does it feel good for you every single time?" Jamie asked.

"Pretty much," Debbie said, and she looked up at Jimmy, waving to him as he stood in a victory pose over the fire.

"I have at least two orgasms every time," Tammy said. "I swear."

"Maybe it wasn't really in," Jamie said. "'Cause there was no way I was going to have anything even close to an orgasm. In fact, I barfed."

There was a beat of silence, then Debbie asked, "What do you mean you barfed? Like, while you were doing it?"

"I got up and barfed in the ocean, then went back to the blanket and finished the act."

"That is so sad!" Debbie laughed.

"It was the beer, not the sex," Jamie said.

"That is just so sad!" Debbie couldn't stop laughing. "Barfing on your first time!"

"Maybe it wasn't my first time. Maybe it wasn't quite in, so it doesn't count or something." Jamie thought of her first attempted tampon, trailing halfway out of her like a strange, white tail.

"Wasn't quite in?" Tammy said. "When you really want to do it, it just slips in. I swear."

"Well, it doesn't always slip in, but it goes in easy enough," Debbie said.

"You have *got* to relax." Tammy pulled a cigarette from the pocket of her sweatshirt and lit it with a red Bic. "You have to go with the flow."

"Ride with the tide," Jamie continued the quote from a Carly Simon and James Taylor song.

And then Tammy and Debbie began singing "Mocking-bird" with Tammy doing the Carly part and Debbie doing the James part. They were bumping their shoulders against Jamie, clapping their hands, and were so involved with the singing that each batted her eyes shut every time she held a note for more than a second.

Flip seemed to have forgotten about Jamie since they returned to the campsite. He was sewn together with Brett and Jimmy: the three of them bouncing off one another and the invisible web that bound them into a three-foot radius surrounding the fire.

"Sing with us!" Tammy poked Jamie in the side.

Jamie smiled and rocked her body back a little as if she

would start singing. She wanted to fake the fun, like forcing a smile, in the hope that it would bring a genuine fun feeling, but she was so stunned with an empty nonfeeling that she couldn't even pretend.

Around three in the morning, the girls organized the sleeping bags, the exposed parts of which were already wet with a velvety layer of dew. They zipped Debbie's and Jimmy's sleeping bags together as one, so it was like a sleeping bag double bed; and they rolled up Tammy's and Brett's sleeping bags, so they could take them down to the beach to sleep. Jamie's and Flip's sleeping bags remained where they were, in the dirt, near the fire. Flip peed on the embers, stretched, burped, and then climbed into his sleeping bag and slipped into unconsciousness.

Staring past the glow of the grill, Jamie could see that Debbie and Jimmy were having sex. Jamie tried to make out Debbie's face; she wanted to know if it really felt good to her, if it was truly as wonderful as she had said.

The fire turned to dust and the night settled cold on Jamie's nose and cheeks. Flip made small choking sounds and jerked in his sleep, as if he were receiving an occasional electrical shock. Debbie and Jimmy were a giant, still mound, like a green and brown waterproof bear.

Jamie was awake. She wanted to go home and lie snug beneath her chenille bedspread and stare at the light wedging under her bedroom door, reminding her that her father was wandering around the house in his pajamas, or eating cheese and apple slices in his office while he typed up business plans for huge corporations that were mere ideas to Jamie, names that she heard across the dinner table. Her desire to be home was so great that she thought that even if her naked mother scooted into bed with her and talked about things she shouldn't be revealing (that her father was a flirt, that Renee was immature for her age, that marriage could be tiring) she would be happier than she was at that moment. More than anything, Jamie wanted to wake up in the morning to the thick, smoky smell of breakfast cooking. Breakfast was the least-complicated meal in her household; her mother was always happy to make it and everyone, even Renee, was happy to sit at the kitchen counter and eat it.

Jamie imagined that she could rewind time and restart at any moment she chose. She would stop just before the trip to Disneyland, on a day when she and Flip kissed for two hours on the beach. He didn't touch her within the bounds of her bathing suit, she touched only his back; it was thrilling.

7

In the week before Flip left for Hawaii, Jamie and Flip had sex seven times. Each time, Jamie lay on the backseat of the VW bus or on a bed (his or hers, depending on whose parents were out of the house), lifted her legs into flesh triangles, and waited for something to happen while Flip bounced himself against her. Intercourse was no longer uncomfortable or scary to Jamie, it was simply something she willingly endured. Often Jamie found herself bored during sex and so she invented a little song that she repeated in her head to the rhythm of Flip's movements. *I am in love, my heart soars to Venus, even as Flip pummels me with his penis.* As Flip increased speed, so did her song, so that by the end Jamie was merely imagining sounds pushed together into solid Germanic words, like in the final round of the camp song "Do Your Ears Hang Low." *Iminlove myheartsoarstoVenus evenasFlipummelsme withispenis.*

At the end of their final encounter before he left for his family vacation, Flip said, "When I get home we're going to go totally crazy, okay? *You* are going to be on top!"

The idea of being on top haunted Jamie from that moment on. What would she look like sitting there? What exactly would she do? These were Jamie's thoughts as her parents walked into the house with her cousin Jan, who was carrying a large, blue, plastic suitcase.

Jan had acne that looked like hot pepper flakes that you shake from a can in a pizza parlor. Jamie knew the acne wasn't Jan's fault, or her choice, but she held it against her anyway. And she blamed her for the intricate silver headgear that was attached to her mouth like scaffolding for Barbie. And her clothes, which had been purchased at Ames (pronounced *aim-zez* by Jan) and were so thick and raspy that you could have lit a match by scratching it across her knee. And her unyielding size—Jan was Betty's height with a few extra New Hampshire pounds packed on.

Betty had left New England when she went away to college. In the years since college, she had returned to her family home only twice: once for her sister Ginny's wedding, and once for her father's funeral. So the only time Jamie saw Jan was when her aunt shipped her out for an annual summer visit, or on the occasional Christmas when she, her mother, Ginny, her older brother, Donny, and her father, Fritz, flew out for a week. Because Jan and Jamie were the same age, Betty and Allen gave Jamie the job of host. Because Jan believed that everyone in California was hipper, prettier, and wittier than everyone else in the world, Jamie and her friends were like celebrities to Jan.

Renee was still away at Outward Bound, so her bedroom and the guest bedroom were both unoccupied. But Jan wanted to sleep in Jamie's room, as she always had, in Jamie's double bed with Jamie. As soon as she said this Jamie flashed on an image of herself and Flip having sex in the bed, the gritty stains he left behind, the tennis-shoe smell of his sweat on her pillow.

Allen had paused at the stair landing with Jan's suitcase dangling like a giant anvil from one hairy hand. Betty, Jan, and Jamie were clustered at the base of the steps, looking up toward Allen.

"So should I put it in Jamie's room?" Allen asked.

"But I kick in my sleep now," Jamie said. "Put it in the guest room."

"I don't care if you kick." Jan spoke in the slow drawl of a hound dog, if a hound dog were to speak. "We always sleep fine together."

"I'm different now," Jamie said, and she knew it was true. "I'd worry about kicking and I wouldn't be able to sleep."

"But you've always had so much fun in bed together," Betty said. "Staying up late telling secrets!"

Jan clapped her hands and did a little jump. Betty trained her eyes on her daughter; Jamie could read her mind and was not pleased with what her mother was saying.

"We did always have fun but this summer is different. I worry more; I'll be nervous about the kicking." Since she had started having sex, Jamie's sense of space, of the invisible barrier between herself and others, was more acute, more sensitive to invasion. She did not want Jan's body rolling near hers in her bed. No matter what.

"I could sleep on the floor next to your bed."

There was a hollow silence. An invisible thread cast out from Jamie's heart and hooked into her father's heart. He felt the double tug, the signal to pull her up out of the water.

"I'm going to put you in the guest room, Jan," Allen said.

"That way Jamie will sleep well and she'll have more energy to entertain you this week."

"You could get in bed with her at night," Betty added, "have your girl talk, and then, when you start falling asleep, you could move into the guest room."

"Great!" Jan said. Even when enthusiastic, Jan couldn't shed the hound-dog twang.

Everyone knew Jan would eat thirds at dinner that night; to her a single serving was always dished out three times over. Betty cooked mashed potatoes, dried corn chowder, and steak. She called it New Hampshire food, the food of her childhood, but really, it was the kind of food Jamie's friend's mothers prepared (although not the kind of food her mother's friends prepared). There was white bread with butter on the table. Jamie ate half the loaf, Jan ate the other half. According to Betty, white bread fell into the same food group as doughnuts, so was as coveted by Jamie as a chocolate eclair.

Betty shoved a few family questions at Jan, who answered in such a flat, vague way that Jamie wondered if Jan even knew the people Betty was asking about. Later, when Betty was bubbling over the color of her nephew Donny's eyes, and why hadn't any of her children gotten those eyes, Jan said, "I guess I never noticed the color of his eyes."

"Well, what have you noticed about him?" Betty took a sip of wine as if to cover for her abruptness.

"I don't know," Jan said.

"Anything you can tell us about your brother?" Allen asked.

"Donny's got a big truck. And it bumps a lot."

"Probably got a gun rack on the back, right?" Allen said.

"Probably," Jan said. "But I don't remember."

"Now that he's seventeen, I bet he's never around," Betty said.

"No, he's around all the time," Jan said. "Mom always tells him he should leave the house for some air every now and then."

"Did Jamie tell you she has a boyfriend?" Betty asked. "I think he's seventeen, too."

"He is," Jamie said.

"Cool," Jan said.

"He's in Hawaii with his family for two weeks," Jamie said, "so you won't get to meet him."

"Flip's seventeen?" Allen asked.

"Yeah," Jamie said.

"No one told me he's seventeen. How old are you?" Allen was hunched over his plate, holding a forkful of mashed potatoes midair.

"She's fourteen," Betty said.

"And you have a seventeen-year-old boyfriend!" Jan said.

"How come no one told me he's seventeen?" Allen asked.

"Well, he drives, Dad," Jamie said. "So you'd have to know that he was at least sixteen."

"He's very cute," Betty said. "He doesn't wear underwear."

Jamie and Jan both turned their heads and stared at Betty. Betty delicately forked a bite of steak into her mouth.

"How do you know he doesn't wear underwear?" Jamie asked.

"You can tell," Betty said. "His shorts are always sagging down and you can see that he's not wearing underwear. Sweetheart, I don't care that he doesn't wear underwear."

"I know you don't care," Jamie said. "I just think it's weird that you'd notice."

"Your mother's a noticer," Allen shrugged. "She notices things."

Jamie wondered if her mother had noticed that she'd started having sex. She had certainly noticed when Jamie sprouted breast buds; she had pointed it out to Allen, the last to know, at the dinner table one night. And once, around the time Jamie was thirteen, she came into the bathroom while Jamie was in the tub and noticed that Jamie had started to grow pubic hair. When Jamie's hips widened and her belly flattened, Betty noticed and bought her new bathing suits. Her father was right. There were few things Betty didn't notice.

"So, does Donny have lots of friends?" Betty asked Jan.

"I'm his friend, I guess," Jan said.

"What do you do together?" Betty asked.

"Last night we went to the movies."

"In the truck that may or may not have a gun rack?" Allen asked.

"Yeah," Jan said.

"What did you see?" Posing this question, Jamie later realized, was like opening the hatch in a submerged submarine. Jan took the family through the remainder of the meal with the first half of *Logan's Run*. She was still not near the end when Betty served pound cake and vanilla ice cream for dessert. The final scene approached as Betty cleared the table and started the dishes. Just as Jan reached the end of the film, Allen pushed back his chair and announced that he had to retire to the record room to file some new albums.

So there Jamie sat, feeling like Edith Ann in a dramatic

high-backed chair, alone with her cousin, whose mouth flapped open and shut, open and shut. Jamie ran her finger along the scars in the table to the rhythm of Jan's voice (the table that she had always thought looked like a charred picnic table and that her father, in a fit over the charred picnic table observation, claimed, "cost as much as a god-damned hillbilly house in Mississippi and if your mother weren't so hell-bent on donating my earnings to what she considers the artisans of the world, we'd be sitting at a decent fucking table with turned out legs and not this slab of cinders she calls a table"). Jamie's finger stopped moving when Jan's voice shut down.

"Wanna go for a swim?" Jamie asked.

"Wait, I've gotta tell you the end," Jan said. "You'll love it."

Twenty minutes later, Jan was in the guest room putting on her suit. Betty, Allen, and Jamie congregated in the kitchen.

"But your dad and I are going swimming with Leon and Lois." Betty had the same tone as Renee when she and Jamie fought over what to watch on TV.

"So you tell her we can't go swimming," Jamie said.

"Why can't they swim with us?" Allen asked. "The kids always swim with us."

"You can't go naked in front of her," Betty said. "She'll tell everyone in town."

"What do you care, you're never there!"

"Please, Allen," Betty said. "People don't show skin in New Hampshire, even in the summer."

"And you're going to tell Leon he can't swim naked? The schmuck doesn't even own a suit. He doesn't even own underwear."

"Just like Flip," Betty said.

"Flip probably *owns* underwear," Jamie said. "And, really, I don't know if he wears it or not."

"He doesn't wear it," Betty said. "Which is fine with me. I mean, most people didn't wear underwear until sometime around the First World War."

"No way," Jamie said.

"If Leon swims naked, then I'm swimming naked," Allen said. "I mean, if she sees one schlong, what difference does it make if she sees another?"

"Allen," Betty said. "She's been in Swiftwater since birth. She might go her whole life without ever seeing a penis."

Jan waited on Jamie's bed while Jamie put on her suit. She didn't pretend to look elsewhere; she just stared at Jamie. Jan was already in her suit, which made her look like a giant, blue egg. Jamie couldn't recall seeing anyone her age in a one-piece suit. She knew that girls wore them for swim team, but she had never been on a swim team, nor had she ever gone to a meet.

"So I guess your stomach doesn't get tan," Jamie said.

"I don't tan anyway," Jan said. "But maybe I can borrow one of your suits later and try to tan."

Jamie could not stop herself from imagining the inner-suit view of Jan's massive white and pimply butt folded into her bathing suit and filling it like pancake batter. Her fat crotch would be wedged apart, a spandex taco, as she pulled the waist up.

"I don't think my suits will fit you," Jamie said. "Maybe you can borrow one of Mom's."

* * *

Jamie paused at the French doors leading out to the pool. The sticky, arm-pit smell of marijuana puffed up the air. She wasn't sure if Betty cared if Jan saw her smoking or not, so she blocked the doorway as best she could and shouted a warning.

"We're coming out!"

"Well, come on, then!" Betty yelled, as she handed a roach to Lois, who smashed it into a rock.

Betty was splayed against the boulder, butt folded up, creating a gap at the small of her back, breasts flung to either side like fighting kids who had been separated. Lois sat cross-legged at Betty's feet. She looked like a scarecrow closed up to be put into storage.

"So this is Jan," Lois said softly.

"Jan," Betty said. "People in California don't wear bathing suits when they swim in their private pools. So don't be shocked, okay?"

"Uh . . . " Jan pulled her chin in. She turned her head toward the bushes on her left, her eyes flitting to and from Betty's breasts.

"If you want to swim naked, you're welcome to do so. No one will judge you here. All bodies are beautiful bodies."

"Except the ugly ones," Jamie said. "Like Johnathan, the man who looks like Moses in *The Ten Commandments*, or Judith Tisch, whose body looks like the Grinch's without the green hair–"

"Jamie!"

"It's true."

Lois sat up tall and sucked in her already hollow stomach. Her mouth was a straight line across her face.

"It's not true," Betty said. "Everyone is beautiful."

Music popped into the air, and ten beats later, Allen and Leon wandered out of the house. They were each in rib-knit jock straps. Leon's jock was yellowed like the walls in a smoker's house and Allen's was a purply-gray; it was clear that both jocks had originally been white. Jan turned to them, then turned away, her face searching the bushes, the lawn, the blue and red skyline. Jamie could not help but stare at the abstract form made by the jock straps on their crotches. They were twin white elephants, albino armadillos, the letter *T* beside another *T*: *TT*? They were anything but two, hairy, grown men wearing worn-handkerchief-colored jock straps.

"Sweetheart," Allen said, and Jamie looked up at his face, surprised to find him there. "Run to the poolroom and get us some towels. I forgot to get towels."

Jan was so close behind Jamie, Jamie could hear her breathing as they walked into the poolroom, a closet-sized room with no windows and two doors: one that went out to the backyard and one that went into the house. Jamie pulled four towels off a shelf and turned to leave. Jan was in the doorway.

"It's okay," Jamie said. "It's just bodies. They're just naked."

"But your dad and his friend aren't naked."

"That's so you wouldn't see their penises, okay? They did that for you so you wouldn't be embarrassed, being from New Hampshire and all."

Jan looked at Jamie like she was drowning. But how could she be drowning? Jamie thought. This wasn't her dad, this wasn't her family, how dare she drown when Jamie herself didn't have the luxury to do so.

"Just get over it. I mean Get. Over. It." Jamie squeezed

past her and headed toward the pool. By the time Jamie reached the water she was almost running. She dropped the towels on a rock, relay style, then kept going until she hit the diving board. Once on the board she was truly running until her feet were bicycling in the air like Wile E. Coyote in *The Road Runner* when he doesn't realize the road has ended and he's suddenly run himself off the edge of a cliff.

Halfway through Jan's visit, Betty and Allen went to Ojai for the day, leaving Jamie to tend to Jan on her own. Jamie invited Debbie and Tammy over to help. They were hesitant, as neither wanted to give up her time with Jimmy or Brett. Jamie argued that if she could go without Flip for fourteen days, surely they could spend a day or two without their boyfriends. Finally they agreed, and when Jamie hung up the phone she was no longer sure that she wanted them to come after all; friendship, Jamie thought, shouldn't have to be operated with guile.

Immediately after meeting her, Tammy declared that she wanted to try on Jan's clothes. Jamie decided that if Jan was stupid enough to let her, then she deserved whatever followed. Tammy knocked on the outside of the suitcase.

"This thing is like a rock," she said.

"I think they put elephants on them," Jan said, "to make sure they're sturdy."

"When would you ever have to worry about an elephant stepping on your suitcase?" Tammy asked.

"I dunno."

"Is this how they dress in New Hampshire?" Tammy held out a turtleneck shirt with acorns printed on it.

Debbie pulled out a pair of pants that appeared to have been made out of burlap, or the wiry straw stuffing from an old chair.

"Do these itch?"

"You wear long underwear under them in the winter," Jan said.

"But it's summer," Debbie said.

"Yeah," Jan said. "I packed them just in case there was a cold spell."

"Don't light a cigarette around those pants," Jamie said. "They're probably flammable."

Debbie and Tammy collapsed on the bed in laughter. Jan stood beside the suitcase and sort of hee hawed.

"I'm putting those on," Tammy said, and she grabbed the pants from Debbie.

Jan grinned as Tammy pulled on her clothes. Scrawny, blond Tammy looked clownish, mean, in the huge, stiff pants. She rolled up the hem so the pants wouldn't drag on the floor and slipped on her pink Candie's mules.

"You look ridiculous," Jamie said.

"I think you need a smaller size," Jan said.

"I need a cigarette." Tammy pawed through her purse and pulled out a pack of Marlboro Light 100's. "Want one?" she asked Jan.

Jan looked to Jamie as if Jamie could give her the answer. Jamie looked away. She hated the flightless dodo bird feeling she had when presented with the onus of Jan.

"Are you going to smoke?" Jan asked Jamie.

"What?"

"Are you going to smoke?"

"Not those gross things." Jamie waved her hand. "But you can smoke if you want. I won't tell."

"Do you smoke other stuff?" Jan asked.

"All the time."

Tammy and Debbie pursed their lips so as not to laugh. Jamie still hadn't tried pot, even though it crowded the seashell ashtrays that were scattered around the house and by the pool; even though Tammy and Debbie had taken to smoking it every now and then with Brett and Jimmy.

"Yeah," Tammy said, "Jamie smokes pot *all the time.*"

"Whoa," Jan said.

"Wanna try some?" Debbie asked.

"I dunno."

"I'll smoke some now to show you how," Tammy said.

"I'll do it, too," Debbie said, jumping off the bed and hopping from one foot to the other in a spastic dance of anticipation.

"But aren't you tired of smoking pot?" Jamie said. "Don't you think it's getting old?"

"No," Tammy said. "Let's smoke pot, *again.*"

Jamie felt dirty as she dug through the ashtray on the night table next to her parents' bed. Pulling out a half-smoked joint seemed just as invasive as peering at the vibrator she accidentally found one day in the back of her mother's underwear drawer. But her need to be bolder, braver, bawdier than Jan pushed her ahead. Jamie took the joint and a pack of matches to the pool, where Tammy, Debbie, and Jan were waiting. Tammy had let Jan's pants fall to her ankles; she sat against a rock in her underwear.

"I got tired of holding them up," she said.

"Here." Jamie handed her the joint and the matches.

Tammy put the half cigarette in her mouth, lit it, and took a pittering puff that barely inflamed the tip. She handed the joint to Debbie, who pulled a little harder but didn't get enough smoke to exhale. Debbie passed it to Jamie, who pursed her lips as if she were smoking but was really holding her breath. Jan took the joint from Jamie, wrapped her wet lips around it, and pulled so hard that it burned halfway down. She was like a soft dragon as she hissed out the smoke. Tammy grabbed the joint from Jan and pulled on it just as Jan had. She was seized with a coughing fit that turned her face red and teared up her eyes. Debbie took another hit, which she coolly held in before slowly exhaling. Then Jamie really inhaled, sucking it in fast and hard, until her lungs felt like they were being scraped with a nail file, and she coughed. They passed the joint until it was the size of a child's tooth. Tammy and Jamie coughed at each round. Jan was still and mighty like a rock.

Tammy flicked the tab of the joint into the bushes, stepped out of the puddle of Jan's pants around her ankles, peeled off her tank top and bra in one swift motion, slid out of her underpants, and dove, naked, into the water. Jan watched her the way people watch fireworks.

"Can anyone see back here?" Debbie asked.

"No way," Jamie said. "The whole layout of the pool was planned around–" Her mind had ended.

"What?" Debbie laughed.

Jan watched Tammy swim laps, rolling from her belly to her back to her side.

"I dunno," Jamie said.

"No one can see, right?"

"My parents swim naked all the time."

"But they don't care if people see them. That's what their style is."

"Style?" Jamie smiled.

"Can people see us?" Debbie was still laughing.

"No. It was plotted that way. The place. The place of the pool is the place where no one sees." Jamie looked at Debbie and erupted in laughter.

Debbie stripped down and Jamie followed. They jumped into the pool, one after the other. Jan had not moved.

Swimming naked felt better than Jamie had imagined. The water was alive; it swam against her, tickled, tingled. It was nothing like a bath—it was not passive, or restful, or soft. Swimming naked was motion, action, sensation. Tammy and Debbie were noise and movement. They were a kaleidoscope that sings.

Jan was mute.

Jan stared.

Jan breathed through her mouth.

Every couple of minutes Jamie forgot that Jan was there.

On the rock.

In her clothes.

Every couple of minutes Jamie saw Jan and remembered that she was there.

On the rock.

In her clothes.

It was as if Jan were a thought too ill-fitting for Jamie's long-term memory.

Debbie was hungry. She pushed herself out of the water like a mermaid emerging from the sea. Sheets of wetness glided down her back, off her thick black hair, tailed off the crack of her butt. She left a wet trail as she walked naked into the house. Jan was still looking at the French doors when Debbie emerged from them several minutes later.

"There's nothing good to eat in this house," she said. "Let's go out."

They all wore shorts and tank tops, except Jan, who had on dungarees and a brown T-shirt. The sidewalk wasn't wide enough for the four girls, so Jan fell behind. When the sidewalk narrowed further, from a bush, or bulging-rooted tree, one of the girls stepped ahead so that they formed a diamond. They walked to the Fig Tree, a restaurant built around a giant fig tree, on which lived two wallabies. There were interior glass walls forming a cage, and a net that enclosed the top of the massive tree. The wallabies looked like miniature kangaroos. They were the size of small monkeys and hard to find. If you didn't know they were there you could have an entire meal without ever noticing them.

The girls were seated at a table whose end abutted the glass wall. Jamie sat closest to the wall, Jan was across from her, Debbie was beside Jamie and Tammy was across from Debbie.

"I'm having French dip," Debbie said to the waiter, who was college-aged, thick-haired, smiley.

"Me, too," Jamie said.

"French dip and fries," Tammy said.

"You don't have to say fries," Jamie said. "It automatically comes with them."

"But you don't have to have the fries," the waiter said.

No one asked Jan what she was having.

"Three French dips *with* fries," Tammy said, and she handed him all four menus.

"Three for the four of you?" he asked.

"No, for the three of us." Tammy pointed at herself, Debbie, Jamie.

"Anything for you?" The waiter stared at Jan, who was looking out the glass wall.

"Jan, do you want a French dip?" Jamie asked.

Jan looked at her and nodded.

"Four French dips," Jamie said.

Jamie, Debbie, and Tammy began laughing when the waiter walked away. Jan had yet to turn away from the glass wall. Then, suddenly, she yelped and pushed her chair back.

"There's something hell'a big in that tree!" she said.

The other three couldn't stop laughing.

Jan had brought her wallet—a red plastic square with a yellow plastic apple on the front—but had forgotten to put money in it (her cash was hidden in the lining of her suitcase). Jamie had three dollars that she took from the cookie jar where her mother kept grocery money—the French dip was only $1.75, but she threw all three in. Debbie didn't have any money with her, so Tammy, whose father handed her a twenty-dollar bill every time she walked out the door, paid the rest of the tab.

"I'll pay you back," Jan said to Tammy.

"I don't care," Tammy said. "Easy come, easy go."

Just as the girls approached the door, their waiter dashed up.

"Hey," he said.

"Hey," Tammy said.

"What are you girls doing later?"

"Why?" Tammy asked.

Debbie and Jamie were holding in laughter. Jan looked bewildered.

"Some friends and I are having a party at Devereux tonight."

"Who's Devereux?" Jan asked Jamie, her voice sounding as if it were dubbed in at the wrong speed.

"It's a beach," Debbie snapped, "not a person. A beach."

"Kegger," he said.

"What time?" Tammy said.

"Ten," he said. "And bring any cute friends."

"Cool," Tammy said, and she sauntered toward the door.

"See ya tonight," Debbie said.

"Yeah, see ya," Jamie said, though she knew that even *her* parents wouldn't drive them out to Devereux beach at ten o'clock at night, and there was no possibility of Brett and Jimmy driving them to a party hosted by college boys.

They paraded out the door, Tammy in front, Jan stumbling in back. Jamie was smiling, seeing herself from what she imagined was Jan's perspective, thinking how cool they were, fourteen-year-olds who had been asked by a college boy to go to a kegger. Just when they reached the sidewalk, the waiter ran out behind them.

"Hey, one thing," he said.

Like pigeons in a row, the girls cocked their heads toward him.

"Don't bring the retard." He jutted his chin toward Jan, turned, and walked back into the restaurant.

Debbie and Tammy each placed a hand over their mouths—

they were smiling in horror. Jamie's stomach thumped like a giant heartbeat as she reached out and grabbed Jan's forearm.

"We're not going to that party anyway," she said. "Tammy was just flirting."

"Yeah," Debbie said, half-smiling, "*he's* the retard."

"I don't care." Jan's cheeks were bulging tomatoes, her eyes were wet, flashing butterflies. She turned and galumphed off in the direction of home.

Tammy exaggeratedly mouthed *Oh My God*. Debbie was still trying not to laugh. Jamie ran ahead and caught up to Jan. Jan shrugged Jamie's hand off her shoulder.

"Hey," Jamie said. "I'm just trying to walk with you."

"'Kay," Jan said, and she slowed.

They walked side-by-side; Debbie and Tammy were two sidewalk squares behind them, whispering and giggling. Jamie despised them both. And although it was the first time she had had such strong distaste for her friends, Jamie wasn't surprised by how easily the feeling had come to her, as if it were something she had been working toward all along.

"When are your parents going to be home?" Debbie asked. They were at the turning point for Tammy's house, paused on the corner.

"They're probably home by now," Jamie said. "I'll see you guys later."

"Later," Debbie said, as she and Tammy turned the corner and walked away.

Jan remained silent for the rest of the march home. As Jamie expected, the car wasn't in the driveway when they approached the house; Allen and Betty hadn't planned on returning until late that night, after dinner at their favorite restaurant in Ojai.

"Do you know how to play Rummy 500?" Jan asked.

"Yeah," Jamie said.

"Wanna play?"

"Yeah, sure." She would have played anything her cousin wanted.

Jamie and Jan sat at the kitchen counter with a package of Oreos, a carton of butter pecan ice cream with two spoons, and a deck of cards. They played Rummy 500 until their bottoms were sore and their stomachs were churning from too much sugar.

"Let's have popcorn and cocoa for dinner," Jamie said.

"That's so crazy," Jan laughed.

Jamie made popcorn in a saucepan that sounded like it was screaming when she scraped it back and forth along the iron burner. Jan melted butter in another saucepan, then added parmesan cheese and garlic powder before pouring it over the popcorn. In a third saucepan, cocoa brewed. When everything was ready, they poured the popcorn into a bowl and took it with their mugs of cocoa into the TV room. Jan plopped down just beside Jamie on the couch, thigh to thigh. *The Gong Show* was on and they both laughed. Jan screamed each time a contestant was gonged. The first couple times, Jamie looked at her cousin and laughed at her lumbering figure: mouth open, hands pushing down on her thighs as if it would give more force to her scream. Then Jamie joined in, bellowing each time the gong sounded, releasing something inside her—the weight of too much air, it seemed, for she felt so much lighter after screaming. By the end of the show the girls were throwing popcorn at the TV following each gong. Jamie thought it was more fun than any beach party she'd ever been to.

That night, lying in Jamie's bed together whispering, just as Betty had hoped they might do, just as they had done when they were younger, Jamie drifted easily off to sleep. When she awoke the next morning, she didn't mind that Jan was still beside her.

8

Holy moly does that girl eat," Betty said.

"She's not fat," Jamie said.

They were driving away from the airport. Jan had just boarded her plane. Allen wanted to stay and watch the jet lift off but Betty insisted on leaving so she could go home and pack for their trip to Yosemite with Lois and Leon.

"She's big," Betty said, "and it's a pain in the ass cooking for big people."

"You didn't have to cook," Jamie said. "She would have had cookies and milk for dinner."

"Since when did you become Jan's ally?" Allen was driving; he eyed his daughter in the rearview mirror.

"I dunno. I'm just sick of people making fun of her. She's nice. She's a nice person and she'd never hurt anyone the way people hurt her."

Allen and Betty looked at each other, half-smirking, the way parents in a sitcom might look at each other after a clever comment at the dinner table. Sometimes Jamie felt the imbalance of her sister's absence. Without Renee the family was a wobbly tripod with Jamie as the shorter third leg.

Betty bought two books for Jamie for the camping trip: *Love, Sex, and the Family: A Guide for Young Adults,* and *Our Bodies, Ourselves.* Jamie sat calmly on the edge of her bed, slouched in the middle, knees knocking, feet out, when Betty handed her the books. But really she wanted to scream like she had at *The Gong Show*–to throw the books across the room like giant kernels of popcorn. Jamie was convinced that Betty had somehow sniffed out her loss of virginity and was trying to help her through it. Jamie liked when her mother showed an interest in her; she was always happy to find her sitting in the theater during plays at school; she loved when Betty asked about her friends– who was hanging out with whom, who was popular, who had slipped away. But the attempted entrance into her body made Jamie shudder; if she'd had quills, she'd have raised them. Jamie left the books on her bed and packed *Fear of Flying,* which she had stolen from her mother's room and which she didn't want Betty to know she was reading for fear of having to discuss Isadora's sex life in the book.

When they pulled up to their campsite along the Tu-olumne River, they found Leon lying on his back across a rock, arms folded behind his head, a toothpick bobbing out of his mouth like a tiny baton conducting an orchestra. Lois was sweeping the dirt of the campsite with a stick that had wide, serrated leaves bound to it with a vine.

"Oh, you brought Jamie," Lois said.

"She's too afraid to stay home alone and her boyfriend's in Hawaii," Betty said as she unpacked the car.

Jamie walked to the river to pretend she wasn't listening. She wondered why Lois had to begrudge her mother the joy of having her children around. Was it because the only person Lois had was Leon, whom Jamie often imagined as some sort of stink bug, wafting his noxious smell wherever he went?

"Didn't her friends want to stay with her?" Lois asked. Jamie could still hear them.

"I think they're drifting apart," Betty said.

"We're not drifting," Jamie shouted from the riverbank. "They're busy with their boyfriends!" It was painful for Jamie to hear her life narrated by her mother—Betty was so matter-of-fact about everything: Jamie's fears, her friends, her love life. It was as if these huge chunks of Jamie's life, the stuff that defined her summer, were mere details to Betty, as insignificant as a pair of flip-flops discarded on the first of September. And it wasn't that Betty had the facts wrong, perhaps she and Tammy and Debbie were drifting, but who knew how long the drift would last? Tammy and Debbie were her best friends, Jamie thought; they'd drift back together soon enough, like rafts floating down the same slow-moving river.

There are bears in Yosemite, and deadly stinging scorpions, and rattlesnakes, and of course Jamie imagined that the woods were filled with violent ax-wielding men and flashers who would specifically seek out girls sleeping alone in pup tents. So before dinner, Jamie dragged her sleeping bag from the pup tent that was set up for her to her parents' tent, which had flaps that rolled up to reveal net windows and a roof the shape of a circus tent roof. Jamie put her bag next to her parents', then pulled both bags as far back from the flap-door as possible. The inside of the tent smelled like the inside of a garage: moldy and dusty, with a hint of the stink of a freshly tarred road. There was a burning kerosene lamp hanging from a hook in the center of the tent. When Jamie looked at it she imagined the inflamed tent collapsing around her in a blanket of fiery death. She knew she wouldn't sleep until she had witnessed the snuffing of the lamp flame.

After dinner, after Lois, Betty, and Jamie had washed the dishes in the sink of the public bathroom, after Leon had extinguished half of the campfire by peeing on it while yodeling (which made Jamie wonder if everyone with a penis used it to pee on fire), after Allen had fetched sticks and carved them to points for roasting marshmallows, Betty pulled out her guitar. Her voice was beautiful and full, a gift that neither of her daughters had inherited. Leon stared at Betty as she sang, her face glowing orange from the firelight. His lips were pulled slightly, like he wanted to smile, but wouldn't. For several minutes he was frozen, a half-burned marshmallow hanging lopsided off his stick as he watched Betty. Allen and Lois were talking quietly about meditation, they were sharing their mantras, revealing ones that worked and ones that had failed. Jamie reached over and plucked the dangling marshmallow from Leon's stick. He looked at her for a second, then looked back toward Betty, nodding his head with the beat. Jamie wished Renee were there so she'd have someone to eat marshmallows with, someone to nudge when she said, "Do you think Mom has a crush on Leon, the man with the floppiest penis our backyard has ever seen? Or is it just that he is in love with Mom?"

Betty was not in the tent in the morning.

"Where's your mother?" Allen asked Jamie, waking her up.

"Maybe she went for a morning hike." Jamie flopped onto her stomach and tried to go back to sleep.

"Was I snoring?"

"Yeah."

"She probably moved out because of my snoring."

"Yeah, maybe."

"BETTY!" Allen called out from the sleeping bag.

Betty stuck her head in the tent.

"What are you screaming about?"

"Did you sleep here last night?"

"I went into Jamie's tent."

"It's not my tent." Jamie sat up. "I won't sleep there."

"You were snoring again," Betty said.

"What'd you use for a sleeping bag?" Allen asked.

"The blankets from the car."

"You walked to the car in the dark?!" Jamie asked.

"No, I put them in there before we went to bed in case your dad started snoring. What's the big deal? I slept in the other tent, okay? Now come out and have breakfast."

"What's for breakfast?" Allen smiled at Betty like he was flirting.

"Cooked, hot Grape-Nuts," Betty said.

"Ever eat a pine tree?" Jamie asked with an Appalacian twang. "Many parts are edible."

"What's that from?" Allen asked. "It sounds familiar."

"Euell Gibbons," Jamie said. "He says it in a commercial for Grape-Nuts."

"You're reciting commercials? You should be reciting poetry, or Shakespearean sonnets, for godsakes."

"Nothing wrong with reciting commercials," Betty said.

"There's something very wrong with reciting commercials," Allen said. "Maybe you should have homeschooled them."

"Come eat Grape-Nuts," Betty said, and she threw back the flap from the tent and walked away.

The third day in Yosemite, Allen, Leon, and Lois woke up early to hike to the top of Half Dome, a giant amphitheater-shaped rock, high up on a mountain peak. Betty decided to take Jamie to the hot spring swimming hole she had read about in *Mother Jones* magazine. A hot spring sounded good, as the Tuolumne River was as chilly as ice water, turning Jamie's ankles and feet white, like flesh socks, when she waded at the rocky banks.

Jamie wore her bathing suit under her shorts and T-shirt, and stuffed a thin, white towel into her mother's backpack. Betty wore blue jean cutoff shorts with no underwear and a mossy green tank top with no bra. They both had on hiking boots that made their feet look oversized and lumbering.

The hike was short but steep, up a mountain trail full of switchbacks, like a circular stairway that had been flattened wide. A sturdy, middle-aged couple on their way down stopped to chat with Betty.

"It might not be appropriate for your daughter," the man

said. He looked like the men in the Grecian Formula ads: slick gray hair with a swooping side part.

"Really?" Betty asked.

"Nudists," he said, with a knowing grin.

Betty and Jamie carried on up the mountain, Betty smiling blissfully from what Jamie imagined was anticipation of a naked swim.

Soon they approached an arch of bushes and overhanging trees. They walked through the arch and found themselves on a large, sloping sheet of orangey rock, pressed against a sheer rock wall. In the nook where the rock wall met the rock floor was a deep, rectangular pool. There were five people in the pool, mostly standing and talking. Everyone appeared younger than Betty, older than Jamie. Everyone was naked.

"Who fills that pool?" Jamie asked.

"Maybe I *should* have homeschooled you," Betty said.

"What?"

"It's a hot spring. There are streams flowing under all this rock, and the water from those streams seeps out into that pool. The water probably formed the pool."

Betty peeled off her shorts. Then, slowly, she lifted off her tank top. A dark-haired, square-faced man turned away from the woman who was speaking to him and smiled at Betty. He had pronounced canine teeth that made him wolfish. Betty returned the smile, then sauntered to the edge of the pool and stepped in. The water came up to Betty's chest. Her massive breasts floated like buoys. The Wolf pushed himself toward her; Jamie wondered if he was terribly short or floating on his knees, for his eyes were level with Betty's nipples.

"How's it goin'?" he asked Betty.

Jamie turned away from the scene and busied herself by digging through Betty's backpack, pulling out her towel, and lying on an empty spot in the sun. There was a small breeze that chilled her, but when she lay flat the breeze was gone. Eventually Jamie slipped off her shorts and shirt so that she was wearing only her black, crocheted bikini. Jamie's skin was brown as a nut, with deep tan lines that seemed to have been drawn with a straight edge. When an outline of white peeked out along her breasts or thighs, she adjusted her suit so that it disappeared, thus reinforcing the exactitude of her tan. Jamie hadn't slept well the night before, so she had no trouble falling asleep with the sun lighting up the inside of her eyelids a glowing pink, and the drone of voices drifting from the pool and settling around her ears like a lullaby.

When Jamie awoke, the sun had sunk into the valley, leaving her in a puddle of shade. There was no one around, no towels strewn hither and yon; she was alone. An eerie chill shot across Jamie's skin, but then she spied Betty's backpack and knew that her mother couldn't be far. The air had drastically cooled and a steamy fog was rising off the surface of the water. Jamie wanted to jump in the pool to warm up but was afraid of water snakes hiding in the cracks of the stone wall. She walked to the edge of the water and was contemplating it when she heard her mother's braying laugh. Seconds later, Betty and the Wolf emerged from the brush. They were each wearing shorts, hiking boots, and no shirt.

"Hey!" Betty said.

"Hey."

"This is Dog Feather," Betty said. "He took me up to this ledge where there's an amazing view of the valley."

"Dog Feather?" Jamie dipped her toe into the water, swung her leg back and forth.

"My grandfather was a tribal elder," Dog Feather said. "He named me after watching me grasp the dog's tail and yank out a handful of hair. When I opened my tiny fist, the hair was arranged like a perfect feather."

"Isn't that a wonderful story?" Betty said.

"So you weren't named until you were old enough to grab a dog's tail?" Jamie asked.

"I was about four or five days old," Dog Feather said. "I started grabbing the day I was born."

"Are there snakes in here?" Jamie asked.

"Not usually," Dog Feather said, and he sat down on the rock floor, looking up toward Betty, who was standing right beside him.

"Dog Feather is a Pomo Indian," Betty said.

"Full-blooded," Dog Feather added.

"If there are snakes," Jamie asked, "do they bite?"

"They're more afraid of you," Dog Feather said.

"Go in," Betty said. "It's like a warm bath."

"What about leeches?" Jamie asked.

"Only in the river," Dog Feather said.

"Salamanders?"

"Yeah, there are salamanders, but they don't do anything. They just look at you."

"No harm in being looked at," Betty said, and she giggled in a way that made her breasts jiggle.

Jamie jumped in, then turned and hauled herself out. The water was warm and silky, but she felt too alone in there—the only target for whatever might be lurking. Dog Feather sat on the rock beside Betty. They both smiled as they chatted, and nodded their heads at the same time. Jamie dried off with the towel and put on her shirt and shoes. The wet swimsuit made her colder than she had been before she jumped in.

"It's cold," Jamie said. "Let's go."

"Just a minute," Betty said, continuing to chat with Dog Feather.

"My suit is wet and I'm cold." Jamie would rather have had Betty's invasive personal attention than witness her mother flirting with a sharp-toothed Pomo.

"Can you wait a few minutes?"

"I'm freezing. I wish I were in Hawaii with Flip."

"Well, you're not. So relax." Betty's face was poised like a knife in the direction of Jamie.

"Fine," Jamie snapped, and she decided that when she was a mother she would never flirt in front of her children, she would never let them feel the tenuousness of love and marriage, the dangers that lurked, waiting like land mines that could blow the family apart.

"Where are you staying?" Betty asked Dog Feather, her face instantly relaxing.

"Wherever I land at sunset," Dog Feather said. "Last night I slept up here on this rock."

"We have an extra tent," Betty said. "You should stay with us tonight."

"Are you talking about my tent?" Jamie asked. "Is that the extra tent?"

"Well, you won't sleep in it!" Betty turned to Dog Feather and added, "She's fourteen, she's got a boyfriend who's seventeen, but she's afraid to sleep in a tent alone."

"I'm not afraid of the tent." Jamie tempered her voice lest her mother blurt out more personal details that Jamie preferred remain in the family.

"Well, you're afraid of a million imagined threats to your safety, and you won't sleep in the tent, so Dog Feather might as well use it."

"Fine," Jamie said. Unlike her parents, who seemed willing to discuss any subject in any forum, Jamie preferred to give in than to publicly argue with her mother.

"Beautiful," Dog Feather said.

Dinner that night was lively. Everyone, except Jamie, seemed sparked by the presence of Dog Feather. Betty asked Dog Feather about life as a Native American, what he ate growing up, what he wore, where he slept. Dog Feather claimed he'd never slept in a bed in his life and he didn't understand why the white man had beds. He also said that because he was born on a piece of stretched calf skin in the dirt, he wasn't circumcised until he was an adult. Jamie didn't understand what calf skin had to do with a flap of skin on his penis, but everyone else seemed to get the connection as they oohed and aahed, their faces scrunched with curiosity. Allen wanted to know if Dog Feather received any government money for being Native American.

"It's so little," Dog Feather said, "that I pass my share on to my mother, who has greater need."

Lois and Betty both gasped and Betty put a hand on his forearm as if to thank him on behalf of mothers everywhere.

Leon asked Dog Feather if he knew any secrets to growing female marijuana plants. Indeed, Dog Feather seemed to know everything about growing female marijuana plants—so much, in fact, that Leon dug out a pad of paper and a pen from the glove box of his car so he could take notes.

After dinner there was a marijuana tasting: Dog Feather's versus Leon's. Jamie sat on a log eating marshmallows out of the bag, watching the adults' faces change from excited alertness into the melted, buttery look of being stoned. At one point Dog Feather reached his big hand back to pass Jamie a joint. She took the joint, stood, walked over to Allen, and delivered it to him.

"You didn't start smoking, did you?" her father asked.

"No. Dog Feather gave it to me."

"But haven't we smoked with Fred?"

"Flip?"

"Yeah, I remember seeing him smoking."

"He did, but I didn't. I don't smoke."

"Good," Allen said, lifting the twisted cigarette to his mouth. "Don't smoke."

"You don't have to tell me that. I already don't."

"I know. That's good. Don't smoke."

"I don't."

"Good."

"And I probably never will." Jamie was happy to tell her father she didn't smoke. She wanted him to see her as a good girl–she wanted to see herself that way.

"Good," Allen said with finality.

Betty went to the car and fetched her guitar. She sat on a log playing, picking and strumming. Leon stood, pulled Lois up, and the two of them started dancing, Lois with her hands winding around her tiny head like flaccid snakes. Then Dog Feather danced, a body-bending rhythmic thump that didn't follow the music and looked like the way the Indians danced in black-and-white movies. Allen stood to dance, holding his arms out to Jamie to join him.

"No thanks, Dad," she said. "I gotta go to bed."

Allen looked disappointed, but Jamie simply walked away and ducked into the tent. The fact that she was on a camping trip with her parents already, in her mind, defined her as a friendless freak. And although she loved dancing, Jamie couldn't help but imagine Tammy or Debbie or Flip, even, looking down on her dancing with her dad and thinking she was a freak beyond freaks, one of those geeky kids who are like oddball parent replicas. Like Bobby Chillings, who was always in math classes with Jamie and who built model freight ships with his dad and started most sentences with the words, "When my dad . . ." Or Jamie's old best friend from sixth grade, Julie Freemore, whose mother would pick up an extension and talk with them every time Julie and Jamie were on the phone.

After a couple chapters of *Fear of Flying*, Jamie put down the book and stuck her head out the flap of the tent to see what was happening around the campfire. Dog Feather, still dancing, caught Jamie's eye and winked. It was a wink that she would have read as friendly only a couple of months earlier. But after the loss of her virginity, and after having read half of *Fear of Flying*, everything in Jamie's world seemed to have a slippery, horny undertone. The next morning they had to be out of the campsite by noon. Jamie was looking forward to it. Dog Feather would return to the stones he had slept on before and Jamie would never have to see his wolf face again.

9

Dog Feather spread his legs so wide that his knee knocked Jamie's knee. Betty was turned around in her seat so she could talk to Dog Feather in the backseat. Allen drove silently and Jamie stared out the window. Betty had invited Dog Feather to stay with the family in Santa Barbara and he had accepted. In her excitement, Betty rambled a monologue that included the to-do list for when they returned, item seven being to change the sheets on the guest bed where Jan had slept and remake the bed for Dog Feather.

"I can't sleep in a bed," Dog Feather said. "I sleep only on dirt and rocks. . . . Although I have slept on wood floors as they're almost as hard as rocks."

"Amazing." Betty smiled and shook her head.

The guest room was carpeted and there were rugs over most of the wood floors. The only clear, open, hard surfaces in the house were the wood floor in the kitchen and the wood floor in Allen's study.

"You could sleep out by the pool," Jamie said.

"Under the stars, what a beautiful idea," Dog Feather said.

"I'm putting your backpack in my study," Allen said. He was grumpy after the long drive and not nearly as excited as Betty about having Dog Feather in the house. Dog Feather followed Allen out of the kitchen toward the study off the living room. Jamie sat at the counter watching her mother whip eggs for late-night omelets.

"Don't you want to go to bed?" Betty asked.

"But we never had dinner."

"You said you don't want an omelet."

"I'll have cereal."

Betty handed Jamie a box of Cheerios, a spoon, a bowl, and a carton of milk.

"I bet he'll sneak up onto the couch," Jamie said.

"What?"

"I bet Dog Feather will end up sleeping on that leather couch in Dad's study."

"He's an Indian, not a Labrador," Betty said. "He chooses to sleep on the floor."

"I don't believe him."

"Why would he lie?"

"Sugar."

Betty passed the sugar bowl and Jamie spooned out three small piles onto her cereal.

Dog Feather and Allen returned to the kitchen. Allen sat on a stool; Dog Feather stood behind Jamie and began massaging her shoulders. Jamie froze, with a spoonful of Cheerios midair, and stared at her mother.

"You're very tense," Dog Feather said.

Jamie's eyes darted from her mother to her father. Allen was half asleep, his head flopped into his wide hand, watching the omelets cook. Betty was looking over her daughter's head at Dog Feather's head looming somewhere behind. A rope of anger wound around Jamie's gut as she saw that her parents would not save her from Dog Feather's blatant molestation.

"You think *she's* tense, you should meet her sister," Betty laughed.

"I'm going to bed now." Jamie slipped out from beneath Dog Feather's hands, picked up her cereal bowl, and dumped it in the sink with a violence no one seemed to notice.

Betty was driving, Allen was in the front seat, and Dog Feather and Jamie sat in the backseat again, like siblings. They were on their way to the airport to pick up Renee, who was returning from Outward Bound. Flip was coming home from Hawaii that same day. Betty had asked Jamie to put off seeing Flip for a couple of days in order to let Renee get used to the idea that he was her boyfriend.

"Mom," Jamie leaned up between the two front seats, "can I at least talk to him on the phone?"

"Not in front of your sister."

"Well, why can't I go to his house and see him? I'll tell Renee that I'm going to Tammy's or something."

"Don't you want to spend time with your sister?" Allen asked. "You haven't seen her in six weeks."

"But I haven't seen Flip in two weeks! Two weeks is, like, torture—you don't know how this feels!"

Betty and Allen laughed.

"We know how it feels," Allen said.

"It is good to honor your sister with your presence," Dog

Feather said. Allen and Jamie stared at him as if he had just told them he had soiled himself.

"Dog Feather's right," Betty said. "You should honor your sister with your presence."

"I'm not sure she'll feel so honored," Jamie said.

"Just visit with your sister for a couple days," Allen said. "You can see Flip soon enough."

Renee looked different: tanner, ropier. The muscles on her narrow, long arms had ridges and shadows. The top of each calf looked like it had a fist in it. Her black eyes were huge. She sat in the kitchen eating everything that was placed before her and telling stories: rapelling down a cliff, the bear that ran by her when she was walking across a footbridge, the kid who had an asthma attack and had to be helicoptered out, her five days alone with a compass and backpack, that she hadn't had processed white sugar in sooo long and she couldn't believe how good it tasted. Dog Feather asked as many questions as Betty. Renee startled every time he spoke, as if he were an apparition.

"So," Renee finally spoke to Jamie. "What have you been doing, Farrah?"

"Farrah?" Dog Feather asked.

"She calls me Farrah," Jamie explained.

"Something about her hair," Allen said, "but I don't really see it."

"Still going to Slut Beach?"

"I thought you went to Butterfly Beach," Allen said.

"That's Slut Beach," Renee said.

"Honey, do you want more syrup on your waffle?" Betty asked.

"I'll have more!" Dog Feather held his plate up to Betty.

"So what's the latest news of Slut Beach?" Renee asked.

"Why do you have to use that word?" Allen asked. "It's such an undignified word. *Slut.* I mean, who uses that word?"

"My friends use it," Jamie said.

"Her friends are it," Renee said.

"Look how honored she is by my presence," Jamie said to Dog Feather.

"She's honored," Betty said. "She just doesn't know how to show it."

"What do you mean I'm honored?" Renee said. "I'm not honored by Farrah!"

"Do you want to know what I did while you were gone?" Jamie said.

"Not really," Renee said. "I was just asking to appear polite."

"Girls," Allen sighed.

"You know when I had you two so close together I thought you'd be built-in playmates for each other," Betty said.

"I wore all your clothes while you were gone," Jamie said.

"You did not. Mom! Did Jamie wear my clothes?!"

"No! Jamie, why are you telling her that? It's not true."

"But look how upset she is. Isn't it sad that she'd be so upset if I just wore her clothes? I mean, who cares about clothes!"

"Clothes have no meaning," Dog Feather said.

Allen sighed and rubbed his eyes with the heels of his palms.

"That's right," Betty said. "I should send you two off to

live with Dog Feather, that way you'd understand the real value of things."

"Dog Feather seems to live here," Jamie said. "And we're already here."

"No, I mean on the reservation!"

"Mom! I just came from six weeks of Outward Bound! You think I need to go live on an Indian reservation?! Please!"

"You should go live on an Indian reservation," Jamie said. "You're dark enough."

"Jamie!" Betty said.

"What the hell does dark have to do with it?" Allen asked.

"She looks like an Indian."

"Native American," Dog Feather said.

"I can't believe you'd think that saying that I look like an Indian is an insult. Mom, do you hear how prejudiced she is?"

"I didn't say it was an insult. I just stated a fact."

"Why did I ever come home? I can't think of anything to make my summer more miserable than to come home to you, Farrah!" Renee's voice trembled and her face twitched. Normally this would have softened Jamie, eased her, but something about Dog Feather's presence in the room pushed her away from sympathy. Besides, it seemed entirely unfair that her reward for tending to Renee's feelings by not seeing Flip was to sit and suffer Renee's poison arrows.

"I'm leaving." Jamie hopped off the stool. "I'll be at Flip's house if anyone needs me."

"Flip who?" Renee looked around at the faces watching her: Betty, with her lips pursed, shaking her head; Allen, who was exhaustedly slouched onto his palms, elbows propped on the counter; and Dog Feather, whose mouth was cracking into a smile.

"Flip who?!"

"My boyfriend," Jamie said. "Flip Jenkins."

Jamie walked out of the room, but she could hear Renee in the kitchen saying, "I don't believe her."

And then Dog Feather said, "When a girl becomes sexually active, she never lies about who her lover is."

Jamie paused in the hallway waiting for the next breath, the next word. From anyone. When it didn't come, she dashed out of the house and ran, in red and orange flip-flops, the two-mile distance to Flip's rambling, woodsy house.

When Flip opened the front door Jamie was flushed with the urge to cry. She didn't know if she was overwhelmed by simply the sight of Flip, or if her anger at Dog Feather was floating to the top of her emotions, an oily scum shifting over her flooded heart. She remembered Flip's description of his worst date: a crier who told him she loved him. And so she swallowed the walnut that pulsed in her throat, smiled, and hugged her boyfriend without a tear.

Flip drove Jamie home at ten o'clock. He wanted to pull over so they could have sex, since they had spent the evening at his house sitting in the family room with his parents looking at the photos of Hawaii that had been developed at the one-hour drive-through booth. To Jamie it seemed unnatural to see pictures so quickly after they were snapped—as if a decent amount of time should pass in order to officially make something a picture-worthy memory.

"Let's go to the beach," Flip said. "We can do it in the parking lot."

Jamie looked at Flip, studied his face. So far they had had only boring sex–sex that left Jamie feeling hollow and cardboard–and yet she loved him. She still wanted to press her body against his so hard that she could imagine passing through bone and gristle and nestling somewhere deep below his skin. But she had a sudden pang of pain for Renee, guilt for leaving her sister so far behind while she, herself, sailed forward with Luscious Lester, the un-official captain of high school. It just didn't seem right that she'd tell Renee about Flip *and* have sex with him all in the same night.

"I should get back." Jamie hoped Flip would still love her even if she wouldn't stop at the beach for sex. She hoped he would still love her even when he met Renee and found that she was more jagged than smooth. Jamie was afraid that she and Flip were peaking and she never wanted any-thing–her sister's ill wishes, her guilt about maturing more quickly than Renee–to run across that peak, to break it off or dull it down into a nub.

"But no one even called for you," Flip said. "You'd think if they wanted you back they'd call or something."

"I hate Dog Feather," Jamie said.

"I still don't get it," Flip said. "Is he a cousin or something?"

"No." Jamie didn't want to explain–the truth was like an embarrassing stain on the seat of one's pants. "He knows a lot about pot."

"Cool," Flip said.

When they pulled up to the house, Flip turned off the engine and cranked up the emergency break. It was obvi-ous to Jamie that Flip liked being at her house. He liked

getting high with Betty and Allen. He liked Betty's cooking. He liked the pool. He was so comfortable there that
even if Jamie wasn't home, if she was out grocery shopping
with her mom or helping Allen pick out a birthday present for Betty, he would still hang around, eat, swim, watch
TV. But with Renee home, Flip's occupation of the house
might create the tension of avoidance: Renee avoiding Flip,
Jamie avoiding Renee's glare, Allen and Betty avoiding the
conflict altogether.

Jamie thought it was strange that she felt close enough
to Flip to let him touch her body (all over) and to touch
his body (all over), yet there was still an awkward formality between them. She had always thought that when
people were in love everything was easy, normal, but
happier. Like the way things often were when she was
hanging out with Tammy and Debbie. But being in love
wasn't like that. Jamie often felt like she had to figure
things out—how she should act or what she should say.
For example, she couldn't find a way to explain to Flip
her relationship with Renee and why his presence in the
house just then might be somewhat like the presence of
the stray dog Betty once brought home. Allen, Renee,
and Jamie had taken circuitous routes around the house,
cutting out into the backyard, or through the garage, in
order to avoid running into the dog, which had a boxy,
rock head, leonine body, and the glare of a mind reader.
(Allen finally insisted Betty return the dog to the pound
when the dog eviscerated a seagull and presented it to
Betty as a gift.) Her parents always seemed to be their
normal selves together—talking to each other while one
was on the toilet and the other was brushing his teeth,
laughing at jokes only the two of them seemed to get.

But her parents didn't seem in love the way she and Flip were; when her father went away for long business trips, Betty didn't appear to miss him. Maybe, Jamie thought, you could relax into your complete self only when the crazy, buzzing, drunk love had faded. Maybe it was the love itself, its constant presence and intensity, which made things awkward in the first place.

"So, should I, like, pretend that I remember your sister from school?" Flip asked.

"I guess," Jamie said. At that moment the light in Renee's room went out.

"Think your parents will want to get high? I haven't had any doobage in two weeks."

"I dunno," Jamie said, and the light in her parents' room went out.

"So, are we going in?" Flip leaned forward and examined Jamie's face.

"You know," Jamie stared at the house, "I think everyone's asleep. The lights are all out."

"Let's have sex in the pool." Flip slapped his hand against Jamie's crotch and began rubbing as if to call a genie out of a lantern.

"Let's just wait until tomorrow." Jamie couldn't possibly feel comfortable having sex with her sister brooding upstairs and Dog Feather lurking somewhere.

"You're torturing me!" Flip opened his door and stepped out.

Jamie hesitated, one foot out of the bus. There was no way she could prevent Flip from coming inside, she decided. She hoped that Renee planned to stay in her room, door shut, for the night.

"You comin'?" Flip asked. Then he laughed, "I guess we won't be cummin' tonight, will we?"

Jamie got out of the car and led Flip into the dark house. "Try not to wake anyone up," she whispered.

Flip looked around, as if they were breaking in. He gave Jamie a double thumbs up with pursed lips to indicate silence. Neither said a word until they entered the kitchen.

"I'm starving," Flip said. "Any Nutter Butters?"

"Yeah. You want milk?"

"Of course!" Flip said.

Jamie went to the pantry and pulled out the package of Nutter Butter peanut butter sandwich cookies. She got a glass from the cupboard and filled it with milk. She felt like her mother, zooming around the kitchen like she was on a track: pantry, cupboard, fridge, island, pantry, cupboard, fridge, island.

Flip and Jamie were dipping cookies into a glass when Dog Feather came in wearing a batik sheet bound around his waist.

"Dude," Flip said. "You're the Indian!"

"Native American," Dog Feather said, and he shook Flip's hand.

"I'm Flip."

"I know."

"Whoa, how do you know, man? You like one of those people who knows things?"

"What?" Jamie said.

"You know. Those people who read people's minds."

"But if he read minds, how would he know you're Flip?" Jamie asked. "I mean, it's not like you're sitting there eating Nutter Butters thinking, 'I am Flip, I am Flip.'" Jamie stopped herself from laughing at Flip. She would never want to embarrass him.

"Got any spleef?" Flip asked Dog Feather. "I've been away with my parents for two weeks and I'm dying, man."

"I'll get my pipe," Dog Feather said, and when he left the room Flip looked at Jamie and mouthed, *Fuck yeah.*

Flip and Dog Feather sat at the barstools while Jamie stood at the other side of the island and watched them smoke a pipe.

"So," Dog Feather said, "are your parents cool with you guys having sex?"

"Jamie told you we're having sex?" Flip asked.

"No!" Jamie said.

"I just know," Dog Feather said. "I *am* one of those people who sees things."

"It's a guess," Jamie said. "You just guessed."

"It's so cool that you can read us like that," Flip said.

"But he can't!" Jamie imagined herself giving Flip a Three Stooges head bop and slap. She wanted him to awaken from the marijuana fog and look at Dog Feather with the same yellow glare as she.

"You should honor your parents and tell them about this beautiful thing that's happening with you two," Dog Feather said. "Sex is nothing to be ashamed of."

"I'm going to bed." Jamie looked at Flip, who was squinting as he sucked in deep, his lips pursed around the stem of the pipe.

When he finished, he passed the pipe to Dog Feather. Flip's eyes looked torpid and dull; he had an aimless smile.

"I'm going to bed," Jamie repeated, more sweetly this time. "Do you mind letting yourself out?"

"Nah, I can get myself outta here." Flip blew her a kiss before turning to watch Dog Feather repack the pipe.

Jamie left the kitchen wishing the day were already over: Renee's horror subsided, Flip's postvacation horniness settled, her post-Flip-vacation awkwardness dissipated, and Dog Feather's revelations forgotten and ignored.

Jamie hadn't been under the covers for five minutes when her mother slowly opened her door.

"Jamie?" she whispered. "You up?"

Jamie refused to answer.

"Jamie?" Betty delicately walked across the room and sat on the edge of the bed. "Jamie, honey?"

Jamie's eyes were shut. She was afraid to move.

"Jamie," Betty nudged her daughter's arm. "Wake up."

"Huh?"

"Sweetheart, I want to talk to you about your sexual relations with Flip."

"Mom!" Jamie rolled over, away from her mother. "We've already talked about this, remember?"

"I'm not mad, honey."

"Dog Feather's making it all up, Mom. He's a crazy red-blooded Indian."

"Red-blooded? Aren't we all red-blooded?"

"His is redder 'cause he's crazy."

"Jamie, your father and I aren't mad. We just want to make sure you're using birth control."

"Mom, I don't want to talk about sex, I don't want to talk about pleasing myself, I don't want to talk about what Flip and I may or may not be doing." Jamie shut her eyes and shot up a quick prayer that Flip wouldn't try to sneak into her bedroom just then.

"Just tell me you're using birth control."

"God, I hate Dog Feather!"

"Honey, he has nothing to do with this. Your father and I are the ones who want to know."

"Mom! It's not like I even like sex, okay? I mean, we're not doing it that much and when we do do it, it's not like it feels good or anything, okay?"

"Oh, sweetheart! I want it to feel good for you. I want you to be having beautiful orgasms."

Jamie couldn't speak; she struggled for even breaths. Betty leaned in and went for her arm. Jamie wanted to scream and push her away. The paradoxical effect of Betty's desire to wade into Jamie's body was that sex, to Jamie, didn't seem like a joy to sneak off to. Rather, it felt like a crossover into her mother's life. The only people Jamie knew who enjoyed sex or drugs were the people who weren't allowed to indulge: Tammy, Debbie, all the boys at the beach. Was the thrill in those things simply because they were forbidden?

"Please Mom," Jamie finally said, "please just let me do this on my own."

"Sex is a beautiful, magical thing, honey. But pregnancy isn't. So just tell me you're using birth control."

"I'm using birth control. Good night."

"Are you on the pill?"

"Diaphragm. Okay?"

"What size? I have a diaphragm, too. Wouldn't it be funny if we were the same size?!"

"Mom, I really need to go to sleep."

"I'm a ninety-five."

"Good for you, Mom. That sounds about the size of a Frisbee."

Betty laughed. "A Frisbee! That's funny. I'm going to tell your father you said that."

"Please don't tell Dad any of this."

"But that's funny. A Frisbee! So I take it yours isn't a Frisbee."

"More like a yarmulke for a guinea pig."

Betty laughed again. "Oh, you are so funny! I wish I could tell your sister this but it would just make her mad."

"Mom, please don't tell anyone. Especially not Dog Feather."

"Okay, sweetheart. It's between me and you."

"Me and you," Jamie said, and her mother leaned down and kissed her once, quick, right on the lips.

My parents found out I'm having sex," Jamie told Debbie and Tammy. They lay three in a row on their stomachs facing the ocean. Tammy's top was untied; she stayed down low to cover her breasts.

"How did they find out?" Debbie asked. She was smiling.

"Dog Feather."

"How'd he know?" Tammy tied her top, then propped herself up on her elbows.

"He guessed, and they believed him."

"Why didn't you just say it wasn't true?" Tammy asked.

"I dunno. They don't care so there didn't seem to be a point in lying."

"They don't care!" Debbie was laughing.

"They're nudists," Tammy said. "Of course they don't care. I mean, did you think they'd really care? Did anyone think they'd care? I mean, they're not even Christian!"

"I kinda hoped they'd care." Jamie tried not to sound defensive; she didn't want to try this case with Tammy, who seemed to feel that the only way to get away with bad behavior was to filter it through Christ. Jamie just wanted to complain. "I mean, you'd think a person would care that their daughter, who *just* turned fourteen, is having sex with a seventeen-year-old boy."

"They don't care if you smoke pot, so why would they care about sex?"

"My father actually does care if I smoke pot. And I don't smoke it."

"You have," Tammy said.

"Once. That day we hung out with Jan." Jamie felt a flush of embarrassment when she remembered how hard she had tried to be cool in front of Jan.

"You could smoke every day if you wanted to," Debbie said.

"I dunno," Jamie said. "Having sex just seems like something to care about."

"I think it's cool that they don't care," Debbie said.

"It's grossing me out," Jamie said. "Every time Flip brings up sex I just see my mother sitting on my bed asking me what kind of birth control I'm using."

"No way!" Debbie said.

"Yes. And then she told me—"

"What?" Debbie sat up and crossed her legs.

"I can't even say it because it's so gross."

"You have to tell us." Tammy sat up too.

"I don't know if I can say it aloud."

"Just say it and get it over with," Tammy said.

Jamie sat up, looked out at Flip, who was riding a wave, his hands in karate position, mouth open, knees bent. He wiped out, then popped up from the foamy water, smiling.

"Say it." Tammy demanded.

"She told me she wears a diaphragm too, and that it's a size ninety-five."

"That is so gross," Tammy said.

Debbie laughed like she was wheezing.

On day nine of Dog Feather's stay, Allen emerged from his study and said he was taking the day off work. Betty pushed a waxy smile across her face.

"We're going to the natural history museum today," Betty said. "You don't want to come, do you?"

Allen looked over at Dog Feather, who sat at the counter eating seven-grain oatmeal with sliced strawberries that Betty had made for him. He wore Allen's leather slippers. Jamie was standing on the other side of the counter next to her mother; she refused to sit beside Dog Feather.

"Are those mine?" Allen looked down at the slippers.

"The floors are cold in the morning," Betty said, "and he has only one pair of shoes."

"So those are my slippers?"

"They remind me of the moccasins my grandmother

sewed for me when I was just a small boy." Dog Feather looked up from his oatmeal.

"Did she use a seal bone needle and the skin of an elk? Did she chew the thread from whale fat?" Jamie laughed, but no on else did.

"You know, I'll go with you to the museum," Allen said. He sat at the counter and poured himself a bowl of cereal.

"Jamie's not even coming," Betty said.

"How do you know I'm not coming?" Jamie said.

"You just said a couple minutes ago that you've probably been to that museum three hundred times."

"I've been three hundred times because I like it there."

"So you're coming too?" Betty wasn't even trying to look pleased.

"No," Jamie said. "I'll stay home."

"Come," Allen said.

"Why don't you stay home with her," Betty said. "She never has father-daughter time."

"Yeah, Dad," Jamie said. "It will be like when we were in Indian Maidens."

Dog Feather looked up.

"Don't say Indian," Betty said.

"That's what it was called," Jamie said. "It was Indian Maidens."

"What's Indian Maidens?" Dog Feather asked.

"It was a father/daughter club," Allen explained. "I think it was through the Girls Club of America. Or maybe it was the YMCA."

"They should call it Native American Maidens," Betty said.

Allen rolled his eyes.

"I don't understand why *Indian* is a bad word," Jamie said.

"The people in India are Indian," Dog Feather said.

"So, you can be Indian too."

"But I'm not from India," Dog Feather said. "I'm from the United States of America. My people were the first people here. This land belongs to my people."

"*This* land belonged to the Chumash, not the Pomo." If she were Chumash, Jamie thought, she'd start a tribal war against Dog Feather.

Betty slurped her coffee while staring at her daughter. Allen ate his cereal while looking alternately into the bowl and down at his slippers on Dog Feather's feet. Dog Feather smiled at Betty.

Renee walked into the kitchen. Since returning from Outward Bound she had spoken to Jamie only to discuss their mutual dislike of Dog Feather. Renee poured a bowl of cereal and sat on a stool on the other side of Allen.

"Renee," Jamie said.

"Farrah," Renee said.

"Do you think it's bad to say *Indian*?"

"Indian."

"See," Jamie said, "that wasn't so awful. I mean it's not like saying *fuck* or *shit*."

"Or *motherfucker*," Renee said.

"Or *mother shit fucker*," Jamie said, and she and her sister laughed while Allen and Betty looked at each other with bemused smiles.

"Sweetheart," Allen said to Renee, "do you want to go to the natural history museum with us today?"

"No."

"You can look at the Indian exhibit," Jamie said. "You know, those life-sized models of Chumash *Indians* picking up acorns, making fires, shooting arrows at mountain lions."

"She's too old for the museum," Betty said.

"She's younger than you," Jamie said.

"Yeah, Mom," Renee said. "Like, *twenty years* younger."

"No, I mean there's a window," Betty said. "The museum is for the very young or the somewhat old."

"Maybe Dog Feather's too old but not old enough. I mean, like, how old are you?" Jamie said to Dog Feather.

"In human years," Renee said, and Jamie laughed.

"Younger than the moon, older than the sparrow," Dog Feather said.

Allen lifted his eyebrows like he was waiting for more. Betty smiled.

"Come on!" Jamie said. "Sparrows have probably been around longer than humans. So you're saying you're like, over two hundred thousand years old?"

"How old are you really?" Allen asked. "Did you go to college?"

"Will you all just leave Dog Feather alone!" Betty said. "He's younger than Allen and I and older than you kids."

"So you know his age and you're not telling?" Jamie asked her mother.

"Your mother is very wise," Dog Feather said.

"Yeah, she's wise like the owl, right? Or is it wise like the slumbering wolf?" Jamie said.

"Are you old enough to vote?" Renee asked.

"Enough!" Betty said, and her face turned stiff, like a cat watching a hamster.

Allen, Renee, and Jamie convened in the kitchen after Betty and Dog Feather had left for the museum.

"Dad, you don't have to stay home for us," Renee said.

"I didn't really want to go," he said. "I was just trying to be included."

"I say you kick Dog Feather out of the house," Jamie said.

"Yeah, Dad," Renee said. "It's your house. Mom's your wife."

"He makes your mother happy." Allen sighed.

"Well he's making me miserable!" Jamie said. "And he's making Renee miserable too. So that's two unhappy people versus one happy one."

"And Dad," Renee said, "you seem unhappy too. So that's really three unhappy people versus one happy one."

"Dad, he's wearing your slippers! You love those slippers!" Jamie said.

"All our friends seem to like him."

"Yeah, 'cause he's got good pot," Renee said.

"Face it, Dad," Jamie said, "if he weren't an Indian, I mean if he were a Mexican or something, no one would have anything to do with him."

"How can you say that?!" Allen asked.

"It's true, " Renee said.

"If he were a Mexican," Jamie said, "Mom would hire him to clean out the flower beds, not take him to the museum."

"She's right," Renee said. "You need to evict him."

"I'm going to look through his stuff," Jamie said, and she marched out of the kitchen. Renee followed; she placed one hand on her sister's shoulder, making a chain between them. Allen didn't move from the stool, but he also made no indication that he minded if his daughters rummaged through Dog Feather's things.

Dog Feather's backpack was propped against the wall in Allen's study. His sleeping bag was on the floor next to the couch. There was a small zipper pouch at the bottom of the backpack. Jamie went there first.

"Maybe you should put on gloves," Renee said.

"For fingerprints?" Jamie asked. "You think he's going to fingerprint his backpack?"

"Your hands are always so greasy," Renee said. "You don't want to get caught, do you?"

Jamie unzipped the pouch, pulled out a folded wad of bills and handed them to Renee.

"One hundred thirty-seven dollars," Renee said, after a quick count.

"Hey Dad!" Jamie yelled out the door. "He's got a hundred thirty-seven dollars!"

Next Jamie pulled out a credit card with the name Anthony Mirello; a student ID for Essex City College in Newark, New Jersey, for Anthony Mirello; a membership card for the Italian Students' Union, also for Anthony Mirello; and a New Jersey driver's license with a photo of Dog Feather and the name Anthony Mirello.

"Dog Feather is a murderer!" Jamie handed the cards to her sister.

"You're such an idiot!" Renee said. "He's a liar, not a murderer."

"He murdered Anthony Mirello and assumed his identity!" Jamie laughed. "Look!"

"Dad!" Renee yelled. "Dog Feather is really Anthony Mirello!"

"OR ELSE HE KILLED ANTHONY MIRELLO!" Jamie was cracking herself up.

Allen showed up in the doorway.

"What are you screaming about?"

Renee handed him the four cards.

"Anthony Mirello," Allen said. "Funny name for a Native American."

"He's busted!" Renee said.

"You think Mom would let anyone named Anthony Mirello mooch off her for nine days?" Jamie asked.

"No way," Renee said.

"Maybe his mother was native and his father's a Mirello," Allen said.

"He said he was one hundred percent Pomo Indian," Jamie said. "He tells everyone that he was born on the reservation and that his dad didn't even speak English, he spoke only Pomo."

"Mom is going to die!" Renee said. "He is totally busted!"

"Don't tell your mother," Allen said.

"Dad!" Renee said. "We have to tell her. She's being duped!"

"Yeah, Dad. I mean, like, what if Flip wasn't really a surfer dude, what if he was in the KGB or something? I'd expect you to tell me."

"Don't worry, Farrah," Renee said. "You have to have *intelligence* to work in intelligence."

Renee avoided Flip when he was at the house and mentioned him only if she had a neat little quip to put him down. Jamie had grown so used to Renee's sharp tongue that she heard it as a distant murmur, the way a very old man hears his nagging old wife.

"Oh, when's Dog Feather's birthday?!" Jamie asked.

Allen read the license. "He's twenty-three. Your mother said he was twenty-nine. At least that's what he told her."

"He is *such* a liar!" Renee said.

Allen handed the cards back to Jamie, who shoved them, along with the money, back into the pouch where she found them. Then she unzipped the largest pocket, felt through some gritty clothes, and pulled out two magazines: *Knockers* and *Penthouse*.

"Gross!" She dropped the magazines on the floor.

Renee looked down at them with her head pulled back and her mouth half open.

"He's a pervert too!" she said.

"He's not a pervert." Allen leaned down and picked up *Knockers*.

"Dad!" Renee said. "How can you touch those!"

Allen flipped through the pages.

"Dad!" Renee's voice was shrill. "Do not look at those! Do not look at those in front of us! That is wrong!"

Allen laughed. "I'm just glancing," he said.

"That's gross," Jamie said.

Allen shoved the magazines back into the backpack, put one hand under Jamie's arm, and led her out of the study.

"Don't tell your mother any of this," he said.

"But what are we going to do?" Renee followed them out. "I mean, he's a liar. He's probably already gotten into your checking account and stolen all our money and–"

"He's probably convinced Mom that she needs to sign over the house to him. I mean, you know how she is about *things*–"

"Yeah," Renee said. "Mom thinks *things* have no value, so she probably did give him the house–"

"Like your slippers, Dad, I mean, she already gave him your slippers!" Jamie said.

"Girls!" Allen said. "I'll take care of it, don't worry."

Renee was usually the first person awake in the house, but the next morning, the day after they discovered that Dog Feather was Anthony Mirello, Jamie woke up earlier than her sister. She went downstairs, glancing at her father's closed study door as she turned toward the kitchen. Betty was at the kitchen counter in her red kimono bathrobe, reading the paper.

"Good morning," Jamie said.

Betty turned the page and sighed.

"Mom? Are you making anything good this morning? I'm dying for some waffles."

"Huh?" Betty didn't look up.

"Are you making breakfast?"

"No, no. You can cook if you want to."

"But you've been making all these great things for Dog Feather and I haven't been that hungry and now I'm really hungry and this is the day you're not cooking?"

Betty put the paper down and stared at her daughter.

"What are your plans for today?" she asked.

"I dunno. Go to the beach with Flip. Hang out with Tammy and Debbie maybe. What are you and Dog Feather doing?"

"He left." Betty picked up the paper and scowled.

"Why'd he leave?"

"It's the Indian way," Betty said.

"Native American way," Jamie said.

Betty rolled her eyes.

"He wasn't a real Indian," Jamie said.

Betty put down the paper and stared at Jamie.

"You're such a skeptic. You get that from your father."

Jamie said nothing.

"Of course Dog Feather was an Indian." Betty picked up the paper again.

"Dog Feather? Who would really name a child *dog* feather?"

"I don't want to hear what you have to say, unless it's something kind and generous. Just because someone is named something that you think is silly doesn't mean he's not a valuable person. *All* people are worth being nice to, whether they're Native American or Jewish or Christian or Buddhist or–"

"What about the Jews for Jesus? Dad always says they're morons."

"You should be kind to morons too! Kindness is not something you should dole out according to whom you think is or isn't worth it!"

Betty stared at Jamie to drive in her point, then handed her a receipt for $3.99 for a keychain purchased in the Yosemite Valley Country Store.

"You spent three ninety-nine on a keychain?!"

Betty grabbed the receipt, turned it over, and handed it back to Jamie.

"It's Dog Feather's receipt," Betty said. "He wrote a note on the back."

"Why didn't he just use a piece of paper?"

"I'm sure he was trying to save trees by using a receipt instead of fresh paper. We should all follow his example."

"I'm not going to write letters on the backs of receipts!"

"Jamie, just read the note."

"My Friends," Jamie read aloud, *"The winds have changed, the time has come, and this feather must blow on to another journey. Thank you for you kindness and hospitality. The sunshine of your generosity will carry me far in this journey. Peace, Dog Feather."*

Betty looked at her daughter, waiting for a response.

"Mom," Jamie said, "I know you don't like it when I'm critical, but even you have to admit that Jan could write a better note than this."

"What's wrong with that note?"

"The *winds have changed?!* The *sunshine of your generosity?* That's so corny. And he uses the word *journey* twice. I mean, *journey*? Does he think he's Christopher Columbus or something?"

"For godsakes, he's a Native American! Give the guy a break!"

Betty's eyes welled and glassed, and suddenly Jamie understood that it wasn't Dog Feather who needed a break, but her mother. And she gave it to her.

10

Renee was angry because her mother wouldn't take the film from the pictures she had taken at Outward Bound to the Quik-Photo drive-thru booth where they'd be developed in a few hours. She had been home twelve days and still had no photos to prove what she had gone though. The reason Betty wouldn't take Renee's film to the drive-thru booth was that they were having a party and she was wholly focused on that.

"Honey, this party's for you, in part," Betty told Renee.

Betty talked to her daughters as she passed by them. She had been walking through the kitchen to the backyard and into the kitchen again in an endless loop. Each time she swooped by there was something different in her hands. Candles on her way out, wet towels on her way in, aluminum tubs that would be filled with ice and drinks on her way out, two pairs of Jamie's flip-flops on the way in.

"Naked Leon and Lois and all your other naked friends are not my idea of a party for me," Renee said.

"There'll be other kids too," Betty said "The same kids who were at most of our parties last summer, and all the kids who were at the last party. Those cute boys who are around your age, Mitch and Paul, they'll be here. And the pretty Layman twins."

"Flip will be here," Jamie said.

"Flip should be named Flip-Flop," Renee said, "because he has the brains of one."

Jamie started to tell her sister that flip-flops were Flip's favorite type of shoe and that Flip had once told her (in a drunken slur) that anyone who wore flip-flops was in a way advertising their love for him, Flip, without the flop; but she realized the story would not work in Flip's favor. Besides, there was no point in trying to proselytize Renee into worshipping the greatness of Flip. She was as stuck on hating him as Jamie was on loving him.

Allen came into the kitchen through the garage; he was smiling, excited.

"I got it!" he said. "They're setting it up right now."

Betty walked to the back yard and peered out. Jamie and Renee hopped off the kitchen stools and followed their mother. There were three men walking down the hill carrying a box almost as long and wide as the pool.

"What is it?"

"You'll see," Allen said. "It's a present for you kids."

"We're too old for a swing set, Dad," Renee said.

"I know," Allen said.

"We're too old for a geodesic dome too," Jamie said. That year, geodesic domes had been erected all around town. There was one at the elementary school, one at the East Beach playground, one at the drive-in movie theater where the family often went on Sundays for the Swap Meet. There was also a giant one built as a house near Isla Vista Beach with triangular windows seemingly scattered at random, and a front door that contained the only right angle on the house.

"It's better than a geodesic dome," Allen said.

Renee walked out past the pool and gardens to get a better look, then ran back to tell Jamie they were assembling a trampoline.

"Why'd you tell her?!" Allen said. "I didn't want Jamie to see it until it was completely set up."

"What about me?" Renee asked. "You didn't care if I saw it before it was set up?"

"You ran off before I could stop you," Allen said. "Did you see how big it is? It's industrial-sized, the kind of trampoline they have for circuses."

"Let's go!" Jamie said, and she ran to the trampoline with her parents and sister following. Betty climbed up with the girls and the three of them jumped while Allen signed papers on a clipboard, which had been handed to him by one of the workers.

When the men left, Allen climbed on and the family jumped together. Betty's short hair flipped up and down like a darting bird. Renee smiled for what seemed like the first time since she'd been home from Outward Bound. Allen took Betty's hands and the two of them jumped together, laughing and hooting. And then Renee took Jamie's hand and broke into Betty and Allen's grip and suddenly they were all connected in a bouncing, grinning circle. Jamie thought it was a perfect moment; painful almost, in the realization of its perfection. Her sister was happy to be among them (sweetly holding Jamie's hand like she had when they played twins), her parents were happy with each other, everyone had their clothes on, and no one was high. Jamie shut her eyes for a second and made a wish that the party would be canceled and they would spend the rest of the day, and even into the night, jumping. The trampoline was long and flat and seemed like a perfect place for a picnic dinner. And why not sleep on a trampoline, Jamie wondered, four in a row tucked into sleeping bags on the elastic platform, hovering over the biting, multilegged things that lurked in the grass.

The jump-party ended when Rosa (who cleaned the house on Wednesdays) and her husband, Jesus (who took care of the pool and gardens and whose name everyone except Betty pronounced *Hey-soos*), came out to the backyard. Betty had hired Rosa and Jesus to help serve food and clean up after the party. Rosa and Jesus were probably the same age as Betty and Allen, but they had a smiling, deferential manner that made them seem much younger. And they dressed younger, too, Rosa in clothes from JC Penney that were always a season behind whatever was in fashion—all of it from the Juniors department, as nothing from the women's department would have fit. Her hair fell to the top of her behind when it was out of a braid, which was rare. Jesus dressed like a surfer in ripped jeans, T-shirts, and shorts. That night he wore a clean, ironed, button-down shirt tucked into his jeans. Jamie imagined Rosa looking at him in their bedroom (a bedroom that she always thought would have a gilt-and-white bedroom set, like those she had seen in the windows of cheap furniture stores in Los Angeles) and telling him that he had to look nice for the party: no holes, nothing untucked, and no legs showing. Rosa spoke English and Jesus didn't, so she did all the talking.

"Miss Betty," Rosa said, "where do you want us to start?"

For several seconds the family remained connected in the circle. Then Betty dropped her hands, Allen followed, and they both climbed down from the trampoline. Betty took Rosa and Jesus inside, while Allen went to the bar at the pool. Because of the shrubs that surrounded the pool area and the fact that the lawn was downhill from the pool, Jamie could only see her father when she jumped up. She and Renee watched him at the bar, setting up glasses and pitchers, slicing lemons and limes. It was like watching an old-fashioned movie; his movements seemed jerky from the missed beat of the down jump that put him out of sight.

About five minutes before the guests were scheduled to arrive, Flip phoned Jamie.

"Put your diaphragm in," Flip said.

"But we're having a party." Jamie was in her father's study, whispering into the phone. She looked down at the folders arranged in a fan on her father's desk and read his block print on the tabs: McMahon Furniture, Wilson Leather and Fur, Cal Worthington.

"We'll totally sneak off," Flip said. "I mean, shit, we've done it only three times since I've been home and I'm starting to get a little edgy, you know."

His words felt like a threat. The image of Flip with older, prettier, tanner girls clunked around Jamie's brain like a stone in an empty soup can.

"Okay, I'll put it in," she said.

Upstairs in the bathroom, with the diaphragm sliding out of her hand like an oiled rodent, Jamie wondered how she would feel about Flip if they were alone on an island. Would the thrill of being with him still shiver across her skin if no one else knew they were together—if there weren't an entire society of teenage girls who envied her position? Would she love Flip if she didn't know that her sister had once had a *Tiger Beat*-style crush on him—a crush that never even pretended to hold the expectation of reciprocity? Would she love him if she didn't have the constant emotional cushion of Tammy and Debbie on the other side of her soiled sheets? Her deflated, orgasmless sex with Flip had become a joke with the girls, a source of such great fits of laughter that Jamie often found herself wishing things were worse than they actually were just for the hysterics it would bring to her girlfriends. Jamie found she couldn't separate the experience of Flip's popularity from the experience of loving Flip. It was like falling in love with a billionaire—would *he* be the same man, the type of man you'd fall in love with, if he didn't have his money?

The adults congregated at the shallow end of the pool, near the bar. The kids crammed around the table of food that had been set up near the deep end. It was so crowded that from the kitchen the pool was invisible; all one could see was bodies, many naked, some half-naked, and a few clothed. Renee took Paul and Mitch to the trampoline. Flip and Jamie followed. Renee was far more bold than she had been the last time they had seen these boys, at the pool party that kicked off the bicentennial summer.

"You're different," Paul said, tilting his head and smiling at Renee.

"I went to Outward Bound," Renee said, as if that were an answer everyone should have understood.

"She's a mountain mama," Flip said. Jamie cringed as she anticipated Renee's knifed tongue working over that phrase as soon as Flip went home.

Eventually, most of the kids were on the trampoline. Jamie felt carsick as she watched the near-collisions and the near-ejections off the trampoline. She was certain that someone would land headfirst on the ground and be killed, or worse, paralyzed. The previous summer, a boy at school had dove headfirst off the downtown pier; he hit an old pylon that had been burned to a stub in the pier fire two years earlier and was paralyzed from the neck down. Everyone who knew him well said he'd be better off dead, and Jamie believed them.

"Renee!" Jamie stood on the ground, waiting to catch anyone who might fall. She reached up and tried to grab her sister's ankle as Renee jumped face-to-face with Paul.

Renee kicked Jamie's hand off.

"Renee," Jamie said, "we've got to come up with some rules here or someone's going to get killed."

Renee stopped jumping and looked down at Jamie. Her body bounced and rocked as if she were on a boat as everyone around her jumped.

"Why don't we say only three people on the trampoline at once. I mean, there are . . ." Jamie counted, "eight kids on there now. That's insane."

Renee trained her eyes on her sister to tell her that she was ruining her good time. Paul was listening. He stopped jumping.

"She's right," he said. "It'd be more fun if there were fewer people because then we could do tricks, you know, flips and stuff like that."

"Flips!" Flip said, leaping open-mouthed up in the air.

"Yeah," Renee said. "Let's say only three people at a time, so there's room to flip."

"Fliiiip!" Flip raised a fist in the air as he jumped.

"Cool," Paul said.

For a second Jamie was disappointed that she wasn't getting credit for the call for safety. Then she decided she didn't care; she didn't need credit, as long as there would be no death or paralysis.

"Well?" Jamie said.

"Well what?" Renee said.

"Tell everyone to get off and set up the three-person rule or something."

Paul stuck two fingers in his mouth and whistled the way men whistle for New York City cabs in movies. Everyone stopped talking, but no one stopped jumping.

"Only three on at a time!" he yelled.

"THREE AT A TIME!" Renee added.

Flip jumped off and stood beside Jamie.

"I wish Dog Feather were still here," he said. "He was the coolest Indian dude ever. And he had way better doobage than your parents."

"He wasn't really an Indian," Jamie said. "I already told you that."

"Let's eat," Flip said. He took Jamie's hand and pulled her away from the trampoline toward the pool.

At the food table, they dipped tortilla chips into Rosa's homemade salsa. The salsa was so good and crisp that Jamie imagined picking up the bowl and drinking it down like Chunky Soup. Flip stared at the naked women, smiling.

"Your mom has the best tits of the party," he said.

"Don't start that again!" Jamie picked up another chip.

"That lady over there looks like she's from *National Geographic* or something. I mean, her tits are like empty wet plastic bags."

Jamie looked over. He was right, but she didn't want to discuss that woman's breasts or anyone else's with him. She didn't want to be forced to think about her naked parents and their naked friends on Flip's terms, which were, as she understood them, solidly sexual.

"I'm gettin' kinda horny looking at all these naked old ladies."

"They're not that old," Jamie said. "And please don't get another erection for my mom."

"Some of them are totally foxy. I mean, none of them are as foxy as you, but they are still foxy, you know, like the way they're just walking around and shit. Why don't you go naked?"

"No way."

"All these old men would be looking at you and I'd be, like, Yeah, she's totally with me, man."

"I don't think anyone would notice me." Jamie's experience of life with her mother was that if Betty was in the room, that's where people looked.

"Your dad's got a hella long dick, man." Flip nodded in the direction of Allen.

"Flip! Please! I don't want to look at my dad's dick!"

"But it's right there! I can't help but look at it!"

"Look at something else."

"What?"

"See that baby." Jamie pointed to Lacey, who was wearing her red bandana-print swimsuit and sitting on her naked father's lap. She was trying to suck on a slice of orange, which kept turning in her hand so that she had more peel in her mouth than fruit.

"What about her?"

"Last time they were here, at the beginning of the summer before we were going out—"

"Yeah?"

"Her dad just threw her off the edge of the pool into the water 'cause he thought she could swim."

"No way."

"I swear. I caught her and pulled her out. It was freaky."

"Totally."

"Wanna swim?"

"Let's go hide out somewhere and have sex first."

"Uh . . ."

"We can go to the far end of the yard. No one will see us. Everyone's here or at the trampoline. No one's going to walk all the way back there."

"Why don't we go to my room and lock the door?"

"It's so much more cool outdoors. I mean, it's like real. Natural."

Flip took Jamie's hand and led her away from the pool. She grabbed a handful of chips and ate them while they walked out of the pool area, past the trampoline, past a row of hedges that outlined the grass, through a stand of fragrant eucalyptus trees, to the wooden fence that was so far back and so hidden from the house that the only way to see it was to walk all the way to it.

"Koala bears eat only eucalyptus," Flip said.

"They explode in fires," Jamie said.

"Koalas explode in fires?"

"No!" Jamie couldn't stop laughing. Flip laughed too. "Eucalyptus! Remember the Banana Road fire?"

"Yeah." Flip was still giggling.

"Dad drove us to the top of East Camino Cielo that night and we parked the car up there and watched the eucalyptus exploding."

"That must have been way cool."

"It was beautiful," Jamie said, and she popped her last chip into her mouth just as Flip leaned in for a kiss.

"Wait!" Jamie chewed fast and swallowed. "Okay. Now."

Jamie's back was flat against the fence slats. Flip leaned into her, hard and deep as if he were going to iron her with his chest and crotch while he kissed her. Jamie imagined splinters in her back and how that detail would add to the story she would later tell Tammy and Debbie. In her head she narrated each move Flip made, edited it, and rewrote it if it didn't sound interesting or funny enough.

And just as Jamie was noting the repetitive drumbeat that Flip used when fluttering his hand in her crotch, she unexpectedly felt as if she were burning like a eucalyptus fire. A spectacular, beautiful eucalyptus fire. A fire so rich with heat and flames that Jamie couldn't escape into the running narrative in her head—she was suddenly centered in her own body, like a stacking cup that fit perfectly into the cup outside it.

Flip lifted Jamie's right leg, put himself inside her, and the fire spread, exploding like ignited oil.

And then, in an instant, Jamie understood why sex was such a big deal; why it made marriages and broke them up again; why most graffiti in public bathrooms was about sex; why Dog Feather read *Knockers* and loved Betty's breasts; why Allen loved Betty; why Leon hung around the house like a mosquito you couldn't pin down long enough to catch; why Tammy and Debbie thought they were in love; why Flip wanted to do it right then and right there.

A plunging shudder ran through Jamie; she lost vision and her knees buckled. She feared she might gasp, or weep,

or laugh. But she didn't. She went limp in Flip's arms. Flip
kissed Jamie's forehead, which was covered in dewy sweat,
like a layer of velvet. He told Jamie he loved her. She said
she loved him too. And she knew, right then, that she'd be
happy to be alone on an island with Flip, with no audience
to help discern her feelings. He alone could sustain her. The
orgasms would sustain her. Sex like this was better than
having colorless sex that led to neon stories. It was better
than cracking up with her friends.

They stood there, bodies suctioned together, as still as the air.
Flip's skin smelled musky, like sun-induced sweat, and astringent,
like the eucalyptus. The music from the party sounded far away,
as if it were music from another town, another era. For the first
time, Jamie actually felt connected to Flip and she wondered if
that connected feeling was the soul of true love. And then she
heard the hooting laughter of her mother, and the gauzy cloud
of love cracked open and plunged her back to reality.

"We better check on the trampoline," Jamie said. "Make
sure everyone's safe."

"Cool," Flip said, putting his hand around Jamie's waist
as they walked. The song "Love Roller Coaster" came on
and Flip started bobbing his head like he was dancing. Jamie
laughed.

"Ohio Players," he said.

"Yeah," Jamie said. "You know that album cover with the
girl smothered in honey?"

"I know," Flip said. "Everyone says she died from lack of
oxygen."

"You don't believe it?"

"Yeah. Right. And her death scream is on the album."

"It's so creepy that they'd keep her dying scream on the
song, don't you think?"

"Ah, to be fourteen again," Jamie's seventeen-year-old boy-friend said, and he gave her a paternal peck on the cheek.

"Hey, there's this girl at school and her dad's a record producer and he told her it was true."

"Yeah," Flip said, "right."

As they approached the trampoline, ten-year-old Franny, whom Jamie thought looked far larger and more mature than she had last summer, was loading one-year-old Lacey up for a jump. There were three big kids already jumping.

"Hey," Jamie said, "don't put her up there, she could get trampled and killed."

Flip reached up and took Lacey off the trampoline, an act that made Jamie bite her lip to hold in a love-struck sigh.

"I'm babysitting," Franny said. "They're paying me a dollar an hour."

"That's good," Jamie said. "But, listen, don't put her up there when the big kids are jumping." Jamie liked the sound of her voice as she said this, the gentle authority.

Two kids climbed down and Franny climbed up with Lacey. Jamie's job was done, she felt, so she wandered away with Flip, their arms loosely draped across each other's backs.

Jamie and Flip settled on a poolside boulder. They sat side-by-side, talking while staring down at their tangled-together bare, brown feet. Almost twenty-five minutes passed like this, and when they finally looked up the pool was quiet and empty, like it had been closed.

"Where is everyone?" Jamie asked Jesus, who was walk-ing by with a tray of empty glasses.

Jesus smiled and nodded his head toward the trampoline.

"Let's go," Flip said, and they jogged down the hill.

The trampoline was covered with naked, jumping adults.

Betty was near the edge, her giant breasts heaving and plummeting. Leon was right in front of her, his eyes following the bouncing breasts, his teeth showing. More adults were congregated around the trampoline. They were laughing, shouting at the jumpers, cheering as if they were watching a football game. Rod was jumping with Lacey in his arms. Jamie worried that she'd be knocked out of his grip, sent flying in the air. Perhaps Lacey's mother, Bridget, was worried about this too, for she reached up to Rod and yelled at him to hand the baby down.

"This is so fucking cool," Flip said. "I wish my parents were like this."

"Believe me, you do not want to watch your parents jumping naked on a trampoline." Jamie looked back up to the trampoline and saw that Bridget was now jumping with Rod. This was the first time she had seen the married couple within the same frame of vision. They always seemed divided by an expanse of room, or water, or lawn. And now there they were, hand in hand, jumping together.

"I think the trampoline unifies people," Jamie said to Flip.

"That's such a totally cool way of looking at it," he said, and he leaned forward and latched his lips onto Jamie's, his tongue flickering in her mouth. Jamie looked up to see if either of her parents witnessed this kiss, but they were oblivious. Everyone on the trampoline, in fact, was oblivious; they seemed to be caught under an invisible net of naked drunkenness. Jamie thought that if she slit her throat and ran around the trampoline with her head dangling off her neck by a string, none of these people would have noticed.

Jamie and Flip walked back to the pool where the kids had begun to congregate. They stood, the way normal parents might, at the edge of the pool, surveying the scene.

Renee was sitting on the base of the diving board with Paul. Jamie wondered if they had kissed; and if they had, could it possibly have felt as good as what she and Flip had just done against the fence? The Layman sisters and a few boys were gathered in the shallow end working out the rules to a game of Marco Polo. The furry-headed Olsen boy was standing on his head on the end of the diving board. He lived with his parents and four cats on a yacht and was homeschooled by his father. Each time Jamie saw him, he seemed more feral than the time before.

And then Jamie noticed it: a bandana floating in the deep end. She couldn't get the words out when she realized that it was not a bandana; it was Lacey, facedown. Jesus was nearby, picking up wet towels; Jamie turned to him, gasping and pointing at Lacey in the pool. Before she could take another breath, Jesus dove into the pool and pulled the baby out. He thrust her to the side of the pool, jumped out, and kneeled over her. Jesus slipped his right hand under Lacey's neck and her head flopped back like a baby doll's. He plunged his mouth over her, covering Lacey's entire face, it seemed, and puffed out two quick breaths. Then with his thick, dark fingers, Jesus rapidly thumped Lacey's chest, just where her mounded belly met her ribcage. Jamie watched Jesus's eyes—they were steady, black marbles. He was moving with the fluid efficiency of a machine: mouth to chest to mouth to chest. Jamie wondered if Jesus had done this before, in Mexico, perhaps. And then Jamie wondered why she was thinking about Jesus and why wasn't she screaming or running for more help, or thumping *her* hand on Lacey's chest while Jesus blew into her mouth and nose.

None of the kids, it seemed, had noticed, for the debate on the Marco Polo rules continued. Flip was no longer standing beside Jamie; he was running toward her with a group of naked adults. Jamie saw her mother's face: white, rigid, her mouth in the shape of a scream.

Renee was on the poolside phone and she was crying. Allen took the phone from her. It was so quiet, even with all the people present, that Jamie could hear everything he said: a one-year-old girl, yes, someone is giving her mouth-to-mouth. Rod and Bridget were kneeling beside Lacey. Bridget was rubbing the baby's feet and hands, talking to her, telling her to wake up. Rod tried to give Lacey mouth-to-mouth but he couldn't breathe, he said, so Jesus resumed the job.

Lacey was limp and still. She looked rubbery, fake.

Allen sent the kids away when the ambulance arrived. They went into the house and Jamie watched out the living room window as men in white jumpsuits loaded the weightless Lacey doll onto a white stretcher into the back of the ambulance. Rod and Bridget were behind her. They were wrapped in towels and were naked beneath them. Betty, in a towel herself, handed Rod a bundle of clothes with shoes on the bottom. He looked at them blankly, as if he wasn't sure what to do with them, then pulled them against his chest and climbed into the ambulance. The men in jumpsuits shut the doors and the ambulance drove away. Left behind on the street was a yellow leather sandal–Bridget's, Jamie presumed. Her mind would not think about Lacey, would not enter the room that held the visions she'd just taken in. Instead, her thoughts were stuck on the yellow sandal: how Bridget would limp around the hospital with one unshod foot; what she'd look like in the hallways; if anyone would notice the skinny woman with one shoe.

The kids stayed in the living room, herded together, each

person recounting exactly what they were doing when they realized what was going on. Renee started crying small, tight tears. Jamie looked at her and felt she should cry with her, but she was too aware of Flip beside her, too aware of herself standing in the center of the room watching everything with a dreamy detachment. Flip rubbed circles on Jamie's back; he sniffed. Jamie was taken by the gesture, enraptured by the sniff, which may have indicated the edge of a cry. And then, unexpectedly, she was listening to her own, weak, whimperings—a sound that reminded her of the sounds of sex. With horror, Jamie realized that as Lacey was on her way to the hospital, Jamie's thoughts were on standing up against a fence and doing *it* with her boyfriend. Her mother had spoken often of karma and Jamie wondered what bad karma would befall her for her lack of proper focus on the tragedy that had just occurred.

The police pulled up in two cars that, like the ambulance, they parked in the middle of the street. One car had two men, the other had only one. All three men were big, bulky, and slow-moving. They ambled toward the house.

"You get the door," Renee said to Jamie, "and I'll warn Mom and Dad."

"They should probably get dressed to talk to the police," Jamie said.

"No duh!" Renee said, running out of the room to fetch their parents.

Jamie brought the police into the living room and asked them to sit. The ten kids in the room stared at them.

"Why don't you guys go into the TV room," Jamie said, and Flip jumped up and corralled the kids, like a pack of dogs, into the TV room.

It seemed like forever before Allen and Leon entered the

living room. Allen was in jeans and a white T-shirt; Leon had on shorts and a button-down shirt. They looked like normal, reasonable people. And then Betty wandered in wearing cutoff jean shorts and nothing else. All three police officers shifted and sat up in their seats as they stared at Betty.

Renee ran into the room holding the gauzy, Mexican blouse that Betty had been wearing earlier that day.

"Oh," Betty said, as she took the blouse and pulled it on over her head.

"Let's go." Renee took Jamie's arm and led her into the TV room.

Someone had taken a poll while Jamie and Renee were out of the room.

"Do you believe in God?" Paul asked.

"Yes," Renee said.

"I don't know," Jamie said.

"Then you're agnostic," Paul said.

"Okay," Jamie said.

"And you're a believer," he said to Renee. "You, Kathy and Pam Layman, and Franny."

"What's everyone else?" Renee asked.

"Mostly agnostic, and some atheists."

Ten-year-old Franny said, "I think we should pray even if you guys don't believe."

"If we pray," Paul said, "we need to pray to an all-encompassing god, a nature god, or a spiritual god."

"Like the human spirit of all things," said Daniel, a precocious eleven-year-old boy with a long, girly hair like his father's.

"The Chumash Indians have four gods," Jamie said, "celestial gods that live in the sky."

"I'll pray to those dudes," Flip said, and he nudged Jamie with his elbow.

"They're Sky Eagle, Sun, Coyote, and Morning Star," Jamie said.

"You're so lame," Renee said.

"I think that sounds cool," Paul said, and Renee blushed. "Raise your hand if you're willing to pray to the Chumash celestial gods."

Everyone raised their hands except Franny.

"Who do you want to pray to?" Paul asked.

"God," she said. "The real one."

"Okay, so you pray to him and we'll pray to the Chumash gods."

They gathered in a circle with the ottoman in the center. The Game of Life was sitting on the ottoman leftover from when Jamie and Renee had played that morning after breakfast. It occurred to Jamie then how odd it was that in the Game of Life there was no such thing as drowning or death, even.

Paul spoke: "We are gathered here to pray for the life of Lacey, and we are begging the Chumash celestial gods . . ." Paul turned his head and stared expectantly at Jamie.

"Sky Eagle, Sun, Coyote, and Morning Star," Jamie said.

"Sky Eagle, Sun, Coyote, and Morning Star," Paul repeated, "to look down and make sure that Lacey is okay."

Paul nodded his head to indicate that he was finished and everyone, including Franny, said amen.

The phone rang; Renee and Jamie looked at it but neither answered. A few minutes later Allen came into the TV room with Mitch and Paul's dad, Robert, and the Layman sisters' dad, David.

"Kids." Allen lifted his hand and wiped at his eyes. Jamie had never seen her father cry and was so stunned and saddened by the sight that she could think only of him and not of the event that had caused his tears. He took a handkerchief from his pocket, blew his nose, and waved his hand to indicate that he couldn't speak.

"Lacey's dead," Robert said, and he put his hand on Allen's shoulders and rubbed it back and forth a little. Most of the kids in the room started crying. The Layman girls immediately turned to each other and leaned in, head to head, like mating swans. Franny reached over and clutched the wild Olsen boy to her chest. He shut his eyes and his body went still in a way that Jamie had never seen in him. Mitch was slumped in a chair, staring out, mouth open, eyes a watery smear. The girly-haired Daniel rubbed his eyes with his fists, crying the way a cartoon baby might. Jamie imagined text floating out of his mouth spelling WAAA. And Paul was entwined with Renee. Renee appeared to be crying on his shoulder, but the stiffness in her back, and the awkward right angles of her arms, made Jamie wonder if her sister were faking her tears as an excuse to be held. Flip put an arm around Jamie's waist, but she didn't turn to look at him. She was now focused on her father, who was really crying, shoulders bobbing, tears flowing down his face, small sounds coming out as he tried to speak. Robert held Allen square at the shoulders and looked at him intently, as if he were waiting to hear what Allen had to say. Jamie's heart hurt in a way she had never felt before—a churning thrombosis in the center of her chest.

Jamie looked away from her father, out the window to

the empty pool. She thought of the last swim party when she had held Lacey in her arms; she remembered the feel of Lacey, the weight of her. How could it be, Jamie wondered, that that warm ball of squirming flesh would no longer exist, was now only as real and permanent as a memory?

11

The next day Flip broke up with Jamie.

Over the phone.

While his friends were in the room waiting for him to drive them to the beach.

"Can't we work this out?" Jamie said, and she covered the mouthpiece with her hand so he couldn't hear her cry.

"Things are so heavy at your house right now," Flip said. "I'm just going to stay away for a while and let you work it all out, cool? I mean, shit, you don't want me around anyway."

"But I do." Jamie let the snot drip down to her upper lip. She didn't want him to hear even a sniff.

"No way, man. You don't. I know about these things. That was some gnarly, heavy shit that went down yester-day. I mean, a baby fucking died. Totally died. Doesn't even exist anymore. Is not part of this planet, you know?"

"Yeah."

"There's just no way we can stay together after that. At least not for a few months. I mean–" And then Flip yelled to his friends, "HOLD THE FUCK ON, I'LL BE OFF IN A MINUTE! So what was I saying?"

"Uh," Jamie choked. She knew Flip was dumping her but she truly could not recall what he had just said.

"Okay. So. Later. Right?" Flip said.

"Yeah. Later."

Jamie hung up the phone, went to the freezer, and pulled out a carton of butter pecan ice cream. She would never have ordered butter pecan at Baskin-Robbins or at Thrifty's Drug Store, where you could get a single cone for a nickel and a triple for fifteen cents, but it was Allen's favorite, the only flavor Betty ever thought to buy. Jamie was glad no one was in the kitchen. She wasn't ready to repeat the news she had just heard on the phone. She didn't want to see her mother's face as she looked at her, knowing that her daughter's heart was broken. And she was glad she hadn't made plans with Tammy and Debbie that day because she particularly didn't want to hear what they had to say—that of course Flip wouldn't want to date a girl whose parents were so into naked swimming and smoking pot and not being Christian that a baby actually died in their pool.

Several minutes later Jamie was still standing at the open freezer, eating the butter pecan with her fingers wedged together like short, thick chopsticks. She couldn't recall what she had been thinking the previous minutes; she knew only she hadn't been crying about Lacey or fretting about Flip. It was as if the chill from the ice cream were a shot of novocaine to her heart. She was temporarily numb to the drilling pain she knew was hovering somewhere nearby.

Allen walked in carrying three giant plastic bags from Kennedy's Marine World. He put the bags down and looked at his daughter.

"Why don't you use a spoon?"

"I don't really want any," Jamie said. "I was just tasting it."

"So taste it with a spoon."

"A spoon's not worth the time."

"Not worth the time? Of course it's worth the time. Utensils are always worth the time."

Jamie closed up the ice cream, put it back in the freezer, and took out a handful of quarter-sized peanut butter cups that her father always kept in the freezer. Allen brought home a white string-tied box of them every week after his visit to the shrink, whose office was next door to a gourmet market. Allen was often the only one who ate the peanut butter cups; the boxes frequently piled up until Betty would send them home with Rosa and Jesus.

"Peanut butter cup?" Jamie held her hand out to her father, who plucked two, peeled off the brown paper wrappers, and popped them in his mouth. Jamie dumped her handful on the counter, unpeeled them all, then ate them one by one—dropping each, whole, into her mouth. Again, she felt comfortably numb.

"Where's your mom?"

"Don't know."

"Where's your sister?"

"TV room. Watching *The Newlywed Game*."

"Help me with these bags."

Jamie picked up a bag and followed Allen to the pool-room. On one wall were shelves with towels, pool toys, deflated rafts. On the other wall was a bar that hung the long way across the room. The bar had a couple of wetsuits from the summer Renee and Jamie took surfing lessons and all the wire hangers from the dry cleaners that Betty did not want in the closets but that Allen refused to let her throw out. Allen opened a plastic bag and handed Jamie an orange life jacket.

"Hang them in order," he said. "Smallest to largest."

Jamie hung the life jacket that was in her hands, then the next one and the next one and the next one. Allen stood and watched as if he were a supervisor on a factory shift. When they were all hanging in order, Jamie counted them.

"Nine," she said.

"You never know," Allen said. "There might be nine young kids here one day."

"I don't think anyone who would fit these larger ones would need a life jacket."

"You can't say that for sure," Allen said. "The Vorstangs have a retarded boy. He'd need a big one."

"Who are the Vorstangs?"

"We've never had them over, but we might one day."

Renee walked into the poolroom from the house.

"What are you doing in here?"

"We're hanging life jackets," Jamie said.

Renee stood beside her sister and stared at the life jackets as if they were a row of dead bodies.

"Pool rule," Allen said. "Everyone under fourteen must be in a life jacket."

"We have a pool rule now?" Jamie said.

"Rule number one," Allen said.

Renee plucked the smallest life jacket off the bar and held it by the hanger a few inches from the floor. She teetered it back and forth and moved it along the ground as if there were a child in it. Jamie thought she could almost see Lacey's face peaking out from the round neckline, or her fat leg-wedges ending in tiny, square feet.

Renee hung up the life jacket and Allen started to cry. Jamie and Renee looked at him, at each other, at their father again.

"Flip broke up with me," Jamie said.

"Flip's an imbecile," Renee said.

"Oh sweetheart." Allen pulled Jamie to his chest. "Let's hope you're never dealt a blow more painful than that."

At her father's words, a shock of grief surged through Jamie's body with such force that she found herself gasping to breathe as she cried with jagged, choking spasms. A few moments later, when Renee reached up and rubbed her sister's back, Jamie was so startled that she almost stopped crying.

Instead, Jamie coughed up some tears and forced herself to continue, just so she could feel her sister's hand.

12

In the middle of the week, Allen and Betty went to Los Angeles to see the King Tut exhibit for the second time. That same day, Renee took off in the mobile home with the Nambine family for another trip to Lake Naciemiento. Renee frequently talked about the Nambine's mobile home as if it were the inside of King Tut's tomb. At breakfast that morning, before everyone had left, Renee suggested to Allen that they get a mobile home. Allen snorted in the back of his throat and laughed. Renee was so angry about the snort-laugh that she barely spoke to Allen and Betty for the rest of the morning. When the mobile home pulled away from the house, Jamie and her parents ran to the curb and waved good-bye to Renee, who hid below the window, line refusing to acknowledge them. This, naturally, threw Betty, Allen, and Jamie into fits of laughter witnessed only by Mrs. Nambine who, with a nervous smile on her face, leaned her head out the window like someone who was car-sick and waved back until they had turned the corner onto the next street. Jamie wished right then that her parents would stay home and hang out with her. She could help her mother cook, and she'd be willing to talk to her about sex or masturbation if that's what Betty wanted. Jamie had even volunteered to accompany her parents to the King Tut exhibit–although she had seen it once before and found the crush of the whispering crowd so overwhelming that she was unable to focus on the glittery objects before her. She would enjoy the two-hour trip to L.A., she thought, being ensconced in the car, safe from Flip, her friends, and the social mirror that would only show the fetid pile of sludge that Jamie felt she had become.

"We have only two tickets," Betty had said, before following Allen out the kitchen door, "and you hated the show last time."

Alone in the empty house Jamie felt spooked. She had visions of fat little Lacey floating in the corners of rooms watching her, her face red and shiny with tears. In the days following her death, no one went in the pool except Leon one night when it was ninety degrees and the Santa Ana winds were blowing like the hot breath of a giant. Allen and Betty sat on a boulder talking to him while Renee and Jamie looked out from the kitchen doors. Lois didn't come with him. When Betty came in the kitchen for a bottle of wine, she whispered to Renee and Jamie that Lois was mad at them because of Lacey.

Jamie thought that being mad at her parents was absurd–Lois should have been mad at Bridget and Rod for not watching Lacey; or at Franny, who had been babysitting; or at Renee for being the oldest one at the pool; or at Jamie herself–actually, mostly at Jamie. Clearly, Jamie thought, it was her fault for not being as vigilant in pre-

venting death as she usually was. If she hadn't had sex
by the eucalyptus trees, or even if she simply hadn't enjoyed the sex, her mind would have been more alert and
focused.

In spite of the fact that she assumed responsibility for
Lacey's death, Jamie repeatedly counted and recounted
the number of capable swimmers at the party. It became
an obsession that grew with each counting. After she had
counted once, she would count again to confirm the first
count. If the second count came out differently, she'd start
the process again. If the second count confirmed the first
count, she'd force herself to do a third count to reconfirm.
Jamie couldn't stop until she had reached an identical count
three times in a row. Once the count was completed, she
would picture all those people in a pyramid (Flip's face
blurred as if he'd been moving while the "picture" was taken
in Jamie's head) stacked at one end of the pool while Lacey
sat at the edge of the other end of the pool. How could it
be, Jamie wondered, with all those people present, not a
single person saw Lacey fall into the water?

After finishing her fourth triple count of the day, Jamie
picked up the phone and called Tammy—a conversation,
even with Tammy, whom she'd been avoiding, would force
her to stop counting.

"It's hot," Tammy said. "We're going to the beach."

"Why don't we swim at your house?" Jamie said.

"My parents are home and my dad doesn't like having
Jimmy and Brett hanging around."

"Why don't just me and you and Debbie hang out at
your pool?"

"What, and, like, tell Jimmy and Brett they're on their
own today?"

"Get out of your creepy house and come to the beach!" Debbie had grabbed the phone from Tammy.

"What do you mean creepy house?" Jamie said.

"You've been in the house since that baby died and, well, I think it's time you went out."

"I want to go out," Jamie said. "I just don't want to go to the beach. I mean, Flip will be there and I don't want to see him." Jamie's heart did a drumroll at the thought of Flip. She had been so busy counting lately that she had successfully quelled the throbbing of her scraped and battered heart.

"There're so many people hanging around it will be easy to avoid him," Debbie said.

And then Jamie heard Tammy in the background say, "Tell her!"

"Tell me what?"

"Nothing."

"What? Tell me!"

"Flip's with Terry."

"Terry who?"

Tammy grabbed the phone again and said, "How many Terrys hang out with the surfers?"

"Terry Watson?"

"Yeah."

"Since when?"

"Since, like, the day after that baby died."

"You're kidding."

"Unfortunately not."

"And you expect me to go to the beach with you and watch Flip with Terry Watson?" Jamie felt a claw in her chest, scratching off the still-soft scabs that had started to form on her psyche.

"She's nice. Don't worry about it."

"She's nice?! She's your friend?!"

Debbie grabbed the phone back. "She's really nice when you get to know her. I don't know why we've hated her all summer."

"We've hated her because she's, like, way too tan for someone with blond hair and her teeth are way too square for a human and way too white and she must weigh, what, ninety pounds? *And* she snubbed us all summer, getting up and moving her towel every time we tried to sit near her at the beach! Additionally, what kind of person would start dating a guy the *second* he broke up with his girlfriend?"

Debbie sighed. "Listen, if you can get past the fact that she's with Flip you'd really like her. I mean, Tammy and I have been sitting with her while the boys surf and I swear, she just cracks us up."

"Yeah, she sounds hysterical." Jamie imagined her internal wounds glistening wet, weeping with shiny viscous tails.

Tammy took the phone again: "Do you want to come to the beach with us, or do you want to wallow at home?"

"I'll wallow, thanks."

"Jamie!" Tammy said. "Don't be so sensitive!"

"My mom needs me," Jamie said. "I gotta go."

Jamie went to the freezer and pulled out the butter pecan ice cream and an already-opened box of peanut butter cups. She unwrapped nine peanut butter cups and dropped them into the butter pecan carton. Jamie ate the peanut-butter-cup ice cream with her achy, cold fingers. It took only a moment to regain the chilly numbing in her heart. When the peanut butter cups were gone, she unwrapped nine more and dropped them into the carton. When the ice cream was gone, she unwrapped the remaining six peanut butter cups and ate them, two at a time, one crammed into each cheek. Jamie collapsed the ice cream carton and the peanut butter cup box and hid them in the bottom of the trash, underneath that morning's soggy cereal and an empty carton of orange juice.

Jamie's stomach was stiff, edgy. She walked into the pantry, opened a box of Triscuits and forced some into her mouth. The salty needles of cracker scratched against the edges of her tongue. Jamie began a count of the people at the pool party, naming a person in her head each time her jaw flapped open. When she'd finished the box of crackers, the tip of her tongue felt inflamed—she imagined taste buds popping out like mini heads of cauliflower. But she had yet to obtain an identical count three times in a row and she needed something else to chew as she counted. So she took the Nutter Butter peanut butter sandwich cookies from a drawer and retrieved the milk from the refrigerator. Jamie drank the milk straight from the carton, holding a mouthful while she popped in half a Nutter Butter and chewed in time to the litany of names. The cookie didn't taste as good as usual, so she tilted the carton, bringing the milk into the triangle wedge of the pour-spout where she dipped the cookie before biting in. Each Nutter Butter was the shape of a giant peanut, each bite lopped the nut in two. There were thirty-two cookies in the pack. Four were missing when Jamie started. Four were suddenly left.

"I ate . . . ," Jamie said aloud, "sixteen?" She was drunk from food. "No, twenty-four, right?"

"Right," she answered, then turned her attention to her next prey.

There was a ceramic bowl of fruit on the counter.

Beside it was a smaller bowl filled with almonds. A silver chevron nutcracker lay on top of the nuts. Jamie cracked open an almond, but the payoff didn't seem worth the effort and she couldn't get a quick enough rhythm for a pool-party count. Jamie picked up an apple, held it in her hand; it, too, seemed wrong. She returned to the freezer, took out a new box of peanut butter cups, pulled off the cardboard that separated the two layers of the box, and ate three from the second layer, allowing her to start the count. When she shuffled around the remaining peanut butter cups, enlarging the gaps between cups, it looked like none were missing. She retied the string around the box and returned it to the back of the freezer.

Was she done? It didn't seem so; she needed one more perfect count. Jamie opened a box of Cheerios and shoveled handfuls into her mouth until she had completed a third exact count. She stumbled into the TV room, the top button of her Op shorts undone, her belly busting out firm and round like a baby's. There was half a Snickers bar sitting on the coffee table. Renee had opened it the night before, eaten half and then set the rest down and forgotten about it. It didn't strike Jamie as odd then, but as she picked up the bar and peeled off the remaining wrapper, the half-eatenness of it seemed absurd. Why not just take the three bites needed to finish it? Why leave anything behind? Who doesn't have room for three inches of chocolate, nuts, and caramel? Jamie finished the Snickers and shoved the wrapper down her shorts' pocket.

The television was on, but Jamie couldn't see. She couldn't hear. And she couldn't feel anything other than a bursting forward, a swirling expansion in her belly. She imagined she had just gained the entire body weight of

Terry Watson. Jamie felt suddenly deformed: a grotesque, plump dwarf. A day at the beach seemed like a fantasy. The beach, Jamie thought, was a place where other people went, people who weren't balancing the contents of their kitchen cupboards in their stomachs. People like Terry Watson, who was so thin there was no line between her ass and thigh. People like Tammy and Debbie who didn't have naked parents jumping on trampolines, or dead babies floating in their swimming pools. People who were never left alone in a house with a kitchen and heartache as their only company.

Jamie wanted to move back to the kitchen and fetch more food but to push herself up off the couch seemed unfathomably difficult. So she counted instead. Before she finished the first count she was asleep, like a drunk with his head on the bar—gone beyond sense and reason, blissful in oblivion.

13

Ten days later Jamie was in the kitchen on the phone with Tammy.

"What are you eating?" Tammy made a light popping sound; Jamie knew she was exhaling her cigarette.

"Cap'n Crunch. I talked my mother into buying it."

"She agreed? I thought she was Miss Carob Health Nut."

"Yeah, but she's also Miss Eat If It Makes You Happy. She doesn't believe in overcontrolling food."

"Can you stop with the Captain Crunch for a second? I can't hear anything but you crunching."

"Cap Nnnn Crunch. There's no *t* on the box."

"I can barely understand you with all that Cap *Nnnn* Crunch in your mouth."

"Well, I can hear you smoking."

"You cannot." Tammy popped her smoke out again.

"This is my sixth bowl," Jamie said. "The box is almost empty."

"So, are you coming or not?" Tammy asked. She wanted Jamie to go camping on the beach with her, Debbie, Brett, Jimmy and a boy named Scooter Ray.

"Does Scooter Ray know you're inviting me?"

"Yeah. He's the one who told me to call you."

Jamie rolled her eyes and let her head drop back. She had spoken with Tammy and Debbie only three times in the three weeks since Flip broke up with her, and each time it had been she who had called them. The last time she had hung up with them she had dared herself not to call again, to simply wait for their call. And here it was, at the beck of Scooter Ray.

"Why doesn't he just ask me out?" Jamie poured more cereal into the leftover orangey milk.

"He's Scooter Ray. He doesn't ask people out."

"His boxers kinda creep me out."

Scooter Ray, like all the boys at the beach, changed into his wetsuit right there, on the sand, in front of anyone who happened to be looking. His boxers were worn so thin there was nothing covering his ass. It was sheer cotton, like netting almost, with what appeared to be string around the leg holes. Sometimes he put a towel around his waist before slipping his boxers off and pulling on his wetsuit. But often he just turned his back to wherever the crowd sat, as if he were aware that everyone had already seen his behind anyway.

"He's totally hot," Tammy said.

"He doesn't speak."

"He dated all these senior girls who are, like, so hot they could get anyone, and *they* went out with him."

"But I don't even know him. Are you sure he knows that I'm me? I mean, like, did he say my name and everything, or did he say 'Call that girl you hang out with'?"

"He knows who you are!"

"Did he say my name?"

"I don't remember."

"So he could be thinking of someone else. Like, maybe if he just described me and said, that short girl with straight brown hair, you thought he was thinking of me, but really he was thinking of Amy Bell."

"He meant you. Okay? So are you coming or not?"

"And do what? You guys will be going off in your sleeping bags and then Scooter Ray and I will be sitting there by the fire and, what? Make out? Have sex?" Every time Jamie thought of sex she thought of the explosion she had felt against the fence with Flip. And when she thought of the explosion she thought of Lacey. Sex thoughts had become a tautological tangle from which she couldn't extract anything but the horrifying facts of that day.

"You could have sex," Tammy said. "I'm sure he'd want to."

"I think I've gained ten pounds," Jamie said.

"I wouldn't know, I haven't seen you in, like, a month," Tammy said.

"You wouldn't recognize me. I'm fat now."

"I want to have an ankle reduction."

"What do you mean?"

"Like, I want my ankles reduced."

Tammy's legs were as skinny as most women's forearms.

"Your ankles only look big because your legs are so skinny. If you put on weight they'd look smaller."

"No way. I'm not gaining a pound. My goal is to go all the way through high school without ever passing a hundred pounds."

"My goal is to not pass two hundred pounds."

"I'm serious. I'm really gonna do it."

"I gotta go." Jamie propped the phone against her shoulder and poured out more Cap'n Crunch.

"So are you coming camping with us or not?"

"If I can lose ten pounds by Friday I'll come. But I'm not making out with some guy who wears boxers that look like my dad's handkerchiefs and who doesn't speak."

"You're so critical! He's cute!"

Betty walked into the kitchen as Jamie was hanging up the phone. She wore a yellow skirt and blouse, orangey suntan-color stockings, and straw-colored pumps. She looked like she was in costume, playing the part of a secretary in the local dinner theater. Jamie ate her cereal and watched her mother put on mascara while looking at herself in a compact. Each time the mascara wand hit her eye, Betty's mouth appeared to unhinge and drop, as if she were singing and holding a note.

"Where did you get those clothes?"

"Wouldn't your sister be happy to see me dressed like this?" Betty put the mascara down and pulled a tube of lipstick out of her purse. She applied the lipstick, smacked her lips together, and made a pucker face into the mirror.

"Where are you going?"

"I've got a meeting with some priests. I'm going to try and get one of them to drive the bad spirits out of the pool."

"Really?"

"Yes, but don't tell your father. He's against it."

"He's against getting rid of the bad spirits?"

"No. He doesn't believe they're there."

"Do you?"

"Don't you?" Betty tucked the compact into her purse and looked at Jamie

"I guess." Jamie sprinkled out a fistful of Cap'n Crunch into the teaspoon of milk that remained in the bowl.

"That's why Lois won't come over here anymore," Betty said.

"I thought she was mad at you."

"She was, but now she's just spooked by the bad spirits in the house."

"I thought you said they were in the pool."

"House and pool." Betty brushed her hands along her skirt as if to smooth it, picked up her slouchy, leather purse, and slung it onto her shoulder.

"Can I go with you?" Jamie shoveled the last few bites of Cap'n Crunch into her mouth. She could feel cereal jammed like yellow putty into her gums and the cracks between her teeth.

"No. I can't drag you around with me when I'm visiting priests."

"But I don't want to be home alone with the evil spirits."

"Cross your arms over your stomach," Betty said. "That will prevent them from harming you or entering your body."

"Mom, are you serious?"

"Yes, I'm serious. You think I'd be looking for an exorcist if I weren't serious?"

"No, I mean are you serious about the hands over the stomach?"

"Arms over your stomach, like this." Betty stacked her arms under her breasts as she squinted down at Jamie's stomach. She reached out, smiling, to pinch her daughter's tiny roll. Jamie jumped back.

"Purse doesn't match the outfit," Jamie said.

"I'll leave it in the car," Betty said.

"What about God?" Jamie asked.

"What about God?" Betty pulled the purse off her shoulder, dumped it back down on the counter, and dug through it like a burrowing guinea pig.

"How can there be evil spirits if there's no God?" Jamie asked.

Betty pulled out a blue tampon box. She opened the box and retrieved a rolled joint and a pack of matches. She didn't speak until she had taken a deep hit off the joint.

"Who said there's no God?"

"You said that," Jamie said. "You've always said that."

"There's no God the way most people think of God." Betty took another hit before she continued. "But there are spirits. Good spirits and bad spirits. The good ones are godly in their power. And the bad ones are . . . well, bad."

"So do you think there are any good spirits in the house?" Jamie asked.

"I'm sure there are. But there are bad ones too, and we have to get rid of them."

"You think getting a priest in here will work?" Jamie asked.

"Of course!" Betty said. "Don't go anywhere. I may need you to help with the exorcism when I return."

Betty dashed out the kitchen door. Jamie pulled the liner out of the empty Cap'n Crunch box and ate the stray squares that had escaped and lay stale at the bottom of the box. She wished, for a second, that her sister liked her so she could have gone to East Beach with her and Lori. East Beach, where she didn't know anyone. East Beach, where the waves weren't big enough to surf. East Beach, where she'd never run into Flip or any of his friends. Or, she thought, if not East Beach with Renee, she'd like to be in Los Angeles for the day with her father. While Allen went to his acupuncturist and Dorey, the shrink he'd been seeing for as long as Jamie had conscious memory, Jamie could have sat in the lobby and read magazines. During his business meetings, she could have joined him at the conference table and silently colored on blank typing paper like she had on occasion when she was a little girl. She had loved those meetings, watching her father hand out mimeographed charts and papers, listening to him tell the Chiefs (as she and her dad called them then) how to make money. It was a secret that Jamie went along with Allen, because he never took Renee. Renee was too fidgety, impatient, needy of things like bathrooms and glasses of water. But Jamie knew how to be invisible.

Jamie looked around to see if she sensed any spirits. The kitchen felt so empty that even she herself didn't seem to exist in it.

The phone rang and Jamie yelped, quickly, sincerely. She answered it while pulling on the cord as far as it would go so she could reach the freezer. It was Tammy again.

"Scooter Ray wanted me to call you and beg."

"Come over," Jamie said. "There are bad spirits in this house and I don't wanna be home alone with them."

"What are you eating now?" Tammy asked.

"Butter pecan ice cream."

"I thought you hated butter pecan."

"I don't hate it, I just don't really like it. Are you coming over?"

"I'm meeting Debbie at the beach. Brett's picking me up."

"I'm not going camping with you guys."

"I think you're blowing it. I mean, if I weren't with Brett I'd totally go for him."

"You're not married. Go for him."

"Talk about loose morals!"

Tammy's words sounded small and twittering, as if a mouse were shouting out from inside the phone. Jamie didn't take note of the criticism—she was starting to tune out Tammy in the same way she tuned out Renee.

"My mother's out looking for an exorcist."

"No way."

"I swear."

"You know, I could sense some bad spirits last time we swam at your house."

"No way."

"I swear."

"Well, they'll be gone by this afternoon."

"Is she getting an exorcist like in *The Exorcist*?"

Jamie hadn't seen *The Exorcist*, but Tammy had told her all about it. She had claimed that the girl sitting beside her in the theater had been so freaked out that she had dumped her popcorn on the ground and barfed in the bag.

"Yeah, like in *The Exorcist*," Jamie said.

"Whoa."

"I know."

"I gotta go. I think Brett's here."

"You think or you know?"

"I think I hear his truck."

"You think?"

"Yeah. I gotta go."

Jamie dropped the phone on the ground and watched as the cord retracted, pulling the receiver toward the wall. It would have been easy to have tricked herself into thinking that a spirit was pulling the cord. But she didn't.

Jamie took the carton of ice cream into the TV room and watched *The $10,000 Pyramid*. (The day before she had been watching the same show, eating out of the same carton of ice cream, when her father had come into the room. "Don't worry, sweetheart," he had said, as he kissed the top of

Jamie's head, "we'll get over this." He had been talking about Lacey but Jamie, for once, hadn't thought of Lacey that morning. In fact, she had stopped doing the triple count. Her thoughts had turned to herself, to what she planned to eat and how fat she feared she was becoming.)

By the time Betty came home from the exorcist search, *The $10,000 Pyramid* was long over and Jamie had watched *Password*, *Treasure Hunt*, *Match Game '76*, and *The Joker's Wild*.

"Helloooo," Betty called.

In the kitchen Jamie found her mother standing with a man who looked as old and shriveled as a troll. She wanted to ask her mother if she had found the man under a bridge. He wore a long black robe and a stiff, fabric hat, like what an organ-grinding monkey might wear. His eyes were a phlegm-blue, like an old dog's eyes. There was a large wooden cross hanging from his neck, the ends of which bulged into bulbous geometric flowers. In his left hand he held what appeared to be a wrought-iron lantern on a chain. In his right hand was a Bible.

"This is Father Telamon," Betty said. "He's going to do the exorcism."

Father Telamon nodded his head up and down and up and down. He shuffled toward Jamie, put the Bible on the counter, and laid a hand on Jamie's shoulder. His fingernails were long and mostly gray, although his thumbnail was black.

"Neh," he said with a heavy accent.

"Father Telamon is from the Greek Orthodox church," Betty said. "They don't speak any English during their services. In fact, I don't think any of the twelve or so members of the church *can* speak English." Betty seemed excited to share this fact with Jamie.

"Amazing," Jamie said flatly. She was glad Tammy and Debbie were no longer hanging out at her house. She didn't want to view this scene through their eyes.

"Neh," Father Telamon said.

"Should I show you around before you start?" Betty's smile reminded Jamie of the stewardesses in the Pan Am commercials.

"Neh," Father Telamon said.

Jamie waited in the kitchen, eating cherries, while Betty took the priest on a tour. She could hear her mother's voice as they entered the dining room, then listened to it fade out as if it were a dimming radio signal as Betty took Father Telamon up the stairs. Ten minutes later, Betty's voice came into the background–the radio signal returned. Jamie wondered if the father had ever uttered a word.

"Look!" Betty entered the kitchen holding up a Ouija board game in one hand and a pack of tarot cards in the other.

"You're gonna play Ouija board with him?" Jamie spit a cherry pit into the hole of her fist.

"*Diablos!*" Father Telamon said, pointing at the game.

"I'm not exactly sure what he said," Betty smiled at the priest before continuing, "but I think we summoned the bad spirits into the house with the Ouija board."

"Renee and I must have played that a thousand times. You think there are a thousand bad spirits in the house?"

"*Diablos!*" Father Telamon repeated.

Betty and Jamie followed Father Telamon outside to the pool. He pointed at a boulder. Jamie and her mother both leaned in and examined the boulder as if something might pop out of it.

Father Telamon snatched the game and cards from Betty

and placed them on the boulder. He put his Bible and lantern on the ground, pulled a small silver vial from his pocket, and dumped the contents on the cards and game.

Jamie never saw him light a match; it seemed as if the flames appeared by magic, licking the game and bending the loose cards into arcs that slowly dissolved to ash. Father Telamon's lantern appeared lit suddenly too. It began to spew more smoke than the burning games. Father Telamon waved the smoking lantern over the flames and chanted in Greek.

"Put your hands in the prayer position," Betty said, and she nudged Jamie.

Jamie placed her palms together and stared at the fire on the boulder. Father Telamon didn't seem aware of Jamie or Betty; he chanted in a way that made Jamie think that perhaps his spirit had gone astray and this noise he was making was the elevator Muzak in his body. Jamie wanted to laugh, but her mother's rigid face told her she wasn't even allowed to smile.

Just when Jamie felt as if her knees would buckle from standing still so long, Father Telamon waved the lantern back and forth and marched into the house, continuing his chants. Betty and Jamie followed him, their hands still folded in prayer, their eyes and heads darting around as they went from room to room accompanied by a trail of pungent, woodsy smoke. Father Telamon even went into the kitchen pantry, opening the boxes of cookies and crackers, and the lid to every spice jar, to smoke out the spirits hiding there. Jamie's mouth dropped open, her body on the verge of cracking apart with laughter. Betty plunged the nib of her pump into the top of Jamie's foot until Jamie's face went still and somber.

Eventually, they followed Father Telamon back out to the pool again, where the Ouija board and tarot cards were a smoldering gray pile, layered like feathery dead birds. Father Telamon walked down to the shallow end of the pool, Bible and smoking lantern in hand, and descended the steps in his robe. He walked until he was hip deep in water, the skirt of his robe swimming up around him like an oil spill. He placed the lantern on the side of the pool and turned to Betty and Jamie.

"Come," he said.

"Should we change?" Betty pointed down at her skirt.

"Ohkee!"

"No need to yell." Betty smiled as she spoke, then turned to Jamie and said, "Remember this for when you go back-packing abroad: the Greek word for *no* sounds like *okay*, and the Greek word for *yes* sounds like *nah*."

"Okay." Jamie smirked, then took her mother's hand as they walked down the steps into the pool–Betty in her yellow pumps and Jamie in flip-flops and shorts. They stopped and stood before Father Telamon. He wasn't much taller than Betty, but somehow, to Jamie, he suddenly seemed huge.

Father Telamon turned toward Jamie and made the sign of the cross on her face, shoulders, and chest with a corner of his Bible while continuing to chant in Greek. Without missing a note in his prayer he handed the Bible to Betty, grabbed Jamie by the shoulder and the top of the head, and flipped her, head back, into the water. Jamie gasped and snorted. The water burned her throat and sinuses. When her head popped up, seconds later, she was coughing and blowing water out her nose. Jamie shook her ears clear, then glared at her mother. Betty refused to meet her daughter's stare; instead, she passed her the Bible and then gazed up at Father Telamon before submitting to him as he dunked her backward into the water. When she emerged, Betty was smiling.

Betty threw rainbow-colored pool towels onto the kitchen floor to absorb the water dripping from Father Telamon's robe, Jamie's shorts, and her own secretary uniform.

"Were we baptized?" Jamie asked.

"We were baptized," Betty said.

"Dad's gonna kill you." Jamie finally let a laugh fly out, and she wondered who would find the baptism as funny as she? Certainly not Renee; Renee would be angry at having been excluded. (When Renee was feeling particularly penned-in by the oddity of the family she would threaten to become a born-again Christian.) Flip wouldn't have found it funny—he loved Betty too much and thought everything she did was cool. But, Jamie reminded herself, Flip would never know since Jamie couldn't imagine speaking to him for many, many years. And Tammy and Debbie? They probably wouldn't laugh. When it came to God they were both as rigid as a cross.

For a moment, while Jamie watched her mother bending over straight-legged, mopping up a trail of water, as the priest sat on the kitchen stool and fiddled with the chain on his lantern, Jamie felt completely alone—stranded in her own, small life like an undiscovered island.

"Don't tell your father we did this." Betty scooped up some wet towels, threw them into a corner and took her place behind the kitchen counter.

"I've barely seen Dad lately," Jamie said.

"I hope you like omelets," Betty said to the priest. Jamie had the feeling that her mother never felt properly connected with anyone unless they ate together. If her mother could cook for the world, there would be no wars.

Father Telamon put down his lantern and smiled. He appeared to be a different man than the troll who had entered the house an hour earlier. This Father Telamon looked like he'd want to play Bingo and do the Hokey-Pokey. Jamie sat on the stool beside him, her legs sticky and wet, the crotch of her damp shorts feeling rashy already.

"Do you mind if I change?" Jamie asked her mother.

"Don't change!" Betty moved in fast motion, whipping eggs, laying out bacon on the grill, buttering toast to be cooked in the broiler. She even pulled out the juicer and began slicing oranges in half, rather than simply pouring orange juice from the carton in the fridge.

"Nothing better than breakfast foods for dinner," Betty said.

"It's only four," Jamie said.

"Early dinner."

"Good," Father Telamon said.

"Why can't I get changed?" Jamie worried about pimples blooming on her behind. Butt acne, Jamie thought, would change the baptism from funny to tragic.

"If Father Telamon is wet, then we'll be wet." Betty trained her eyes on Jamie for an extra second before turning to grab a spatula.

As soon as Betty picked up her keys to drive Father Telamon back to his church, Jamie ran upstairs and changed into dry clothes. The house felt the same as it had before the exorcism: same air, same sunlight, same quietness. She looked in the bathroom mirror and studied her face to see if the baptism had given her some glow that would radiate out her ears, nostrils, or eyes. As far as Jamie could tell, she was identical to the person she had been that morning.

Jamie decided she would break her ban on calling Debbie and Tammy and went downstairs to the kitchen to phone them one last time. Maybe they'd be so curious about the exorcism and baptism that they'd paddle across the sea that seemed to separate them and dock on the island of Jamie.

"Is Debbie home from the beach yet?" she asked Debbie's mother.

"She's here," her mother said. "They've been here all day."

Tammy answered Debbie's phone, giggling.

"Debbie's busy," she said. "I was sent in her place."

"What's so funny?"

"You'd have to be here," Tammy said. "It's too hard to explain."

"So the house was exorcised by this old Greek priest," Jamie said.

"Did your head spin around? Did you vomit pea soup?"

"Is that what happens in the movie?"

"Yeah. It was gross."

"No, he just walked around with stuff burning in this lantern and chanted a lot. But guess what."

"What?"

"I was baptized."

"But you're Jewish."

"Just my dad."

"I know, but I thought your mom was an atheist, so that meant that you're Jewish."

"It means I'm half Jewish and half athiest."

"No. Because one plus zero equals one. So if your mom's nothing, that's zero, if your dad's Jewish, that's one. So Jewish plus atheist equals Jewish."

"Religion isn't math, Tammy. Besides, I think I'm technically Greek Orthodox now."

"That is so freaky."

"What exactly does it mean if you're baptized? Does it mean bad spirits can't enter your body or something?"

"It means if you die you go to heaven."

"So if I hadn't been baptized I'd go to hell?"

"Absolutely."

"You can't say absolutely. I mean, we won't know for sure until it's too late to tell anyone else. I mean, how could anyone ever prove this?"

"God knows. Jesus knows."

"What are you talking about?"

"If you don't believe in it just think of it as insurance, you know, just in case."

"But wait a minute. If it's true, then when my mom and I die, we're going to a different place than my dad and my sister."

"Would you really want to spend an eternity with your sister?"

"No way."

"So you're lucky then. And you'll be with me and Debbie too!"

"How come you guys didn't go to the beach?"

"I dunno. There were no waves today so everyone just wanted to hang out by the pool."

"Why is he called Scooter Ray? Why not just Scooter?"

"I dunno. I gotta go." Voices clacked in the background as if a mob had just entered the room.

"Who else is there? Is that Flip?"

"Yeah, I guess he's here too."

"With Terry?"

"I'm telling you, you'd like her if you knew her," Tammy whispered. "Why don't you just get over yourself and move on."

"Fine. I'll go out with Scooter."

"Too late for that. He's here with Kim Redson." Tammy was still whispering.

"What? He was available five hours ago."

"I know. They hooked up at the beach this morning, then they came over here and they're, like, totally in love already."

"That's insane."

"Well, who knows if it will last through Friday."

"So, is she going camping with you now?"

"Yeah. She said she is."

"Is Flip going?"

Tammy sighed. Jamie thought she could feel the wind from Tammy's breath through the phone lines—it pushed at her as if she'd been hit with a bag of laundry.

"Can I talk to Debbie?" Jamie asked.

"She's busy, Jamie. We're all busy. Why don't you call back later, okay?"

Jamie hung up the phone, then silently swore she would really, truly, never call back. Not for another exorcism or baptism or death even. She sat on a stool, reached for the bowl of nuts, then stopped herself as she tapped out with her fist on the kitchen counter another tally of the capable swimmers at the naked pool party. Jamie was so busy tapping that her mind quickly clogged up—a drain stopped with numbers.

* * *

Betty had picked up Renee from Lori's house on her way back from driving the priest home. Renee was angry when she came home; stomping as she walked, squinting her eyes in a way that lifted her top lip into a snarl.

"How was the beach?" Jamie asked.

"Were you here when this happened?" Renee demanded.

Betty peeled off her wet clothes and let them drop to the kitchen floor. She walked naked into the dining room, then returned with a bottle of wine.

"You went to East Beach, right?" Jamie asked. "Or is Lori allowed to go to Butterfly now?"

"Mom," Renee said. "Don't ever come to Lori's door in wet clothes again, okay? I mean, it was so weird, you might as well have been naked."

"So next time I'll come naked!" Betty laughed and poured a glass of wine.

"Farrah. *Were you here?*"

"Yeah. He baptized me."

"He baptized you? I can't believe it! Mom, you're an atheist! How could you let him baptize her! *I* want to get baptized! I'm the only one in this family who deserves to be baptized!"

"You're Jewish, Rifka; Jews don't get baptized." The sting from her conversation with Tammy hovered in a vague unfocused way, making Jamie feel mean, and so Jamie used the Jewish name, Rifka, which Allen had given Renee at birth, a name the family, at Renee's request, had agreed never to utter.

"You're Jewish too, Shayna Gittle, you dork!" Renee couldn't successfully lacerate Jamie with Shayna Gittle, her Jewish name, as Jamie always found it more funny than humiliating.

"Well, now I'm Jewish and Greek Orthodox, so you can call me Shayna Gittle Stanaslopicus." Jamie could hear her mother snickering as she rinsed the dishes in the sink.

"I'm the only one in this family who believes in God. I should be baptized! I can't believe Farrah was baptized! That is so unfair!" Renee turned and marched out of the kitchen.

"Farrah Gittle Stanaslopicus!" Jamie shouted after Renee, who was stomping up the stairs.

Later that night, after Allen called from Los Angeles to say he was going to dinner with some friends and wouldn't be home till midnight or so, Leon and Lois came over for a swim. Jamie followed them out to the pool, where Betty was floating on a raft, her fingertips dipped in the water as if she were tickling it.

"All clear?" Leon asked.

"All clear!" Betty said.

Leon dove in and swam to Betty. He hung onto the edge of her raft, hands near her falling breasts, and kicked her around the pool. Scrawny Lois watched as she took off her clothes. She stretched up toward the dimming sky, then dove into the pool and swam toward Betty and Leon, like a child trying to catch up to her parents.

"Oooooh yeah," she said. "This is great, it's totally different."

Jamie felt certain Lois was trying to distract her husband and friend from each other.

"Can you feel it?" Betty asked.

"Absolutely. It's beautiful. It's like the difference between night and day."

"Serenity," Leon said, and he pulled himself out of the water and went to the diving board, bouncing up and down as if he were warming up for something.

"It's amazing, isn't it?" Betty said.

"I can't tell any difference." Jamie couldn't believe her mother had taken the bait, was entering this conversation that Lois had cranked up only in order to be seen.

"The air here," Lois said, "was thick. It was rancid. It was just wrong."

"As pure as new life now," Betty said.

"Yes!" Lois smiled. "We're free."

"So," Jamie said, from her perch on a boulder. "Do you think we don't need the life jackets now that the evil spirits are gone?"

Betty rolled her eyes at her daughter.

Lois said, "What life jackets?"

"The ones Dad bought for anyone who's at the house who can't swim."

"I don't think you need them," Lois said. "I mean, there's nothing here to harm anyone."

"But what about the fact that some people, small people, you know, kids, just can't swim?" Jamie was surprised by how angry she suddenly felt toward Lois; as if Lacey's death were *her* fault; as if there were something wrong with *her* that drove Leon to her mother; as if *she* were the reason Jamie was eating like she needed to store food for estivation.

"Yes, but there's nothing here to harm them anymore."

"So you don't think a pool that they can't swim in is harmful?" Jamie asked.

"No," Lois said, and she flipped onto her back and floated.

Betty turned to Jamie, her eyes narrowed, and said, "Why don't you go visit your friends?"

"They're busy," Jamie said.

"Then go get your suit on," Betty said.

"But I don't want to swim."

"Well, don't spoil our fun. We're happy the evil sprits are gone, okay?"

"I'm just saying that I think a baby who can't swim might drown in a pool whether there are evil spirits or not." Jamie wished Renee were there. Surely she'd take Jamie's side in this matter. She wouldn't believe in evil spirits; she didn't even believe in karma!

"That's not true," Betty snapped. "It takes evil to kill a baby."

"Whatever," Jamie said.

Betty rolled off the raft and swam underwater. Leon jumped off the diving board and landed inches from Betty. Jamie imagined his body slithering against Betty's as he went down, then sliding across her again as he popped up for air.

There was an ashy stain from the Ouija board and tarot cards on the boulder next to the one on which Jamie sat. Long, black, sooty marks, the shape of a Jester's collar, licked over the edges of the boulder. Jamie stared at the blackened rock and wondered how that burned mess, the smoky smell that lingered in the house, and the water up her nose at the hand of a trollish Greek man could possibly change anything.

14

A few days later, while her head was floating from a binge of leftover lasagna, cinnamon toast, and peanut butter cups, Jamie's loneliness overtook her resolve and she called Tammy once again.

"Do you and Debbie want to come over and hang out tonight?" Jamie asked. "My parents are at some big party in Los Angeles and they said they'd either be home really late, like four, or they'd spend the night and be home in the morning."

"Sorry," Tammy sighed, "we've got plans."

"Oh. Okay." Jamie stretched the kitchen phone cord and tried to get to the pantry, but it was too far.

"You can come if you want. But, like, it's the kind of thing you never seem to want to do anymore."

"What is it?" Jamie opened the freezer. There was no ice cream. She slammed the door shut and slumped onto the kitchen floor.

"A party," Tammy said.

"Where?"

"Henry's Beach. Near the caves."

"Are Flip and Terry going to be there?"

"Probably. See, I told you you wouldn't want to come."

"No, I'll come."

"Really?" Tammy hissed into the phone as she exhaled cigarette smoke.

"I thought Brett wanted you to quit smoking," Jamie said.

"He did. But he just took it up instead, so now it's fine."

"Cool."

"So are you really going to come with us?"

"Yeah. Who's driving?"

"I dunno. Jimmy or Brett. I guess you could sit in the back of Brett's truck."

"Whatever. What are you wearing?"

"I got a bunch of cute new clothes yesterday at La Cumbre Plaza."

"I haven't gotten any new clothes all summer."

"I know. You've been, like, wearing those same Op shorts all summer long."

Jamie looked down at her Op shorts. They were comfortable, stretched out; they adapted easily to the various expansions and contractions of her stomach.

"What's Debbie wearing?" Jamie asked.

"She got a bunch of new stuff too."

"So where should we meet up? Your house or Debbie's?"

"Come to my house." Tammy spoke in the singsong of boredom. "You can borrow something of mine to wear. Maybe it will snap you out of your depression."

"I'm not depressed." No matter how isolated and sad she felt, Jamie would never have characterized herself as depressed. Renee was the depressive, the one her parents had to worry over and tend to.

"Whatever," Tammy said. "Just come over here and we'll get ready together."

Renee!" Jamie yelled up the stairs toward her sister's room. "Renee! I'm going to Tammy's and then we're going to a party at Henry's Beach."

There was no answer.

"RENEE! I'M GOING TO TAMMY'S!"

Renee's bedroom door swung open. Renee came out and stood at the top of the stairs.

"You're sleeping at Tammy's?"

"I'm not sure. Probably not, but you might be alone tonight. Is that okay?" For a sliver of a moment Jamie hoped Renee would ask her to stay home. They could play board games, watch television, or even play the imagination games they had made up as children: Ballerina and Little Girl, Indian and Little Girl, Mermaid and Little Girl. Jamie had always been the Little Girl while Renee got to wear the costumes and dictated what exciting figure she'd be each game. But Jamie hadn't minded. She had loved hanging out with her sister; just being with Renee had made Jamie happy.

"I'll be fine, Farrah. Have fun with your skinny little slut friends." Renee returned to her bedroom and shut the door loudly.

Tammy's mother stood at the front door without stepping aside, as if Jamie were selling cookies instead of coming over to hang out with her daughter.

"How are your parents since that ordeal?" Tammy's mother asked. She wore an orange apron over a red dress, like Lucille Ball in *I Love Lucy*, and her brownish-gray hair was stiff and pushed up, not unlike Lucy's.

"They're okay," Jamie said.

"It must be hard for your mother without a church or synagogue to turn to."

"She goes to synagogue with my dad," Jamie lied.

"Oh?! The one up off San Marcos Pass?"

"Yeah." Jamie had never been there and as far as she knew her father and mother had never been there either.

Tammy's mother's face expressed a painful, encompassing pity. She looked at Jamie as if she were about to pet her behind the ears.

"So is Tammy home?" The pity brought out a fierce irascibility in Jamie. She wanted to rage at Tammy's mother, to rip off her own clothes in the spirit of her parents and run pell-mell through the house.

"That's right!" Tammy's mother said. "You girls are having a slumber party at your house tonight. Will your parents be home?"

"Yes. My mom's writing on index cards right now so we can play charades. And my father's planning a popcorn tasting—you know, garlic popcorn, parmesan popcorn, salted popcorn."

"They've really settled down since that accident, haven't they?"

Jamie saw herself tearing out into Tammy's backyard, mounting the diving board, and doing a few spastic naked jumps before yodeling a war cry and flinging herself into the black-bottom pool.

"Absolutely," Jamie said.

"This must be such a hard time for them. I bet they don't have parties like that anymore."

"Nope. My mom put her bathing suits away for the rest of the summer. She said she's never going in the pool again."

"You know, I'd probably do the same thing. Although I can't imagine something like that *ever* happening here." Tammy's mother finally moved back and let Jamie pass into the house.

As she walked up the stairs to Tammy's room, Jamie dragged her hand along the wall in just the way Tammy had shown her never to do. Tammy's mother hated cleaning fingerprints off the paint.

Tammy and Debbie were listening to Janna Winter sing "Love Me, Love Me, Baby." They were snaking around each other and writhing on Tammy's lacy pink canopy bed as if they were having sex with ghosts. When Janna really started moaning, so did Tammy and Debbie: *Yeeeees, love me, love me, baby! Sweet sugah, love me, love me, baby! Yeeeesss . . .*

Jamie felt like her cousin Jan.

The song ended. Tammy hopped off the bed and put on a record Jamie had never heard.

"What's this?" Jamie asked.

"Nazareth," Debbie said.

"You don't know Nazareth?" Tammy said.

"I guess not," Jamie said.

"Where have you been?!" Tammy said.

"I dunno. What should I wear tonight?" Jamie wondered: if she ran home and begged Renee to hang out with her, would Renee agree?

"You can wear my clothes if you want," Debbie said.

"Where are you guys sleeping tonight?" Jamie asked.

"I dunno," Debbie said, "probably on the beach."

"We told our moms we're sleeping at your house." Tammy went to her window and slid the panel open. With her bony forearm she pushed everything on her pink dresser to one side so she could sit there, her head and hand out the window while she smoked a cigarette.

"Let me have one," Debbie said.

"God, you're smoking as much as Tammy now," Jamie said.

"Yeah, once I started smoking pot, cigarettes seemed so . . . so nothing, you know."

"What, are you smoking pot all the time now?"

"You're one to criticize pot smoking!" Tammy said. "Your parents are, like, total potheads!"

"They're not potheads! They're just people who smoke, like you two. And I'm not criticizing, I just didn't know you did it so much." How is it, Jamie thought, that Tammy could think that her mother, who monitored fingerprints, bowel movements, and milk consumption, was preferable to Jamie's parents, who only wanted everyone to be happy?

"I guess Jimmy's been a bad influence on me," Debbie said, and she and Tammy laughed.

Jamie looked through their new clothes while they smoked cigarettes.

"These are cute." Jamie held up a pair of jeans with heart-shaped back pockets.

"You can wear them," Tammy said. "If they'll fit you."

Jamie took her shorts off and pulled the jeans on, unzipped. She lay on the bed and sucked in her stomach as she struggled with the zipper.

"There's no way you can do that alone!" Tammy tossed her cigarette out the window and hopped off the dresser. She held the zipper together.

"Debbie, help."

Debbie flicked her cigarette out and jumped down to help. She weedled the zipper up while Tammy held the two sides together and Jamie pressed down her stomach with her fingertips.

"Suck, Jamie! Suck in!" Tammy said.

"I am!" Jamie said, just as Debbie pulled the zipper to the top.

Tammy and Debbie looked at each other, heads pointed toward Jamie, eyes pointed toward each other.

"I gained some weight, okay? It's no big deal." Jamie struggled to sit up, then settled for pivoting off the bed and standing.

"Even your boobs look bigger," Tammy said.

"I think you look fine," Debbie said. "It's just we're used to you being smaller, you know? I mean, like, it's not like you're fat now, it's more that you used to be so small and now you're like . . . I dunno, regular?"

"I bet your boobs are going to get as big as your mom's," Tammy said.

"Don't say that," Jamie groaned. "I don't want all those pervy boob-men hanging all over me."

"Wouldn't it be funny if Jamie had those big, whopping boobs? I mean, like the boob shelf. Like in a magazine or something." Tammy looked directly at Debbie as she spoke.

"Can you stop talking about my mother's boobs?"

"I wasn't talking about your mother's boobs," Tammy said. "I was talking about yours!" And at that, Tammy and Debbie fell into razor-edged laughter.

*   *   *

Brett and Jimmy picked up the girls in Brett's truck.

"I'm not going to sit in the back all by myself," Jamie said.

Tammy and Debbie had already climbed into the cab with Tammy nestled between the boys and Debbie on Jimmy's lap.

"I'll sit in the back of the truck with you," Jimmy said, and he slid Debbie off his lap and slipped out of the cab. Debbie huffed, as if her feelings were hurt, then cocked her head at Jamie and smiled.

"Isn't he the sweetest guy in the world?" she said. Jimmy rolled his eyes and hopped into the back of the truck with one quick jump, as if he were pole-vaulting with his arms. Jamie climbed in after him and they scooted, side by side, against the back of the cab.

"So whatcha been doing?" Jimmy said, as they rolled out of the driveway.

"Not much," Jamie said. She looked back at the cab window and saw that Debbie was turned sideways in her seat, as if she wanted to keep an eye on them. Jamie shifted so she wasn't sitting so close to Jimmy.

"Flip told me about the baby."

"He did? God, I would have told you but I guess I haven't seen you in a while."

"Yeah. It's terrible what happened."

"Oh. Yeah. It was terrible."

"Flip was really broken up about it."

"Really? He never said that to me."

"Well, you broke up with him right afterward."

Jamie looked at Jimmy; the wind was blowing back his hair into a mane around his face. She thought she heard him wrong.

"You mean *he* broke up with *me* right afterward."

"No. He said you broke up with him."

"Well, then *Flip* is a *flipping* liar!" To Jamie, the humiliation of having been dumped seemed far less shameful than the act of having dumped someone, over the phone, within twenty-four hours of a horrifying death.

"He said you said that you were too sad to be with anyone, and, like, right after you broke up with him he happened to run into Terry at the beach, and she was really comforting to him in his time of need, you know?"

"She was comforting? Did he actually say 'time of need'?"

"Yeah, she lost a cousin who was a baby or something, so she really knew what he was going through."

"I wasn't *too sad to be with him*," Jamie said. "I was so sad that I actually *needed* him."

"Really?"

"Yes. And he wasn't very comforting to me in my *time of need*."

"Really?" Jimmy seemed genuinely surprised.

"Why would I lie?" Jamie turned away so Jimmy couldn't see that she was on the edge of a cry.

"Why would he lie?"

"So he doesn't look like such a dickhead."

"Yeah," Jimmy said, leaning over to examine Jamie's face. "Are you crying?"

"No," Jamie sniffed.

Jimmy put his arm around Jamie and pulled her in close to him. She could sense that Debbie was watching through the cab window, but didn't look up for proof.

"It's okay," Jimmy said. "You can cry."

And so she did.

When they pulled up at the beach, Jimmy flipped his arm down from around Jamie's shoulder, hopped out of the truck, and extended his hand to help Jamie out.

Debbie looked at Jamie askance, then ran to Jimmy, wrapped both arms around his neck, and kissed him deep and hard.

"Uh, can we, like, go to the party now?" Tammy said.

Debbie unwound her arms, took Jimmy's hand, and headed toward the beach with Tammy and Brett following and Jamie drifting in the back. Jamie thought that the only thing sadder than the fact that she was being left behind was the fact that she was growing used to the feeling–she almost expected it. Jamie felt she was like a hanging thread that had to be cut and recut from the unraveling sweater of her friendship with Tammy and Debbie.

Everyone, it seemed to Jamie, was at the party. It was the kind of party Renee and Lori talked about but would never dare attend. There was a crop-circle-sized driftwood fire with a small crowd standing and sitting around it. Jamie could tell who most people were by the backs of their head: Becca Price, Fran Brendan, Alex Mysko, Scott Rhett, Matty Travis, Donald Sheridan, Simon Blue, Josh Emery, Denis Rhoade, Kindall Blitz, John Stasser, Lindsay Trout, Tracy Walanz, David Greatbeck, Steve McMartin, Boo Landis, Bonnie Louise, Jilly Genna, Claire Stanfare. She wondered if anyone would know *her* by the back of her head. Instead of breaking into the fire circle, Jamie wandered toward the keg that was tucked into a nook on the craggy cliff wall. Flip was standing a few feet from the keg, holding a plastic bag full of stacked plastic cups. Jamie's stomach thumped

when she saw him. She hoped she looked okay, she hoped
he would see her and regret breaking up. She wanted Flip
to beg her to come back so that she could reject him, prov-
ing herself more resilient than even she herself believed,
for who could say no to the near-perfect beauty of Flip
Jenkins?

"Dollar a cup," he said, when Jamie approached.

"Can I just owe you?" Jamie asked, her voice shaky.

"Jamie!" Flip said, "I didn't realize it was you."

"You didn't know it was me?" Jamie felt ill at the thought
that her weight gain had made her unrecognizable.

"No, no, I just wasn't looking. Everyone's buying cups
and I haven't really been looking at faces." As he spoke,
Flip handed out six cups and took in six dollars, which he
shoved into his jeans pocket.

"Can I have a cup?" Jamie asked.

"Yeah, my treat, I *totally insist*," Flip said, as if she'd made
some motion to turn him down.

Jamie took the cup but didn't move toward the keg.

"So, what have you been up to?" Flip asked.

"Why did you tell Jimmy that I broke up with you?"
Jamie surprised herself with the question. "You know that's
not true."

"I totally never said that," Flip said.

"Yes, you did." Jamie realized she was out of patience for
Flip—she wanted to make up for the times she'd been with
him and hadn't been blunt or confrontational out of fear
that it would cause him to flee.

"Look." Flip glanced around as he spoke, never landing
his eyes on Jamie. "That was a really hard fucking time,
okay? Like, it was the hardest time in my whole fucking life.
I mean, I saw a dead baby. Not many people here have seen

dead babies, you know? So, you'll have to fucking excuse me for anything I might have said in the days after that."

"I know it was hard," Jamie said. "But why tell people that I broke up with you?"

"I gotta get outta here," Flip said. He called to Tigger Haus, then handed him the stack of cups.

Jamie felt breathless, almost confused, as she stood alone and watched Flip walk away. Could he not even hear her out, apologize, give a reasonable excuse? Jamie thought that once you had sex with someone, once you'd cracked your body open and joined it to his body, you'd be permanently connected on some level, even if you no longer loved each other. How could Flip act as if his obligation to Jamie was finished, like a completed transaction at 7-Eleven: the money's been handed over, the Slurpee is in the customer's grasp, no one owes anyone anything. Not even a smile.

Jamie got in line for the keg while keeping an eye on Flip. He didn't go far, just to the edge of the fire, where Terry jumped up, took his hand, and pulled him down beside her. Terry scooted onto Flip's lap; he turned around and looked back toward Jamie. Jamie looked away before she could read his expression.

When her cup was filled, Jamie stepped away from the keg and chugged down the beer. Tammy and Debbie were nestled into the fire circle; Tammy leaned into Terry Watson's ear and whispered something that made them both laugh. Jamie's stomach jolted and she knew it wasn't the beer but the fact that Tammy was so cozy with Terry. Jamie had no one to be cozy with—an embarrassment in a social crowd where attachment was the means for identification. If she wasn't Flip's girlfriend or Tammy's and Debbie's best friend, she was essentially invisible. Jamie decided that her invisibility just then was a good thing: If no one saw her, then no one witnessed her humiliating ostracism.

A small crowd cheered a few feet from where Jamie stood; she wandered over and saw that they were watching Bone-Man Deugal climb the cliff. Boys pointed at him with their beer cups, wagering on how far he could go, if he could make it to the top. After only a couple of minutes, Bone-Man fell, skidding down the cliff, hands dragging as if he'd catch something and stop himself. Everyone, except Jamie, laughed. Bone-Man stood and went at the cliff again. The crowd cheered once more. After he fell a second time, the group laughed even harder. He stood and tackled the cliff a third time. Jamie couldn't watch–it was too much like her life, she thought, a continuum of cliff skidding as she clawed at her friends (and her sister, even!), only to slide down below them, scraped and stinging with pebbles embedded in her palms.

Jamie went to the keg for more beer.

"He's like Sisyphus," a tall, sturdy-looking girl said to the guy filling the cups.

"He's got syphilis?" the guy asked.

Jamie tried to recall the girl's name. She remembered seeing multiple pictures of her in Renee's yearbook.

"No. Bone-Man. He's like Sisyphus," the girl repeated.

"Beer?" the guy asked. Jamie held out her cup for him to fill.

"He must not have taken Mr. Zigler's mythology class in eighth grade," Jamie said to the girl, and then she smiled, a little too hard. The girl shrugged and walked away. The guy dropped the tap hose and walked away too. And suddenly, Jamie was alone at the keg. She tossed down her second beer then refilled her cup. When she spied a pack of people with empty cups approaching, Jamie stepped aside.

Tammy was no longer whispering in Terry's ear. Terry was still on Flip's lap, but now she was straddling him, her big feet sticking up like a cadaver's. They were making out. Really making out. As if no one else were around. As if Flip wanted Jamie to know that she wasn't even in his peripheral vision. It seemed that when he had hung up the phone the day he broke up with her, Flip had hung up his feelings as well. Jamie promised herself she would do the same; she wouldn't avoid Flip Jenkins at school next year, she wouldn't care enough to do that.

Jamie walked to a rock perched outside the activity. It was a low, flat rock with circular nickel-sized holes dotting the top—the holes were so perfectly round they appeared to have been drilled. If it had been light out, Jamie would have inspected the holes before sitting to make sure the sea worms, or whatever creatures that inhabited the holes, were no longer there. But it wasn't light out; the moon was a perfect half-circle, and the greatest source of light was the fire or the occasional match being struck to light a joint or cigarette.

Jamie was drunk and she wanted to go home and eat cereal and peanut butter cups, and watch TV with no one to witness her sadness. She wondered: If she were to lose the weight she had gained, or if she were as cute as Terry Watson, would some other boy want her? Or was she unlovable now, surrounded by the halo of a dead baby, destined to a life of spinsterhood with her mother her only friend?

Scooter Ray walked toward Jamie with a cup of beer in each hand. He sat next to her and handed her one of his beers.

"I already have one," Jamie said.

"Then that's your second," Scooter Ray said, and he chugged his remaining beer.

"Okay," Jamie said, although she didn't want two beers.

"Ever been to that long, deep cave down there?" Scooter Ray asked. Jamie's eyes had adjusted to the dim light and she could clearly see Scooter Ray; she had never been this close to him. He was cute the way children are cute: everything neat and clean on his face, nothing too big or exaggerated, snowy soft hair, pouty lips.

"Do you even know my name?" Jamie asked.

"Jamie."

"Yeah." Jamie felt a flush run through her body. Scooter Ray had recognized her even with the weight gain, even with the dead baby halo, even without her friends nearby.

"I even know your last name," Scooter Ray said.

"I know yours too."

"Wanna see that cave?"

"I've been in it. The one you can go in only during low tide, right?"

"It is low tide." Scooter Ray's voice was gravelly and vibrating. Jamie could feel his words on her skin.

"It's low tide right now?" Forget spinsterhood, Jamie thought, Scooter Ray will love me.

"Yeah. Come on."

Scooter Ray picked up Jamie's wrist. She thought he might have held her hand if she hadn't been holding two beers. Jamie took sips from alternating beers as they walked to the cave.

"I think I'm wasted," Jamie said, as she stumbled over some driftwood.

"Me too."

"Why does everyone call you Scooter Ray? Why not just Scooter?"

"My mom's from South Carolina," he said.

"So."

"People have two names in South Carolina."

"Everyone has at least two names. A first name and a last name."

"No, I have a last name."

"Ray."

"Hey, you don't know my last name! It's Smith." Scooter Ray's teeth glowed as he smiled.

"Your last name is Smith? I thought it was Ray." Jamie laughed.

Scooter Ray put his hand on Jamie's forearm and slowed her, as if he were gently pulling a horse's rein. Jamie wobbled for a moment, then regained her balance and stood still, facing Scooter Ray. They were in front of the cave.

"My first name is Scooter Ray. My second name is Jackson. And my last name is Smith." And with that, Scooter Ray Jackson Smith pulled Jamie toward him and kissed her, slow and sweet.

Jamie's arms stuck out like a scarecrow's as she held her two beers aloft. Scooter Ray dug his beer into the sand, then took Jamie's and dug them into the sand beside his.

"C'mon," he said, and he led her into the dark cave.

When she faced the inside of the cave, Jamie could see nothing. When she turned and looked out of the cave the beach had a hazy glow.

"Are you sure there's no one else in here?" Jamie asked. "I mean, I can't see anything. This is like death; it's blacker than when you shut your eyes."

"Anyone here?!" Scooter Ray shouted.

"But animals wouldn't answer," Jamie said. "Do you think there are mountain lions in here?"

"Any mountain lions in here?!" Scooter Ray shouted, and

Jamie laughed because she felt hopeful and desirable–the proof being that Scooter Ray wanted to be with her.

Scooter Ray and Jamie lay on the mucky floor of the cave. Jamie was on her back with Scooter Ray on top of her, running his hands from her breasts to her hips, reading her curves. When Jamie had groaned about getting fat one afternoon, Betty had told her she wasn't fat at all–she was growing more beautiful, replacing the flesh of childhood with the softer stuff of womanhood. With Scooter Ray stroking her, Jamie believed her mother, believed that this new body was better, sweeter to the touch. She was a siren whose call could not be ignored.

The sand was cold, dense: Jamie rolled over so that Scooter Ray was on his back and she was on top of him as they made out. Jamie's mind flitted in and out–she thought about Flip and decided that everything had changed in the past thirty minutes: she no longer cared that he lied about breaking up with her and she had little interest in whether or not he was kissing Terry Watson. With her lips suctioned against Scooter Ray's, Jamie felt so strong and beautiful she could imagine herself chatting with Flip, casually, about the waves or the new Monty Python movie, while Terry Watson silently stood by. And she suddenly didn't care that Tammy and Debbie had cut her out of their lives with the incisiveness of a surgeon removing a giant mole. Scooter Ray would shine the light of his face on Jamie until everyone could see that she existed. And Scooter Ray would introduce her to a whole new set of friends, Jamie thought, people who would care about Jamie just because they knew she made Scooter Ray happy. He probably had a sister who would be Jamie's best friend; or maybe his mother would hang out with her in the same way that Flip had often hung out with Betty. Mama Scooter Ray would teach Jamie how to cook southern-style, show her how to hem her pants so she wouldn't have to roll them at the bottom, and take her shopping at La Cumbre Plaza when her own mother was too busy to do it herself.

Jamie was so distracted imagining her future life with Scooter Ray that she had not been fully aware of the actions that led to her being naked. She also could not remember when Scooter Ray had rolled on top of her, or how it came to the point where Scooter Ray was slicing in and out of her, quietly, quickly. For a second it occurred to Jamie to stop him, only because she didn't have her diaphragm in. But that second passed as her intellect was wiped clean from a surge of stringy, wet, body emotions. And then Jamie was instantly present as Scooter Ray pressed into her, urgently, hard, making tiny whimpering noises that sounded like crying.

Scooter Ray kissed Jamie as wetness pooled between her legs.

"You're cool," Scooter Ray said.

"What do you mean by that?" Jamie nudged Scooter Ray off her; he rolled onto his back so they were side by side.

"I dunno. You're not giggly."

"I think maybe I'm more giggly when I'm with my friends." Jamie slid atop Scooter Ray's warm, slick body; her cheek pressed against the top of his chest. He was as flat and hard as a surfboard.

"Well, I like you without your friends."

"Do you know about the baby that died in my pool?" Jamie felt she had to ask; she thought of Lacey's death as her handicap and she needed to point it out lest it be discovered later and cause even more horror.

"Yeah. Flip did mouth-to-mouth on it or something."

"What?"

"I heard Flip tried to save a baby from your pool. Your parents were all fucked up or something and no one was watching the kids."

"And?"

"And Flip went to check on them and did mouth-to-mouth when he saw the baby."

"Jesus did mouth to mouth," Jamie said.

"Hey-soos as in Jesus? Are you a Jesus chick?"

"No. I mean Jesus, a person, our gardener. He did mouth-to-mouth."

Scooter Ray laughed. "Man, you scared me for a minute. I thought you were like my mom or something. She's a total Bible-lady and she takes all my old clothes to this Mexican church in Ventura, you know, and when she comes back she's always saying 'Praise Hey-soos' and shit like that." Jamie's fantasy of shopping sprees with Scooter Ray's mother fizzled like a dead firecracker.

"Flip didn't do mouth-to-mouth," Jamie said.

"Cool. I believe you."

"And my parents weren't fucked up. Or maybe they were. But it wasn't their baby, it wasn't their responsibility."

"Hey, I'm not blaming you. I'm just telling you what I heard."

"Okay, well then, here's the story: my parents had a party. The baby was being watched by a kid named Franny. The grown-ups were jumping on the trampoline. Flip and I went to the pool and I saw the baby. I screamed, or something, and Jesus, our gardener, jumped in, pulled the baby out, and did mouth to mouth. And the baby died. The next day, Flip called me up and broke up with me." And for the second time that night, Jamie was crying, her floating happiness having plummeted into the muck below her.

"Hey, it's okay." Scooter Ray wrapped his arms around Jamie, real tight, like a boa constrictor, and kissed the top of her head. The longer he held her, the better Jamie felt, until it seemed as though Scooter Ray had squeezed the tears from Jamie and replaced them with the joy she'd been feeling only minutes earlier.

Scooter Ray gently wormed out from underneath Jamie and sat up.

"I gotta get back before Kim starts looking for me." He kneeled into the sand and felt around for his clothes.

"Kim? Kim Redson?" Jamie felt hope streaming out of her–like ghosts flying out of a body.

"Yeah. She's my girlfriend."

"God, I . . . I completely forgot you were with Kim." As she said this, Jamie remembered Tammy telling her that Scooter Ray and Kim Redson had fallen in love. Why hadn't she remembered? Was she so intent on her own internal drama of loneliness, rejection, and eating in solitude that she could no longer keep track of the lives beyond her own? She was like her father, Jamie decided, who when he was immersed in his work couldn't get his daughters' names straight and never knew whether he'd had breakfast or not.

Jamie patted the sand, looking for her clothes.

"We've been together for about a week. She's really serious about this, man."

"Are you in love?" The stain of hope resurged in Jamie's belly. She prayed that Scooter Ray would say that he loved her, not Kim Redson.

"I guess, but being in love doesn't mean I don't have a mad crush on you."

"You've never spoken to me until tonight." Jamie found her clothes and began dressing with shaking hands.

"I thought you were ignoring me."

"No. I just didn't know you." What if Scooter Ray was the perfect boyfriend? Jamie thought. What if her relationship with Flip turned out to the worst thing that had ever happened to her–the thing that prevented her from getting to know Scooter Ray before he met Kim Redson?

"Well, too bad we didn't get together sooner, 'cause now I'm really in it deep with Kim."

"And you love Kim?" Jamie was giving him one more chance to profess his love to her. She and Scooter Ray could avoid each other for a week or so, letting things settle down after he broke it off with Kim, gently, slowly. In person.

"I guess I do love Kim." Scooter Ray reached a hand down to help Jamie up.

"I don't know where my flip-flops are," Jamie said, and she wanted to cry again but held her tears in, sensing that she was verging on the ridiculous.

"I lost my boxers," Scooter Ray said. "They're the only pair I like."

"Maybe it's a sign that you need a new pair." Jamie's voice was high and strained as she tried to shake off her disappointment through forced cheer.

"Yeah, fuck it," Scooter Ray said.

"So we're leaving your underwear and my shoes?"

"Yeah." Scooter Ray laughed. "Let the next person wonder about them."

"God, what if Kim finds out about this," Jamie said. "She'll hate me. Everyone will hate me." Jamie wondered if this was how girls like Taffy Longue got bad reputations: a

series of misunderstandings in which one party thinks she's
sleeping with her future boyfriend, the only person she'll
have sex with for the next two years or so, and the other
party thinks he's getting a wet, instantaneous thrill—an act
never to be repeated or seen again, as fleeting as a sand
sculpture built just before high tide.

"No one will know," Scooter Ray said. He kissed Jamie
on the lips, then took her hand and led her, barefoot, out of
the cave. "Maybe if it doesn't work out with her—" Scooter
Ray didn't finish his sentence.

"Yeah. Whatever." They were out of the cave. Jamie pretended to search the sand for the beers. She wanted to look
anywhere but into Scooter Ray's face; she couldn't bear the
thought of him knowing how hard she'd just landed after
only a few soaring moments with him.

Jamie still held the two beers when they returned to the
party. Scooter Ray gave the top of Jamie's arm a squeeze
good-bye, then slipped away and settled next to the fire,
beside Kim, who brushed the sand off his face and gave him
the look of a mother tending to her rascally son. Tammy
was sitting on Debbie's lap, blowing the smoke from the
joint she had just inhaled into Debbie's open mouth. Jamie
finished off one of the beers, placed the full one inside the
empty cup, and stumbled toward Tammy and Debbie. They
were not more than a few feet ahead, but it felt like miles.
Jamie's feet weren't hitting the sand right, weren't moving
forward the way she intended. Finally she reached them.

"I'm wasted," Jamie said, collapsing behind Tammy. "I
need to go home."

"So go," Tammy said.

"How? I just had sex with Scooter Ray." The words
floated in front of Jamie as she said them; she knew that she

should have trapped them before they hit Tammy's and Debbie's ears.

"You have no morals!" Tammy said. "He's with Kim!"

"I know," Jamie mumbled. "I totally forgot."

"I told you!"

"I know you told her," Debbie said. "You told me you told her."

"Man, Jamie," Tammy said. "You have got to get yourself together. I mean, you're baptized now! You need to act like a good Christian! Christian girls don't do immoral shit like that!"

"Do you know what morals are?" Jamie asked in earnest. Even though Tammy went to church, even though she told Jamie that Lacey was in a better place now that she was sleeping in heaven with Jesus, it had never before occurred to Jamie that Tammy thought there was something better, more pure, in being Christian.

"Of course she knows what morals are!" Debbie said. "And if you ever read the Bible you'd know too!"

Jamie pushed herself up and stumbled away from them, away from the party, to the parking lot of Henry's Beach, toward Brett's truck, which she hoped she could find as her eyes were milky and heavy, as if she were looking underwater in a fish tank that had never been cleaned.

Eventually Jamie stumbled into Brett's truck. Like Bone-Man at the cliff, she tried to mount the truck bed, but instead toppled to the ground. Jamie lay in the gravel for a moment, waiting for the spinning to stop, or at least unify so that her head and body whirled in the same direction. When all felt still, Jamie sat up and put one hand on top of the tire to pull herself up. She remembered the bumper, how easy it is to get into a truck bed when you mount the bumper first. With a few clunky knee bangs, Jamie hoisted herself into the back.

Jamie's clothes were damp from the cave, her feet were cold, and there was sand in her right eye. Lying in the bed of Brett's truck seemed appropriately uncomfortable—as if there were some perfection in having everything feel hard or itchy. Her stomach roiled and Jamie said a quick prayer to the Chumash celestial gods to not let her barf in the truck.

Jimmy and Brett were talking about Brett's weed, where he hid it in the truck. Jamie opened her eyes and realized she'd been sleeping, or passed out, or had simply, somehow, not been present. And then Jimmy spotted her.

"Oh shit!" he said. "Jamie, you okay?"

"Yeah."

"How long you been there?" Brett asked.

"Don't know. Can you take me home?"

"Fucking Tammy will kill me if I leave her here alone and take you home," Brett said.

"I'll take her," Jimmy said. "Give me your keys."

Jimmy rotated his head from front to side, checking on Jamie, who sat beside him in the cab of the truck.

"Let me know if you're going to be sick," he said. "I'll pull over right away."

Jamie nodded and tried to smile.

When they got to the house, Jimmy parked in the drive-way, got out, ran around to Jamie's door, and hefted her up, like a groom carrying his bride. He staggered to the front door and tried to open it while still holding Jamie in his arms.

"Do you have a key?" Jimmy asked. He was panting from the effort of carrying Jamie.

"My sister musta locked it before she went to sleep even though she knows I don't have a key." Jamie tumbled out of Jimmy's arms and landed standing up, leaning into him for support. "Let's go to the backyard."

Jimmy looped his arm around Jamie's back and helped her to the backyard. The glass doors to the kitchen were locked too. Jamie didn't mention the garage door, or the door in her father's study, or the glass doors in the dining room—she knew they'd all be locked; it was Renee's way of punishing Jamie for going to a party that she would never have been invited to.

"I'll sleep in the poolroom," Jamie said. "It's safe enough."

Jimmy followed Jamie around the yard, to the door that lead to the poolroom. The door was unlocked. Jamie stumbled in and sat on the floor, her back against the wall. Jimmy tried the door that went from the poolroom into the house; it was locked.

"Where are you gonna sleep?" Jimmy found the switch and turned on the lights.

"Floor," Jamie said.

"Here." Jimmy yanked the life jackets off their hangers and made a nest on the floor for Jamie.

Jamie crawled across the ground and curled up with her knees pulled toward her chest.

"Blankets," Jimmy said, as he covered Jamie with several towels so that just her face popped out.

"You gonna be okay in here?" he asked.

"Yeah, no problem." Jamie was too drunk to be afraid of

all the things that she would normally imagine lurking in wait for her. She was aware of her current lack of fear and made a note to herself to consider regular drinking as a cure for her anxieties.

"I'll tell Debbie to call you in the morning to make sure you're okay. Okay?"

Jamie knew Debbie wouldn't call in the morning, but it felt wrong to let Jimmy in on that fact. "Thanks," she moaned. Before Jimmy had left the room, Jamie fell (not slowly, the way a leaf falls, but quickly, the way an avalanche falls) into a deep sleep.

15

Although Allen and Betty took pride in the fact that their children weren't monitored or watched like prisoners, they couldn't help but notice Jamie's presence on the family room couch, day after day, eating peanut butter cups and watching TV. Allen decided that Jamie was, indeed, uncharacteristically depressed and that the family should go to therapy together, for who knew what scars the death of Lacey had left behind in each of them. Betty felt that the exorcism and baptism were all she needed, but for the sake of her near-motionless daughter, she agreed to go. Renee claimed that she herself was carrying scars that predated the death of Lacey, scars acquired simply by being in the family. Family therapy would not be right for her, she said, as she needed to be healed *from* them and not *with* them. In an unusual act of paternity, Allen insisted that every member of the family be present for therapy. Dorey, his shrink in Los Angeles, connected them with someone whom she called a "masterful" therapist—a session with this guy, Dorey claimed, should not be passed up. If it didn't work out, Allen told the family, his acupuncturist would give them the group rate on acupuncture for everyone.

* * *

Renee sat in the middle of the backseat of the Volvo, one hand on the edge of Allen's seat and one on the edge of Betty's. Jamie leaned against the window, watching people in the cars that passed and wondering how many other people on the freeway were going to family therapy. A long, velvet-red car cruised along side them. A bald man was driving with a helmet-haired woman beside him. They were as still as the seat itself, both staring straight ahead as if they'd been hypnotized. Nothing, not even a gum wrapper, was in the backseat; and a box of tissue, with one sheet popped up like a burgee, sat on the red ledge behind the backseat. Jamie wondered what it would be like to ride in a car that clean, that quiet, to have a fresh tissue right there if you needed it, to have a life that orderly and organized. The people in the clean car would never have dead babies floating in their pool; they would never have boyfriends who broke up with them with the quick efficiency of canceling a dental appointment. They would never confuse sex in a beach cave with love. They wouldn't even have sisters who hated them. No, tidy people like that probably continued the same tender friendships with their sisters from childhood through puberty and into adulthood.

"I don't see why I have to go," Renee said. "Jamie's the one who's depressed."

"I'm not depressed," Jamie said. "I've never been depressed in my life!"

"No, you're not depressed," Renee said, "you're perfectly happy to sit home eating Cap'n Crunch and watching *Match Game* every single day. I mean, you don't even read anymore!"

"Jamie's problems are everyone's problems," Betty said.

"They're not *my* problems," Renee said. "I don't watch *Match Game* every day."

"Shut up." Jamie stared at the floor, at the balled silver gum wrapper, the hair-laden lint that had collected on the edges of the floor mat, and the three dried french fries from when Allen had snuck the girls out to McDonald's the previous winter. Jamie *had* hardly read all summer; when Flip had been her boyfriend she hadn't had time to read. And now that she had time she couldn't find any books that interested her–nothing seemed as scintillating as game shows. But her problem was not that she watched *Match Game*, Jamie thought; it was that she had no one to watch *Match Game* with.

"Does it have to be group therapy?" Renee asked. "What if someone I know from school is there? What if I know one of the kids in one of the families?"

"If they're there too," Allen said, "you'll have nothing to be embarrassed about."

"We could skip it and go to Family Night at Tammy's church," Jamie said. "It starts at the same time as this."

"Yeah, look how much good Family Night does Tammy–she's not a nasty, skinny, blond bitch, is she?" Renee said.

"No need for sarcasm," Betty said.

"Actually," Renee said, "maybe Family Night would be good. Jamie could just confess or something and not drag all of us into this."

"I'd rather eat dog shit then go to Family Night at Tammy's church," Betty said.

"No need for sarcasm, Mom," Renee said.

"I'm not being sarcastic. I wouldn't go near her family's church."

"How can you say that?" Allen had a slicing edge in

his voice. "You, the woman who had our child baptized in the swimming pool, would rather eat dog shit than go to a church?!"

"Don't start," Betty said.

Renee refused to get out of the car when they pulled up at the therapist's house. Jamie thought it was a boring-looking square house in a neighborhood of similar boring houses. This neighborhood had wide streets; clean, white sidewalks; tidy, trim lawns; small, shadeless trees; and no people outside.

Jamie followed Betty and Allen to the front door. Just as Allen was ringing the bell Renee ran out of the car and joined her family. A man with a square, rubbery face answered the door. He was wearing a shiny tight shirt unbuttoned to reveal a furry nest of brown hair; he reminded Jamie of TV stars.

"You must be Allen and Betty," he said, and he hugged Betty first, then Allen.

"Are we late?" Allen asked.

"Just a few minutes," the man said.

"These are the girls," Allen said.

"Which one is Jamie?" the therapist asked.

"Her," Jamie said, pointing to Renee.

"*She's* Jamie," Allen said, pointing at Jamie. "But we're all in this together. It's not just Jamie I'm worried about."

"Of course," the therapist said, and he leaned down and hugged Jamie. Jamie could smell cologne on his neck and minty toothpaste, which she imagined was caulked in the cracks of his long, yellow teeth. There was something about those teeth that made Jamie want to run from him. Renee must have felt similarly repulsed for when the therapist reached toward her for a hug, she stepped behind Allen and stuck her hand out to be shaken.

"Come meet the group," the therapist said, taking Renee's hand and leading her, and the rest of family, into the house, then down three steps into the sunken living room, where a small crowd was seated, waiting. There were three couches and four chairs arranged in a circle. The couches were orange, flat, with buttons on the seats and backs. The chairs were green, nubby, with bent iron triangles for legs.

"Grown-ups on couches and chairs," the therapist said, "and children on the floor."

Betty and Allen sat in the only open spot, on a couch where another couple already sat. Renee and Jamie sat in front of their parents, their legs crossed and touching at the knee. Jamie scanned the circle to check out the other kids. There were six girls and two boys. One of the girls looked high-school-aged; she wore bright red lipstick, mascara, and a blouse that hung open when she leaned forward on her crossed legs, revealing her woman-sized breasts. The rest of the kids were smaller, younger than Jamie. One boy was black. This was remarkable for two reasons: (1) There were no black parents in the group. (2) There were no black people (that Jamie had ever met) in Santa Barbara. Other than her years-long pen pal from when she went to sleep-away camp near Los Angeles, the only black people Jamie knew were on television: Bill Cosby, Flip Wilson, Huggy Bear from *Starsky and Hutch,* and Rodney Allen Rippy, who sang in the commercial for Jack in the Box.

"Let's start by going around the room and stating our names," the therapist said, "so that Betty and Allen and their kids can get to know us. You all know that I'm Dick."

Jamie's lips pursed as she stifled a laugh. She nudged her sister with her elbow, but Renee ignored her.

Dick put his hand on the knee of the woman sitting

beside him. She was fat but dollish—like a bloated country girl from *Petticoat Junction*.

"I'm Karen," she said. "I'm Dick's wife."

There were two women sitting behind the black boy. One had long, tumbling brown hair. The other had a short, blond pixie cut. The blond one put her hands on the black boy's shoulders as if she were trying to brace herself before speaking.

"I'm Dodie. I'm the wife of Sela and mother of Tugboat." She squeezed Tugboat's shoulders when she said his name.

"I'm Sela," the dark-haired one said, "wife of Dodie and mother of Tugboat."

Tugboat didn't say anything; he was drawing something with his finger in the golden shag rug.

In the middle of the introductions, a waifish girl—about the size of an eight-year-old—stood, turned toward her mother, and raised her mother's T-shirt. The mother watched Dick and didn't seem to notice as her daughter lifted one of her rubbery breasts and shoved it into her mouth. Jamie had seen babies nurse before, but she had never seen someone so large doing it. The mother caught Jamie staring; she smiled and winked. Jamie looked away quickly, scratching her eye, as if that, somehow, would lead the woman to believe that Jamie hadn't really been looking at her overgrown suckling.

"Renee, Jamie," Dick said, "do you have any questions before we begin?"

Jamie wanted to ask why Tugboat was named Tugboat, why the girl was nursing, if Sela and Dodie were really *married,* how old the girl with the lipstick was, and why anyone named Dick wouldn't just go by Richard or Rich or Rick, even. But she shrugged her shoulders and said nothing.

"Jamie," Dick said, "maybe you can start by telling everyone what you've been doing when you're home alone all day and how you feel about what you've been doing."

"Uh . . . ," Jamie swallowed hard. "I'll pass for now."

"You don't need to be ashamed," Dick said.

"No thanks," Jamie said.

Sela said, "Everything is okay here, Jamie. There is nothing you can't tell us. Tugboat told us about his exploration with masturbation and he discovered that what he was doing was fine. That we're all human and everyone masturbates."

"I haven't been masturbating!" Jamie's face flared red as she laughed. No one laughed with her, not even her own family.

"We'll move on to someone else," Dick said. "But Jamie, I'd like you to prepare yourself to share what you've been doing with the group. The only way for you to heal is for you to open yourself up."

"Okay." Jamie forced herself to smile away from the direction of Tugboat. She couldn't bear to look into his face now that his mother had told the group he was masturbating. Was he blushing, she wondered, or had he maintained his focus on the shag rug? Jamie rolled her eyes toward the ceiling and begged the Chumash celestial gods not to let her mother tell the group about her diaphragm or the fact that her breasts came in before Renee's or any other information that Jamie felt should remain in the confines of her own body and mind.

While people took turns "sharing their feelings" Jamie looked around the room and examined faces, skin, hair, and pore sizes. She was so encased in her head that she didn't hear what anyone said until a man with a handlebar mustache and yellow slacks stood up and whined in a girlish timbre that he felt like ripping open his body with a Phillips head screwdriver, tearing out his heart, and hurling it against his wife's sickly face. Dick told the man, Stan, to get the tennis racket, go to the guest room, and return when he had diffused his anger.

"I didn't mean Phillips head," Stan said, as he picked up the racket that had been leaning against a wall, "I meant a standard screwdriver, the one with a tip like a flat tongue."

"Thank you for sharing that, Stan," Dick said. Then he turned to Jamie and Renee and said, "Stan is going to hit the bed with a tennis racket. This is what we do when we feel rage. Do either of you have any rage? Would either of you like to hit the bed with the racket?"

"No, thank you," Renee said. Jamie didn't even answer.

Within the next hour, four different adults left to hit the guest bed with a wooden tennis racket. Then the girl with the lipstick raised her hand and said she needed to hit the bed with the racket.

"What are you feeling?" Dick gave her a rubbery smile.

"Tons of rage," she said.

"Go ahead," Dick said.

She picked up the racket, turned, and looked at Jamie.

"Wanna come?" she asked.

Jamie looked toward Allen for an answer.

"Go, sweetheart," Allen said. "Check it out."

What's your name again?" the girl asked.

They were in the guest room, sitting on the end of the

bed. There was an orange floral bedspread that reminded Jamie of beds in hotels.

"Jamie."

"I'm Pam."

"Are you going to hit the bed?" Jamie asked. Up close, she could see that Pam had acne blooming across her forehead, and that the tips of her teeth were bluish gray.

"No," Pam said. "I was getting bored and just wanted to get away for a few minutes."

"Cool," Jamie said.

"What did you do anyway?" Pam asked.

"I didn't really do anything. I've just been sitting on my couch watching TV and eating all day long."

"Oh, I love doing that!" Pam said. "Do you throw up?"

"Throw up?"

"Yeah, after you eat. Do you, like, eat and eat and eat and then barf it all up so you don't get fat?"

"No. I just eat and eat."

"Oh, you should try barfing. It's so great, 'cause you can eat more and not be so full and it helps maintain your figure."

"Is that what you do?"

"All the time! I'm up to, like, three times a day."

"You're throwing up three times a day?"

"Yeah. Swear you won't tell my dad? He'd kill me if he knew."

"Which one's your dad?"

"Dick! Dick's my dad."

"Dick the therapist?"

"Yeah," Pam said, as she crawled to the top of the bed, untucked the pillows, and lay down. "It's my house. Dick and Karen are my parents."

"Oh." Jamie crawled up and lay beside her. "Is it fun to have a dad who's a therapist?"

"No. Think about the word, okay? Therapist. *The rapist.* Get it?"

"The rapist?"

"If you divide the word *therapist* it comes out to the rapist. That's my dad. The rapist."

"Oh. I guess that's not cool."

"What did you think of Dodie and Sela?" Pam asked.

"Did one of them have Tugboat?"

"They adopted him," Pam said, "from Los Angeles."

"Was he already named Tugboat?"

"No, he was named Michael Paul, but they didn't like that name, they thought it was a name that humiliated women and Afro-Americans."

"I don't get it."

"I'm adopted too," Pam said.

"Where are your real parents?"

"No one will tell me—my *adopted* mom said she doesn't know, but I don't believe her. I think my real mom is Carol Burnett."

"Really?"

"It's a long story, but I have evidence. I'll show you some other time."

"Cool," Jamie said, and she believed Pam; she couldn't imagine that someone this grown, this womanly, would make up fantasy stories like the girls in elementary school, like Tammy, who when she moved to Santa Barbara in third grade, had told the class that her little sister had tumbled down a hill, fallen into a piece of glass that jammed into her eye, and bled to death from her eyeball, when in fact Tammy had never had a sister.

"Have you ever been in a trance?" Pam flipped to her side, head propped up on an elbow, and stared at Jamie.

"No."

"Roll onto your stomach and I'll put you in a trance," she said.

"Will it hurt?" Jamie rolled over.

"No." Pam hopped off the bed and locked the door. "I don't want anyone interrupting us."

"How old are you?" Jamie asked.

"Fifteen," Pam said, and she straddled Jamie's butt.

"You look eighteen, or twenty or something."

"I know." Pam shifted Jamie's shirt up as high as her armpits. "What size bra do you wear?"

"Thirty-two B."

"I'm a D."

"Cool," Jamie said.

"I'm going to unhook your bra, okay? So I can put you in a trance."

"Have you done this before?" Jamie asked.

"Yeah." Pam began running her fingernails up and down Jamie's spine. "My friends and I do it all the time. It feels really cool."

"Was your name Pam when your parents adopted you?"

"I think it was Carol, after my real mother, but my *adopted* mother won't admit that."

"Have *you* gone into a trance before?"

"Yes. Now be quiet so it will work. You have to shut your eyes and breathe really slowly, okay?"

"Okay."

Pam continued to tickle Jamie's spine. Jamie shut her eyes and tried to breathe slowly but found that she was simply holding her breath.

"Now count backward from a hundred."

"Ninety-nine," Jamie began. The counting allowed her to forget about the difficulties she was having with the breathing.

Somewhere around thirty-seven, Jamie petered out.

"You are in a trance," Pam said in a slow robotic voice. "Do not open your eyes until I snap my fingers."

Jamie did nothing, said nothing; she tried not to think about breathing. She thought that if this state she was currently in was a trance, then she frequently went into a trance–she was entranced when she watched TV, or ate ice cream, or read a book, or looked out the car window. Jamie thought that this was just her being quiet. This was Jamie with her eyes shut.

"Now keep your eyes closed and roll over, veeeery slowly."

Pam lifted her body off Jamie's butt so Jamie could roll over, then sat back down once Jamie was in position. Jamie's eyes remained shut and her hands remained by her sides, but she wanted to reach behind herself and hook her bra, which was sitting loose across her breasts.

"You will not remember any of this." Pam slid her hands up Jamie's belly and across her breasts as she pushed her bra toward her neck.

Jamie was nervous and absolutely certain that she was not in a trance. Pam swirled her hands across Jamie's chest and belly as if she were playing with finger paints. There was a ticklish feeling inside Jamie that told her this might feel good. But her racing thoughts didn't linger on the ticklish feeling; they lingered on how strange it was that this girl she had met only an hour ago was sitting on her crotch, rubbing her hands across Jamie's bare chest. And who was this girl anyway? Jamie wondered. Was she insane? If this was what group therapy did for you, Jamie wanted no part of it. These people seemed crazier than she. Jamie wasn't about to make herself throw up; she was simply eating! And Renee was angry and full of rage like Stan, but she never threatened to take a standard screwdriver and rip her heart out! She never threatened to throw her eviscerated heart into Jamie's face! And her parents liked to smoke pot and swim naked, her mother liked to talk to her about sex and masturbation and diaphragms, but they would never have named her Tugboat! And how, Jamie wondered, could she possibly get this loony girl off her body without completely humiliating herself? She was the therapist's daughter! (Or the rapist's daughter?!) That was like being daughter of the boss, or the president, or the school principal! Jamie considered opening her eyes, showing Pam that she wasn't really in a trance, but she was afraid that then she'd be exposed as a liar and a fake. On the other hand, Jamie thought, to not do anything might bring on further deranged exploits!

The door rattled and someone knocked. Pam jumped off Jamie and snapped her fingers. Jamie popped her eyes open, sat up, hooked her bra, and pulled down her shirt.

"Just a minute," Pam said, walking toward the door.

She unlocked and opened the door to her smiling father.

"You girls okay in here?" Dick asked.

"Yeah," Pam said. "Jamie took a turn at the bed too. She was really raging."

Jamie hopped off the bed and picked up the tennis racket that was sitting on the floor.

"Jamie, maybe you want to observe as Pam and I discuss her feelings," Dick said. "Think of our interaction as a model for your relationship with your parents."

"Okay," Jamie said, although she wanted nothing more than to sprint out of the room, away from the rubber-faced man and his daughter, who just then seemed more the rapist than he.

"Pam," Dick said, turning toward his daughter. "What are you feeling?"

"I'm feeling rage."

"Why do you feel rage?"

"Because I was abandoned at birth by you-know-who."

"Pam, we do not know who your birth parents are. We've told you that many times."

"I'm feeling rage because you won't tell me the truth about my birth parents." Pam began to tremble. Dick paused and looked at Pam as if he were analyzing her aura.

"I feel love, Pam." Dick leaned forward and hugged Pam. Pam began sobbing into his shoulder.

Jamie edged toward the door. Dick looked up and smiled, his arms still around Pam.

"Come back here, Jamie! Pammy's okay! Right now we're sharing our love!"

"Cool." Jamie stood three feet from the bed, and began counting the repeats in the floral pattern on the bedspread as Pam and her father finished sharing their love. When they were done, Dick instructed Jamie to sit on the bed, saying that he'd send in her family. Pam held her father's hand and followed him out of the room without once looking back at Jamie.

Betty, Allen, and Renee shuffled into the guest room. Allen shut the door quickly behind him, like he was playing hide and seek. They mustered together, standing at the end of the bed.

"Did you hit the bed?" Renee seemed excited by the possibility.

"No. But that girl, that daughter of that therapist guy"–Jamie couldn't bring herself to say Pam's name–"she told her dad that I did and that I was screaming."

"That's what he told us!" Allen said.

"He said you were wailing," Betty said.

"I swear," Jamie said, "I wasn't wailing and I didn't hit the bed."

"So you're not feeling rage?" Renee asked.

"I don't think so," Jamie said. "Are you?"

"No," Renee said.

"I think I'm feeling kind of freaked out by that lying, makeup-wearing girl."

"I was feeling rage," Allen said. "But then I started feeling bored with listening to everyone complain, complain, complain."

"I was feeling pissed off at you for talking me into this," Betty said to Allen.

"Well," Allen said, "you should feel glad you're married to me and not to all those complainers out there."

"I feel glad you didn't name me Tugboat," Jamie said, and everyone laughed.

"Was that girl screaming when she hit the bed?" Renee asked.

"She didn't even hit the bed, she just wanted to hang out." An image of Pam sitting on her, rubbing her chest, flickered in Jamie's mind; she quickly blinked it away

"She looks slutty," Renee said.

"Don't criticize her," Betty said. "She was adopted."

"Yeah, her real mother is Carol Burnett."

No one seemed to hear Jamie.

"Why can't Renee criticize someone who's adopted?" Allen asked.

"Think how hard it would be to be adopted," Betty said. "It's tragic."

"It's not tragic," Allen said. "It would have been tragic if no one adopted her and she was an orphan."

"At least they didn't change her name to Tugboat," Jamie said, making Renee scream with laughter.

Betty shushed her daughters.

"We're supposed to be working on your rage," she said.

"Yeah," Allen grunted, "why don't you fake cry or something, so your mother won't be embarrassed that you're not raging properly."

"I'll hit the bed." Jamie picked up the tennis racket and hit the spot on the bed where she had been lying in her false trance. Surprisingly, it felt good to hit the bed, like she was hitting that moment away, banishing it with each thrash of the racket.

"Let me try," Renee said, and she did a few whomps on the same spot. Jamie imagined her bashing the ghost of Pam.

"Maybe you girls should take tennis lessons," Allen said.

"Tennis?" Betty scowled. "It's such a white man's sport."

"We're white," Allen said.

"Mom, there aren't any *Native American* sports for us to do," Jamie said.

"There must some sort of Native American sport," Betty said.

"Lacrosse was invented by the Indians," Allen said.

"I want to do tennis." Renee swung the racket in the air as if she were returning a ball.

"Why don't we build a tennis court in the backyard by the eucalyptus trees?" Jamie asked.

"Let's put in a lacrosse field," Betty said. "Everyone has a tennis court, but no one we know has a lacrosse field."

"I'm not competing with the neighbors," Allen said.

"What is lacrosse?" Renee asked.

"Yeah," Jamie said. "If we've never even heard of it, it can't be that great."

"It's an East Coast sport," Allen said.

"I thought it was Native American," Jamie said.

"Who the hell knows," Allen said, wandering toward the door.

"Do we have to come back here next week?" Renee asked.

"Not as long as Jamie stops watching TV and eating all day," Betty said.

"So we don't have to do this again? 'Cause Dad, I swear, these people are really crazy," Jamie said.

"Well, I don't know if we can call them crazy . . ." Allen paused to think.

"Dad! Do we have to go again or not?" Renee snapped.

"Not," Betty said. "As long as Jamie promises to get out of the house, go to the beach, and find another boyfriend."

"I promise," Jamie said.

"Good. Then let's go." Renee marched to the door, opened it, and walked out with the rest of the family following behind.

16

In order to avoid family therapy, Jamie had to ride her bike to the beach daily with Renee and Lori. Renee and Lori never spoke to her while at the beach. They rarely spoke to each other as they lay like twins, their faces turned toward the sun, flipping over every thirty minutes so that they were perfectly and evenly browned–two pieces of carefully watched toast. Jamie didn't mind being ignored at the beach; she enjoyed the time in her head; she imagined she lived a different life, a life where she was skinnier, had shiny hair as thick as a horse's tail, spoke ten languages fluently, and lived in a spacious flat in the center of Paris (where she had been once on vacation with her family).

Renee and Lori always rode far ahead of Jamie on their trips to and from the beach. So it looked as though Jamie were completely alone one day when Brett's truck pulled up alongside her as she was pedaling home on Garden Street. Brett, Jimmy, Tammy, and Debbie were piled in the cab. Debbie was on Jimmy's lap. She had one hand cupped over Tammy's ear, into which she whispered so violently that her head shook, shaking Tammy's head in turn. Jamie stopped and stood, straddling her bike as Brett rolled to a stop. In the back of the truck were Flip, Terry, Scooter Ray, and Kim. Flip was passing a joint to Terry; he looked up at Jamie and lifted his chin real fast, as if he had just hit a Ping-Pong ball with it, as a manner of saying hello. No one else in the back, not even Scooter Ray, looked over at Jamie. Get used to it, Jamie silently told herself, this is how it will be at school in the fall. She turned her head and tried to breathe away the tumbling stones in her gut.

"How have you been?" Jimmy asked, leaning out in front of Debbie.

"Okay. How are you?" Jamie stared at Debbie and Tammy, who were still whispering.

"OH MY GOD," Debbie yelled, as if she had just noticed Jamie. "What are you doing?!"

"Riding my bike," Jamie said.

"WHERE WERE YOU?" Tammy leaned out, pulling Debbie back.

"Why are you yelling?"

Tammy and Debbie fell back into hiccupping laughter.

"They're wasted," Jimmy said. "They were drinking mimosas at Terry's house."

"What's mimosas?" Jamie asked.

"OH MY GOD!" Tammy and Debbie cracked up again.

"Orange juice and . . . shit, I don't know what it is, I wasn't there," Jimmy said.

"I see."

"Throw your bike in the back and get in," Jimmy said. "There's plenty of room."

"Nah," Jamie said. "I gotta go home."

"She's depressed," Tammy said. "She doesn't do anything anymore."

"My parents are having a big party tonight," Jamie said. "I gotta go help them get ready."

"Your parents are always having a party! They're total partiers!" Tammy said.

"Veronica Hale's going to be there," Jamie said, which was the truth. Jamie had been rolling images of the movie star in her head, incorporating her into her beach fantasies.

"Just get in the truck," Jimmy said.

"She doesn't go to the beach anymore!" Debbie said.

"Seriously. I've gotta go home. Veronica Hale's going to be at our house in about two hours." Jamie hoped Flip was listening. She knew he would be impressed by Veronica Hale. And what was the chance that Terry Watson's parents ever had a party with a major international celebrity? Terry Watson might be thin and beautiful, Jamie thought, but she wouldn't be having breakfast tomorrow with Veronica Hale.

"You swear *Veronica Hale* is going to your house?" Tammy asked.

"Yes," Jamie said. "She and her husband, John Krane, are staying in our guest room."

"I've never seen any of her movies but my dad's, like, pissed at her 'cause she was really mean to the soldiers in Vietnam or something," Tammy said.

"Oh. Well, my parents are throwing a fund-raising party for her husband, who's running for Senate. He was in my dad's fraternity in college."

"Can we come to the party?"

"No. You're too wasted."

"Just me and Tammy," Debbie said. "Your parents never care if we're around."

"Yeah, but I don't want you all drunk and goofy–you'll

embarrass me." Jamie had a sudden urge to punish them for having rejected her.

"C'mon! We'll be sober by then!" Debbie said.

"Please, please, please, PLEASE!" Tammy leaned toward the window, grinning at Jamie.

"Fine. Come when you're sober." Jamie hoped that Tammy and Debbie would give Flip and Terry Watson a report of the party with many flattering details about how intimate Jamie's parents were with the Hale-Kranes.

"OH MY GOD!" Tammy screamed. "WE'RE GOING TO A PARTY WITH VERONICA HALE!"

Brett leaned over toward the window and said, "Veronica Hale, really, at your house?"

"Yeah," Jamie said.

"Cool." Brett said. "You comin' to the beach with us or not?"

"Don't say not," Jimmy said, shooting a smiling wink at Jamie.

"Not," Jamie said, but she winked back at Jimmy.

"Later!" Brett said, and he pulled the truck away from the curb, jostling everyone and throwing Debbie and Tammy into screams that Jamie could still hear a block away.

Thirty minutes before the guests of honor were due to arrive, two hours before the party was to start, while Allen was out buying bags of ice, Renee and Jamie sat in the kitchen watching their mother give Rosa instructions on how to be in charge of the Chumash couple that was catering the party. Jesus sat on a stool beside Jamie, also observing Betty and Rosa. Each time Betty said the name Veronica Hale, Jesus smiled.

Betty was in a full-length, sleeveless batik dress that she had bought at an art show. There were large gold hoops in her ears and a gold chain around her ankle. Her leather sandals had a braided toe ring for her big toe. Jamie thought the sandals were cool; Renee said they were embarrassing.

"Mom," Renee interrupted, "you bought a bathing suit, right?"

"Yeah, yeah." Betty waved her hand and rolled her eyes.

"And you told Leon and Lois that they had to wear suits if they swam, right?"

"Honey, don't worry about it. Everyone's wearing a suit tonight."

"I mean, Mom," Renee continued, "he's running for *senator*. You cannot go naked at a senatorial fund-raiser."

"Sweetheart, we know! We bought suits! Relax."

"Maybe we should go back to family therapy and work out the naked swimming thing," Jamie said.

"Shut up," Renee said.

"And listen." Betty turned to her daughters. "Movie stars are very particular about the way their bodies look and they're usually skinnier than normal people. So I don't want you girls comparing yourselves to Veronica Hale, you hear? No matter how good her figure may be, you must remind yourself that you are you and you are perfect in the you that you are."

"A lot of *yous* in that sentence, Mom," Jamie said, and Renee cracked up.

"I'm going to go do some sit-ups before they get here," Renee said, sliding off her stool.

"Don't you dare exercise because a movie star is coming over!" Betty called after her. "You're perfect!"

The doorbell rang and Jamie and her mother froze up, looking at each other.

"Jesus Christ, they're early," Betty said.

Rosa wiped her hands on her apron and headed out of the kitchen to answer the door.

"No!" Betty stopped her. "I don't want them thinking we have some white hierarchy thing going on in this house. You take care of the kitchen and I'll get the door."

Jamie followed her mother to the door and stood right beside her as she opened it. A long-faced man and a beautiful brown-haired, blue-eyed woman stood on the porch.

"Betty?" the woman asked. "I'm Veronica."

Betty shook Veronica Hale's and John Krane's hands and invited them in without introducing Jamie. John and Veronica each carried a soft leather duffel bag, which they dumped on the entrance hall floor.

"Tell Jesus to take their bags up to the guest room," Betty whispered to Jamie.

"But he's Mexican. Shouldn't a white person take them up?" Jamie asked, in earnest.

"Just go get him!" Betty hissed, then rushed over to John and Veronica, who were wandering the living room looking at the paintings.

Jamie helped Jesus take the bags up. There was a fat bouquet of yellow roses on the dresser in the guest room. Betty had never put flowers in the guest room for anyone, not even her best friend from college, not even the president of a company Allen was consulting for, not even her own sister. But for Veronica Hale, flowers were everywhere.

When Jamie came downstairs, Betty, Veronica Hale, and John Krane were standing by the pool. Jamie sat on a boulder and watched her mother rigidly gesturing as she chatted with the couple. Allen came home from the store and joined them, and suddenly everyone, especially Betty, seemed more relaxed. Veronica told Betty and Allen that she loved the pool, she loved the boulders, she loved the landscaping.

"There's a eucalyptus grove way back there," Jamie said, "and there's a trampoline on the lawn."

"You have a trampoline?" Veronica asked Jamie.

"Yeah, down the hill," Jamie said.

"I love trampolines," Veronica said.

Veronica Hale pointed her toes and lifted her arms like a ballerina when she jumped. She was in blue jeans and a puffy-sleeved Mexican peasant blouse that billowed out each time she went up. Jamie jumped with Veronica, facing her, watching her. Veronica didn't talk or look down at Jamie; she simply jumped in a rhythm, staring off into the distance. Jamie felt like she was jumping by herself while watching a movie of Veronica Hale on a trampoline. She wondered if the only way to endure public life as a movie star was to create invisible walls between yourself and everyone around you. Veronica Hale seemed supremely alone, safely separated from Jamie and anyone else who might approach.

While John Krane and Veronica Hale were in the guest room showering and changing, Betty, Allen, Renee, and Jamie huddled together in the backyard.

"I think she's too skinny," Betty said. "I mean, she's had two children—she doesn't look normal."

"Lois is skinnier than she is," Jamie said.

"Lois never had kids," Betty said.

"She looks fine," Allen said. "She seems wonderful."

"Oh, of course she's wonderful to you! Why wouldn't she be wonderful to you? I bet that yellow-aura penis of yours just loves her!"

"Mom!" Renee said. "Don't talk about Dad's penis in front of us!"

Rosa came out to the backyard.

"Miss Betty," she said, "the Chumash are here, but I think you've been duped! That lady in there is no Chumash; she's a Mexican!"

"How do you know?" Allen asked.

"I know my own people," Rosa said, "just like you'd know yours."

"But Chumash, Mexican, they look pretty similar, don't you think?"

"No," Rosa said.

"Is it the people who did the food at the aura reading?" Jamie asked.

"Yes," Betty said. "They're Chumash and they're fabulous. Chumash wouldn't lie about being Chumash."

"Yes, but a *chola* might lie," Rosa said.

"What's a *chola*?" Allen asked.

"Mexican American!" Rosa said. "They lie all the time."

"How can you say that about your people?!" Betty said. "One's people is all that we have in this life!"

"That lady *is* Mexican," Jamie said. "She told me the last time they were here. Her boyfriend is Chumash."

"Well, one Chumash is fine!" Betty seemed near tears. "Just leave them alone and let them cook!"

"Okay, okay," Rosa said. "It's your Veronica Hale party, not mine."

"Jamie probably knows more about the Chumash than that Mexican lady in there," Renee said.

"I probably do," Jamie said. "Did you know that the Chumash believe in four celestial gods?"

"We know, dear, you've told us," Betty said. "Now go get ready for the party."

Debbie and Tammy appeared just as the party was starting. Jamie vacillated between regretting having invited them and being glad to have them witness Veronica Hale hanging out with her parents and their friends. What she really hoped, however, was that somehow, in the absence of their boyfriends, she and Debbie and Tammy would fall into place together and things would be giddy and wonderful the way they had been at the beginning of the summer.

Tammy's father walked into the kitchen with Tammy and Debbie. He glanced out the glass doors toward the pool. It was clear he was hoping to see Veronica Hale.

"This thing black tie?" Mr. Hopkins never looked at Tammy's friends when he spoke to them; it was as if he were avoiding something in their faces.

"I don't think so," Jamie said. "Veronica Hale's wearing a long flowery skirt and a green blouse that's tied up at her waist."

"Tied up at her waist?!" Tammy asked. Tammy was in tight, red pants with a red-and-yellow-striped cap-sleeved shirt.

"Yeah, you know, in a big knot."

"Can you see her belly button?" Debbie asked. Debbie was in Chemin de Fer sailor jeans and a gauzy button-front blouse. She untucked the blouse and tied it around her waist. Jamie was in shorts and a T-shirt. It hadn't occurred to her to dress for the party and it was entirely unlike her parents to either note what their daughters wore or direct their choice in clothing.

"So Hanoi Hale's here," Tammy's dad said. "I got a thing or two I'd like to tell her."

"The party's a fund-raiser for her husband," Jamie said.

"You know, my brother fought in Nam." Tammy's dad nodded his head as spoke, as if he were physically working up to something. "And my father fought in World War Two. Tammy comes from a long line of good American soldiers."

"How's this?" Debbie asked, showing her tied-up shirt.

"I wouldn't let that woman in my house to clean the toilets," Tammy's dad said.

The Chumash man at the stove stared at Mr. Hopkins with dark, hard eyes.

"Do you think I should change into a blouse?" Tammy asked.

"You look fine," Jamie said, "and the party's already starting."

"Don't you girls listen to any of her mumbo jumbo now, you hear?" Tammy's dad ambled toward the door, his giant belly leading the way.

Tammy waved to her father as he walked out.

"See you, Mr. Hopkins!" Debbie called after him.

"My dad hates Democrats," Tammy said. "He told me they're ruining the country, giving away all the money to lazy people and stuff like that."

There was a wooden clanking as the Chumash man knocked his spoon against the side of his pot while watching Tammy as if she were a bobcat.

"Can we please call Jimmy and Brett and let them come to the party?" Debbie asked. "I mean, there are so many people here, no one would notice them."

"No way," Jamie said. "Mom said if we hang around we have to help, pass out food and stuff." Betty had told Jamie that she'd have to help out, but Jamie knew she wouldn't have minded having the boys around too. Jamie didn't want them there because they would have wedged Tammy and Debbie even farther from her; Jamie would be left alone, knocking around the party like a single marble loosed from its bag.

"You girls ready to work?" Rosa pointed to three silver trays on the counter, each with a different appetizer.

"What are these?" Tammy sneered. "They look like slugs on crackers!"

"Go on!" Rosa clapped her hands to move the girls along.

Tammy and Debbie hovered in the vicinity of Veronica Hale. Jamie stood with her back to them, half-listening to an old man with a folded, melted face who talked to her with fishy breath.

Veronica said, "Girls, I won't be having any appetizers at all this evening, so you can stop offering them to me."

Tammy and Debbie hurried off, giggling, to the other side of the pool. Jamie was embarrassed for them.

Betty stood with a cluster of women. Jamie came up behind her and tapped her mother's back.

"What, sweetheart?"

"Anyone want some of these?"

"No, honey. Everyone's had some. Take them over there." Betty paused before turning away; she had just spied Allen talking to Veronica Hale. They were too far away to be heard, but Allen's hands flapped enthusiastically as he gestured. Veronica seemed enraptured; she leaned back laughing, then put a hand on Allen's upper arm as she replied.

"Tell your father he needs to man the bar," Betty said.

"Jesus is at the bar," Jamie said.

Betty looked toward the bar, where Jesus was pouring out cherry-colored margaritas into a row of tall, wide glasses.

"Well, tell him to check on the food."

"I was just in there, everything's fine. Rosa and the non-Chumash Mexican lady are talking to each other in really fast Spanish."

"Christ, Jamie! Tell your father to mingle, tell him it's a big party and he needs to acknowledge more than one guest!"

Jamie wondered what it would be like to love someone as long as her parents had loved each other–to want to be, after so many years, the world's most beautiful woman in your husband's eyes. She had been with Flip for less than a summer–not enough time to ever feel an ownership of his love. And Scooter Ray had lasted for, what, an hour? Not even long enough to develop a jealousy.

Jamie wandered to the far side of the pool where Tammy and Debbie nestled together, their empty trays hanging at their sides.

"Did you see him?" Tammy asked.

"Who?"

"The cute one," Debbie said. "He is so, so, *so* cute."

"I tap-tapped him," Tammy said.

"Yeah," Debbie said, "can you believe she tap-tapped him, as if I'm going to try and compete with her."

"What do you mean you tap-tapped him?"

"She dibsed him," Debbie said.

"You put dibs on a man?"

"Yeah," Tammy said, "or you or Debbie would try to get him first. Do you think your parents would mind if I smoked? I'm dying for a cig."

"There's no way a grown man would be interested in any of us," Jamie said. "I mean, Veronica Hale's here!"

"You don't even know who we're talking about."

"It doesn't matter," Jamie said. "There's no one here who would want us. You don't have to put dibs on some random cute man."

"Of course he'd want us!" Debbie said. "We're young and juicy!"

"God, if I don't have a cigarette soon I'm going to explode. Seriously."

"What about your boyfriends?" Jamie said. "You're the one who's always talking about morals. You're the one who was mad at me for having sex with Scooter Ray!"

"Well, that was very un-Christian of you! You know that!" Tammy said.

"Oh my god, shut up, shut up, here he comes!" Debbie pulled her tray in front of her chest like a shield.

The man was cute in the same way a Ken doll is cute. He had eyelashes like a woman: long, dark, and thick. There were white marks, like a drawing of sun rays, darting out from around his eyes; it seemed he'd been tanned while squinting. He was tall with a flat, broad body, younger-looking than Jamie's parents. And he was staring at Jamie.

"Mmm, can I have one of those?"

Jamie pushed her tray toward him. Tammy and Debbie were silent, watching. Tammy was breathing with her mouth hanging open in a wide O; Jamie looked at her, waiting for her to speak, as she had always been the one who was bold enough to talk to boys and men.

"That's good," he said. "Did you make these?"

"No. Chumash people made them." Jamie shot her eyes toward Tammy, begging her to start talking so Jamie wouldn't have to.

"Chumash, huh."

"Her parents always hire Chumash Indians to cater their parties," Tammy finally blurted.

"Oooh," he said, still staring at Jamie, "you're Allen and Betty's daughter. Are you Renee?"

"I'm Jamie." She wanted him to stop staring. His gaze made her skin prickle, like he was shooting hot sparks from his eyes.

"Are you the older one or the younger one?"

"The younger one, I guess," Jamie said.

"You guess?" he said. "You don't know how old you are?"

"No," Jamie panted. Tammy and Debbie laughed with goofy little hiccups. "I'm definitely younger than my sister." Jamie looked toward Tammy again.

"She's younger," Tammy said. "I can confirm that. By the way, do you have an extra cigarette?"

"I don't smoke," the man said, "and you shouldn't either."

"I do a lot of things I shouldn't do," Tammy said, and she and Debbie cackled and fell against each other.

"Well, Jamie, we'll have to talk again later." The man

winked at Jamie, then walked away, skimming through the crowd like a shark in shallow water.

"I can't believe you just did that," Tammy said.

"Did what?" Jamie asked.

"I tap-tapped him. I put dibs on him. And then you snake him out from underneath me!"

"I passed some food to him! I didn't want to talk to him!"

"She did tap-tap him," Debbie said, "and you can't say you didn't know that."

"I'm not interested in that guy. He's gross. He's a perv." Jamie felt her throat quivering. Then, like in the opening credits of *Get Smart,* Jamie imagined a wall sliding shut between herself and Debbie.

"Oh, right, so since I like him he's a perv?" Tammy faced Jamie, her hands on either hip, the empty tray dangling from one fist.

Jamie felt another wall slide shut in front Tammy.

"I don't know what you two are talking about," she said. "That guy came over here and ate something off my tray. He knows my parents, he asked about me. I'm not about to go off and sleep with him."

"You say that as if you've never gone off and just slept with some guy."

An imaginary ceiling panel slid above Jamie's head.

"You told us yourself about Scooter Ray," Debbie said.

A third wall came down with a thud.

"I was drunk! I honestly forgot about Kim, okay?!" Jamie felt she had to raise her voice for them to hear through the walls.

"You know, ever since that baby died, you've changed,"

Tammy said. "And Debbie and I wanted to, like, forgive you, you know, let it go because we were hoping you'd come back to normal, you know, but you just haven't. You're a different person. You think you're a Christian but you clearly aren't–"

And the fourth wall closed in. Jamie felt boxed away from them, in a different orbit.

"I don't think I'm a Christian," she said.

"It's not even the Christian thing," Debbie said, and she tried to smile. "It's just that you used to be so much fun. I mean, like, we had fun together and now it's like you don't even know how to have fun anymore. You're so serious all the time."

"And you're not interested in the same things," Tammy said. "I mean you used to want to hang out with the surfers, you wanted to relax on the beach and have fun, and now . . . I mean, you show up at the beach one night and you sleep with Scooter Ray? Like, what were you thinking?"

Their voices sounded tinny and hollow, like they were yammering through aluminum pipes.

"Kim found out," Debbie said. "And Tammy and I promised her we'd never talk to you again, you know, out of loyalty to her–"

"Loyalty to her?" Jamie said, her voice echoing in her head.

"Listen, you haven't been around!" Tammy said. "Kim is one of our *best* friends, I mean, we can't even tell her that we're here tonight, it will break her heart."

"How did she find out about me and Scooter Ray?" Jamie asked. It was her final question, the last thing she'd push through the walls to them.

"You've gotta understand," Debbie said. "Kim is with us at the beach, all day, every day. Our boyfriends are best friends. She's part of our group! We can't *not* tell her. I mean, when you were in our group you would have wanted us to tell you, right?"

Jamie could no longer speak, yet there was a way in which she felt powerful and strong. She sensed herself as supremely alone, like Veronica Hale on the trampoline.

"I think it's just easier for all of us if we're officially not friends anymore," Tammy said, speaking more gently. "I mean, we're not interested in any of the same things, our values don't match."

"It's nothing against you," Debbie said, and she put her hand on Jamie's forearm.

"When school starts next week," Tammy said, "let's not pretend we're all friends, 'cause we're not, okay?"

"Do you know who you might hang out with instead?" Debbie seemed genuinely concerned.

Jamie shook her head.

"It's not like we're going to totally ignore you," Tammy said. "I'm just saying let's not act like we're close when we're not, you know?"

"I bet the stoners would want to hang out with you, like, if you told them about your mom's pot and stuff." Debbie said.

Jamie shook her head again, turned, and walked away. She tried to remember the original point of connection with Tammy and Debbie—had it been the beach? Boys? Getting tan? Jamie could no longer see herself as someone who would want to be with them, someone whose world was ruled by tap-taps and loyalty based on proximity. Maybe her father had been right when he had said she should hang out with people who had more solid names: Ann or Carol or Leigh.

Jamie went to the empty trampoline, tossed her silver tray to the ground, and climbed up. She lay on her back and looked up, hoping to find a shooting star on which she could make a wish. The sky seemed still, solid, vast. Jamie imagined that a thick black blanket covered the sky and the pinpoints of light were actually holes in the blanket—holes illuminated from some other side of the universe. How odd, Jamie thought, billions of people on this side of the blanket, yet she was all alone.

Jamie had had so much pain this summer, she thought, that she could actually classify it. Feeling she was alone wasn't as bad as Flip breaking up with her, and it certainly wasn't as bad as Lacey's death. It was worse than her sister calling her Farrah and ignoring her, but really, she was so accustomed to Renee hating her that that hardly registered as a hurt in the list of summer hurts. Jamie imagined herself at school in the coming month. She'd drift down the hallways against the throngs of people like a fish swimming in the wrong direction. And then what? She'd come home from school to a house where her sister wouldn't talk to her, her father was coiled around his work, and her mother was busy filling her days with the things she poured into her life as if she, herself, were a complicated dish that needed more ingredients: ghosts, auras, naked swimming, flirtations.

Jamie sat up as she heard someone approaching. Her mother was wandering toward her, margarita slush dancing from side to side in her glass.

"What are you doing, sweetheart?" Betty asked.

"Just looking at the sky."

Betty climbed onto the trampoline, holding her glass aloft as she hoisted herself up.

"This party is a bore." Betty took a gulp of her drink, then did a bouncing step over to where Jamie lay. She sat cross-legged next to her daughter.

"Maybe you should get everyone to swim or dance or something." Jamie lay back and folded her arms behind her head.

"Nah. Everyone's interested in Veronica Hale. People can hardly talk because they're constantly looking over your shoulder to see where Veronica is. And then, when she joins a conversation, everyone stops talking because they want to hear only what she has to say."

"What about John?"

"John Krane?"

"Yeah, the person the party's for?"

"Oh, he's just a politician. People want to know him only so they can say they know him, you know, they want to be friends with a senator. But really, he's pretty boring. Politics is boring."

"Tammy and Debbie don't want to be my friends anymore."

"Really? Why?"

"They think I'm not interested in the same things they're interested in. And they're right."

"Screw them. They're sweet girls but they'll probably grow up to be idiots just like their parents."

Jamie laughed and rolled in closer to her mother, her head at Betty's knee. Betty dropped her hand and stroked her daughter's hair.

There was a rustling sound and Renee appeared, marching toward the trampoline.

"Jamie?" she called.

"Here," Jamie said.

"We're here, sweetie," Betty said.

Renee approached the trampoline. She looked at her mother and sister, tilted her head as if to ask something, then climbed up and sat on the other side of Jamie.

"What are you guys doing?"

"Mom's bored because people only want to talk to Veronica Hale—"

"Or look at her!"

"Or look at her. And I'm avoiding Tammy and Debbie because they don't want to be my friends anymore."

"Did they say that?" Renee asked.

"Yeah. They said I've changed since the baby died."

"Oh, I hate them!" Renee said. "That is so nasty. They are so mean!"

Jamie stared up at her sister; she was surprised that Renee was so angry on her behalf. Jamie felt an internal easing, as if her sister's fury relieved Jamie from the full load of her pain.

Renee lay down beside Jamie and looked up at the stars.

"She's better off without them," Betty said.

"And she's *way* better off without Flip," Renee said.

Allen approached his family on the trampoline.

"What are you doing?! We've got a party going on here!"

"What are *you* doing?" Betty asked. "Go back out there and schmooze."

"Eh," Allen climbed onto the trampoline, "I'm sick of schmoozing. This party's dull."

"Tammy and Debbie told Jamie that they don't want to be her friends anymore," Renee said.

"Did they really say that?" Allen lay down on the trampoline with his head on Betty's lap.

"Yup," Jamie said. "I'm all alone now."

"Oh, sweetheart," Allen reached his hand up and took Jamie's hand. "You're never all alone. You've got us."

"Then who do I have?" Renee asked.

"Lori Nambine, 'cause I just tap-tapped Mom and Dad."

"You have us too, dear," Betty said.

"Look at that beautiful sky," Allen said.

"I think I see Perseus," Renee said.

"I'm trying to find the Chumash celestial gods," Jamie said, "Sky Eagle, Sun, Coyote, and Morning Star."

"Don't you think you can see Morning Star and Sun only in the morning?" Renee asked.

"You looking for the Greek Orthodox god out there, Betty?" Allen asked.

"Oh, I'm so jealous that Jamie got baptized," Renee said. "That is just so unfair."

"Oy vey," Allen groaned.

"Oh yeah," Jamie said. "It was real fun. Get in the pool in your clothes, then some wrinkled old man throws your head back and all this chlorinated water plunges up your nose–"

"You think there's too much chlorine in the pool?" Allen asked. "I always try to use a little less than what's recommended."

"Gross, Dad," Renee said. "All those naked bodies in our pool and you're using *less* chlorine."

"God, I never thought about it," Jamie said, "swimming in water where all those old vaginas have been, all those wrinkly balls–"

"Jamie!" Renee yelped. Allen and Betty laughed.

"Hey," Jamie said, "anyone wanna jump?"

"I'll jump," Renee stood.

"Why the hell not," Allen said, and he stood and helped Betty up too.

"Put your drink down, Mom," Renee said.

"Okay, okay." Betty staggered to the edge of the trampoline, lay on her stomach, dangled her hand and let the glass drop onto the grass.

"Take my hand," Jamie said, turning toward her sister. Renee picked up her sister's hand without comment, then reached for her dad's hand. Allen took Renee's hand and Betty's hand, then Betty closed the circle by taking Jamie's other hand.

"One, two, three . . . ," Jamie said, and up they went.

Acknowledgments

I would like to thank the following people who have given me tremendous support throughout the writing of this book: Bonnie Blau and Sheridan Blau; Rebecca, Satchel, and Shiloh Summers; and Joshua Blau, Alex Suarez, and the entire Grossbach family of New York. I owe considerable thanks to the writers of the Northway Writers' Project, particularly Lindsay Fleming, Madeleine Mysko, John Sasser, and Tracy Wallace. I am forever indebted to Joanne Brownstein of Brandt and Hochman, and exceedingly grateful to Katherine Nintzel of HarperCollins.

About the author

About the book

Insights,
Interviews
& More...

Read on

Meet Jessica Anya Blau

Lindsay Fleming

JESSICA ANYA BLAU is a graduate of the
University of California–Berkeley and Johns
Hopkins University, where she received her
master's in fiction and where she lectures and
teaches creative writing. In 2005 she was chosen
as a Tennessee Williams Scholar at Sewanee
Writer's Conference. Her stories have appeared
in *The Sun* magazine, *The First Line*, *Washington
Square*, and the *Santa Barbara Independent*,
among other notable publications. *The
Summer of Naked Swim Parties* is based
loosely on her childhood in Santa Barbara.

About the author

Two Jobs I Had and One I Almost Had Before I Realized I Should Write

AFTER COLLEGE, my boyfriend Scott and I had moved to Oakland where we lived in an eclectic Art Deco apartment building near Lake Merritt, a man-made lake in the middle of the city. Our side of the lake hadn't been gentrified yet. There was what we called a Drug-in-the-Box across the street. At a sidewalk level window, people inserted their hand, pulled it out and then walked away. The only thing we ever saw of the dealer was his arm: sinewy, and quick as a biting snake. The building next door contained pay-by-week apartments. Someone called 911 from that building several times each week. The most horrifying call came when a woman dropped her baby down the sixteen-flight stairwell. I went in the building, looked up at the spiral of wrought iron and imagined that ball of sweet flesh plummeting to the marble floor. I still can't look down a deep stairwell without thinking about that baby—he's with me forever.

When the manager of our building died— an old woman who marched out into the hallway each Christmas and plopped down a small, plastic, pre-decorated tree on the radiator—the owner hired me and Scott to manage. We were given a free apartment, and we didn't have to do the maintenance work. Our main responsibility was collecting rents and dealing with tenants. With a building full of the very old, very addled, very strung out on drugs, and very dealing drugs, there was a lot to handle.

A Vietnam veteran, with both a first and last name that sounded like a last name, once asked to use my bathroom when he was dropping off the rent. He peed a deliberate wreath of yellow urine on the seat. An orangey-tanned fifty-year-old crack addict (whose mother paid his rent) once came ▶

> 66 The only thing we ever saw of the [drug] dealer was his arm: sinewy, and quick as a biting snake. 99

3

Two Jobs I Had and One I Almost Had Before I Realized I Should Write *(continued)*

to the door wearing only his Day-Glo green tighty underpants. With his lit cigarette wagging in one hand, he repeated over and over, his brain stuck in a thought-rut, "I want my c-c-c-c-c-c-cable TV!"

I received weekly phone calls from a tenant named Jessie who liked to chronicle all the Jews she had ever met, capping each story with "The redheaded Jews are the *worst* Jews!" At that time I colored my brown hair red, so indeed, unbeknownst to her, she was talking to a redheaded Jew. A redheaded Jew had sold Jessie a car in 1956 that never ran properly. A redheaded Jew had sold her a mattress in 1971 that had springs that could pierce your back. A redheaded Jew had sold her a couch in 1980 and the cushions were too stiff for comfort. I wanted to ask her why she continued to make purchases from redheaded Jews, but didn't dare. When we moved out of the building, I decided, I would tell her I was Jewish. But I never did: moving day was busy, and I had other things to do.

I bought a car from one of the tenants: a drug dealer named Rikki. He wanted ten-thousand dollars for his brand new Saab. When I told him I only had five-hundred dollars he laughed and walked away. Hours later he returned, Jheri curl melting in his sweat. He'd take the five hundred, he said, if I'd give him a ride to the airport.

I traded in the car for another Saab, as each time I drove it I feared I'd be shot—slain through the tinted windows—mistaken for Rikki, who had been running from *someone*.

While managing the apartments, I still needed to find a real job, a career. Someone suggested the airlines (free travel!), so I sent the two largest carriers my resume and was granted interviews—in Dallas and Atlanta—right away.

On the flight to Atlanta, I was seated next to a girl who was also interviewing. She had short blond hair and was cute in the universally accepted meaning of the word.

> **❝ I received weekly phone calls from a tenant named Jessie who liked to chronicle all the Jews she had ever met, capping each story with 'The redheaded Jews are the *worst* Jews!' ❞**

4

"I've only eaten five-hundred calories a day for the past two weeks!" she said.

"Why?" I was astounded. My sister had had anorexia as a teen, and it was so gruesome to witness that I'd never much taken to starvation.

"To fit into the height/weight chart!"

The airlines had sent a packet of information that included a height-weight chart. I am five feet two inches tall. For my height I wasn't allowed to weigh more than 112 pounds. I didn't own a scale so I bought one, and sure enough, there I stood at 112 pounds. One pound more and I'd be too fat for the airlines.

"And I've been doing an hour of aerobics every day!" the girl said.

The only exercise I'd been getting was using the dead apartment manager's left-hander golf club to hit a single ball in the apartment's courtyard.

At the weigh-in in Atlanta, everyone lined up and took off their shoes, then we each stepped onto the scale. There were a few people who walked away teary-eyed.

The interview was done in groups of twenty. My interviewer was a nice-looking man the way politicians are nice looking: neatly dressed, gleaming teeth. We sat in a circle of desks and were given a five-page questionnaire. When my pen didn't flow well, I asked the leader for a new pen. He responded as if I'd demanded a pint of blood, but finally gave one up. When I retold this part of the interview to my father he said, "Jessie, there are some men whose balls shrink up into their stomachs when *you* walk into a room. He was one of those men." I was twenty-two years old and didn't feel comfortable discussing ball positioning with my father, so I said nothing. But, I wondered, who were these men whose balls shrunk up? And, what made me a ball shrinker?

The questionnaire wasn't surprising ("How much weight have you gained and/or lost in the ▶

> 66 One pound more and I'd be too fat for the airlines. 99

Two Jobs I Had and One I Almost Had Before I Realized I Should Write *(continued)*

last ten years?" "What is the most you've ever weighed in the last ten years?"), until I got to the page where I was asked about the quality and duration of my periods, if I had ever been pregnant, and if I had vaginal discharge. There was even a question inquiring about the *color* of my discharge. Crossed out with a ballpoint pen, but entirely legible, was, "Have you ever had sexual relations with someone of the same sex?" I had visions of spiriting away the questionnaire under my skirt, sending it off to Gloria Steinem or the *San Francisco Chronicle*. But Shrunken-Balls had his eyes on me, as if he knew what I was thinking.

Surprisingly, I was called back for a second interview. I declined; I just couldn't fathom working for someone who seemed to be sniffing in my underpants.

If I wasn't going to be a flight attendant, I decided, I would be a buyer at a department store. I could wear fashionable clothes, travel to New York and Europe; I'd be *stylish*. I was hired by I. Magnin in San Francisco, then one of the most exclusive stores in the country. After a preliminary few months on the sales floor, I was to be moved into assistant management, then management, then buying.

I was the youngest salesgirl on Fifth Floor Dresses; the other ladies had been there twenty or thirty years. I was also the only one who was American born. For the most part everyone ignored me, irritated that I seemed to be skimming through a job they'd been at for decades, and furious when I sold more dresses than they. Miss Lena—our first names were always accompanied by "Miss"—was the only one who would chat with me; she liked to talk about Tito, the old country, God and Jesus. When we didn't have customers she went into the fitting room, closed the three-way mirror, got down on her knees and prayed for customers. While she was praying, I would make paper dolls by cutting

> ❝ I had visions of spiriting away the questionnaire under my skirt, sending it off to Gloria Steinem or the *San Francisco Chronicle*. ❞

and coloring the stiff cardboard hold tags. I became singularly focused on these dolls, and would think about them during my lunch hour—how I could draw a perfectly smirking French mouth on the Miss Yvette doll, or how to convey Chinese Miss Chin's choppy stride through the way I drew her legs. The most fun I had was when Miss Lena would actually "play" paper dolls with me. She would laugh with tears in her eyes as we did each person's accent, and she never minded when I took the paper doll of her and tucked it away in the register drawer to pray for more customers.

For management, I was transferred to the more suburban Walnut Creek store. There I planned fashion shows for store meetings, and once taught a group of salesgirls Adelaide's song from *Guys and Dolls* so we could strip as we showed off the new fall fashions. I always joined in.

The best part of the job was talking to my salespeople—all of them had interesting pasts, complex inner lives, some story to tell. There was the sixty-year-old woman with the schizophrenic son. He tried to burn down her house and she had to send him away. "The worst part of it," she told me one day, "is realizing I ignored my healthy son all those years when, really, I should have been ignoring my sick son." There was the beautiful obese woman with a name like a stripper— Coco—whose thin husband was television gorgeous. She once confessed to me that she had to vacuum her living room rug daily into perfect lines—like a fresh-mown lawn. In my office one day, she started sobbing, lamenting that all she had done with her life was sell clothes and have a baby. I said, "But a baby is amazing. You're a *mother*." She looked up at me, wiped her nose with the back of her hand and said, "Jessica, rats breed."

It was while I was managing that I came to realize that if you spend enough time with someone, anyone, eventually you will like them. ▶

> 66 I planned fashion shows for store meetings, and once taught a group of salesgirls Adelaide's song from *Guys and Dolls* so we could strip as we showed off the new fall fashions. I always joined in. 99

Two Jobs I Had and One I Almost Had
Before I Realized I Should Write *(continued)*

My favorite salesperson was a woman named
Deborah, who would be leaving in the fall to get
a PhD. She had pretty blue eyes, one of which
would wander away, as if it were bored, while you
were talking to her. One afternoon, I shared with
her the story of my previous night: I had gone
to meet my father at the crowded, hip bar in the
hotel where he was staying for work that week.
I was wearing a slinky, long gray skirt and
matching top I had bought at a thrift store
in Paris a couple months earlier. The skirt was
so clingy, that I wore control top panty hose—
to streamline what the I. Magnin ladies would
have called my silhouette. I didn't find my father
right away, so I went into the bathroom to pee.
After using the toilet, I walked through the bar
again to look for my father. Everyone was staring
at me with half-smiles and astonished eyes.
I tossed my hair behind my shoulders and slowly
strutted. *My God, this outfit looks good on me*,
I thought, *I have never been hotter!* When I didn't
see my father, I stepped outside to wait for him.
Standing on the curb, I felt a snap of cold air
against my ass. I reached back and realized I had
tucked the back of my skirt into the waist of my
panty hose. Additionally, I wasn't wearing any
underwear, so my fully visible butt was smashed
into the hose like a face against a pane of glass.
Furthermore, there was a hole in the panty hose
over my right cheek. The panty hose were so tight
that my butt flesh pushed out of the gap like cake
rising over the edges of a pan. And because panty
hose never have a hole without a run, certainly the
hole laddered down my thigh, leaving a string of
consecutively smaller dough bursts blooming out.
It was, unquestioningly, deeply embarrassing.

Deborah laughed and then she said, "I don't
know what you're doing here. You should be a
writer."

It's funny—I loved reading, and I had always

> Standing on
> the curb, I felt a
> snap of cold air
> against my ass.
> I reached back
> and realized I
> had tucked the
> back of my skirt
> into the waist of
> my panty hose.
> Additionally,
> I wasn't
> wearing any
> underwear.

thought that being a writer was the coolest job, but it had just never occurred to me that *I* could do it. That week I wrote a story.

A few months later, Scott, who was by then my husband, took a job in Toronto. He had a work visa and I had a wife visa, meaning I was allowed to live in the country and accept their health care, but I couldn't work or go to school. So I got a dog, and named him Moses. I volunteered at the museum. I joined the Y. I had a baby.

And I wrote. And wrote. And wrote.

The first short story I sent out was accepted for publication by a Canadian literary magazine. That small triumph was enough to keep me writing through my daughter's naps, and then, when she stopped napping, twice a week on the mornings she was at nursery school.

When my marriage had to end, I applied to graduate schools and was accepted at Johns Hopkins in Baltimore. Early in my first semester, Stephen Dixon, who was nominated for a National Book Award that year, was talking to my class about paper. "Don't use both sides," he said. "I know it's a waste of paper, but just use the one side. This is your job. You use paper. You're writers."

I felt an internal earthquake. No one had ever said anything like that to me. I had never thought to describe myself with *that* word. But there he stood. Someone in the profession who knew what he was talking about. And he called me a writer.

Even now, I often have a hard time saying I'm a writer. When people ask what I do, I'll mutter something about teaching part-time or taking care of my kids. A couple years ago I ran into a high school friend and she asked me what I do in Baltimore.

"I'm writing," I said, bolder than usual.

"You're riding," she said. "How cool. Do you own a horse?"

"No," I answered. "I don't own a horse." ❧

> " Even now, I often have a hard time saying I'm a writer. When people ask what I do, I'll mutter something about teaching part-time or taking care of my kids. "

"Just Rat One Good Sentence"
The Story Behind
The Summer of Naked Swim Parties

FOUR SUMMERS AGO I was in a writers' workshop with Lynn Freed at Bread Loaf. She is a gorgeous woman with a beautiful South African accent, and when she says the word *write*, it comes out sounding like *rat*. So she said to the group, "Just rat one good sentence. Bring it in tomorrow. One good sentence." I went to my computer and wrote a memory from my childhood of a single moment at a swim party with my parents. It turned out to be two sentences that went something like this: "Leon jumps naked on the diving board. His hairy grown-up body looks slightly melted as he goes up and down, up and down, his penis and balls flying in unison like a long bird attached to its eggs." When I read the sentence to the group the next day, Lynn laughed. She liked it. I left that workshop wondering why I had rarely written about my family in that period of time: the seventies, southern California. My mother didn't shave her armpits, never wore a bra, and always swam naked. My father, who also swam naked, practiced yoga, did pottery on a kick wheel, and made homemade yogurt with exotic fruits like loquat. As a healthy hypochondriac, my father never smoked. He did, however, grow marijuana between the backyard fruit trees, just for my mother. My older sister was angry and embarrassed by the family, and my younger brother, when we could find him, seemed feral.

Later that week, I was chatting with an editor from a major publishing house. She said that I needed a novel, not short stories, for a first book. Then she asked, "Have you started a novel?"

I told her I had the idea for a novel; it was

> 66 I walked out of that workshop wondering why I had rarely written about my family in that period of time: the seventies, Southern California. 99

the family story I'd been thinking about since Lynn's workshop. She asked what the title was, and I made it up as I spoke: *The Summer of Naked Swim Parties*.

So there it was: A title. And an idea even. All I had to do was *rat* the thing. About a year later, after writing everything BUT the novel, I sat down and started with the sentence about naked Leon. It wasn't hard to find the material—I culled chapters from the experiences that had most deeply entered my bloodstream, the stories that were embedded in my bones. I compressed time, juggled sequence, and I took the most tender bits of my adolescent experiences in love, sex, heartbreak, death, and family life and put them all into one fictional summer: the summer of 1976.

There was a buzzing and energy in 1976—it was the bicentennial year, something you were reminded of every time you turned on the TV. The media jingoism seemed to be in strange contrast to the sort of anarchy that was going on in my house as a child. I liked the idea that all the things that were going to happen to Jamie in *The Summer of Naked Swim Parties* would happen in the summer that was supposed to be as wholesome and pure as a television ad for a brand new Ford.

It's odd, but I truly can remember the size, shape, and texture of the naked bodies of my parents' friends and, uncomfortably, my parents. The bodies that are described in the text are pulled directly from memory. My mother didn't have the bold breasts of Betty, but her best friend did. A good portion of the story is like that: the truth, but with a slightly different angle. It's as if I had filmed my life but tilted the camera and blurred in bits and pieces of the lives of the people around me. In some places there are complete replacements—putting someone else's story into my story and making *that* Jamie's story. For example, my family didn't go to group family therapy. We went to regular family therapy, and only once. At that session the therapist turned ▶

> 66 It's odd, but I truly can remember the size, shape, and texture of the naked bodies of my parents' friends and, uncomfortably, my parents. 99

on a camera so she could film how our family interacted. When she momentarily left the room to fetch a pen, I walked up to the camera and flashed my fourteen-year-old breasts. We all erupted into a laughter that never quite let up, and that was the end of family therapy.

But I did, strangely, go to group family therapy many times with my best friend in sixth grade, whose family went once a week. The incidents at group therapy with my friend were almost identical to what happens to Jamie in *The Summer of Naked Swim Parties*.

Religion and faith are used in this book to ice the connection between Jamie and Debbie and Tammy. It is something that sets Jamie apart from her friends and certainly set me apart from my friends as a child. Santa Barbara remains a fairly white, homogeneous town, but it was even more so in the 1970s. My family's Jewishness never seemed particularly interesting, but my friends and their parents liked to point it out, as if we were some alien tribe whose rituals were completely kooky. (We were the only Jews in our neighborhood and the only Jews I knew of in our high school.) Some of the nastier girls in elementary school once let it be known that, unlike them, I'd be going to hell upon my death. And how smart could I really be when I didn't know who the Holy Ghost was? My sister actually had a teacher who regularly called her "Our little Jewish friend." As Allen points out in the book, you couldn't buy bagels in Santa Barbara. My father picked them up from Fairfax Avenue in Los Angeles. I remember Brad B., a cute, blond, goofy-footed surfer, writing in my high school yearbook, "Dear Jessica, Thanks for turning me on to bagels and cream cheese. They're dyno! Love, Brad."

The surfers, surf culture and girls in the book probably exist in more or less the same way today. I was, like the characters in the book, concerned

66 My family's Jewishness never seemed particularly interesting, but my friends and their parents liked to point it out, as if we were some alien tribe whose rituals were completely kooky. 99

more with my tan, my boyfriend and my friends than just about anything else. When I was in college, my father told me he had never expected anything of me other than that I'd be a "beach bunny," and, eventually, a mother and wife. Perhaps my lack of direction was a good thing— it certainly allowed me the time to sit, space out, and commit to memory all the details of my life.

I think this book is ultimately about people searching for connections. Jamie wants desperately to connect to her sister, her friends, her boyfriend, and even her parents. Her parents want to connect to something greater than themselves, but something new, something updated for their generation. Betty also wants to connect to Jamie on the most intimate level—who Jamie is physically, the workings of her body. In writing this book, in processing the memories, I have felt a nice connection with the past, with my parents, with my sister, and even the friends with whom I spent most of my summer days and nights. I can see now that although I often felt untethered, alone, and heartbroken, as Jamie does in the book, I really did have a family to back me up. I hope that in the last scene of *The Summer of Naked Swim Parties* the reader sees that Jamie isn't as alone as she had thought—even her sister is there, like a net, ready to catch her. ❧

Author's Picks
Ten Books That Were Handed to Me by Family, Friends, and Strangers, Which Startled Me with Their Originality and Greatness

MADELINE by Ludwig Bemelmans

My mother bought this for me when I was four. I loved the viney house in Paris. Loved the scar on Madeline's stomach. Loved that Madeline was so small but such a fearless rascal. I named my first daughter Madeline, but it's my younger daughter, Ella, who has the impish personality of Bemelmans' Madeline.

THE PAINTED BIRD by Jerzy Kosinski

Our living room had a wall of floor-to-ceiling books. Every now and then my father would pluck one off the shelf and tell me to read it. I was so moved by *The Painted Bird* that I dreamt about it. Even the painting on the cover haunted me.

SONG OF SOLOMON by Toni Morrison

Every boyfriend I had in college was an English major, and one of them once took a class in Black literature. *Song of Solomon* was his assigned book. I read it on a Saturday. I thought Milkman was the best character I had ever read anywhere.

PARIS TROUT by Pete Dexter

I was in a bookstore in Oakland when I heard a man ask for *Paris Trout*. I thought it was a great title, so I followed him through the stacks. He handed me a copy. It was stunning.

SANCTUARY by William Faulkner

I was discussing *Paris Trout* with my friend Price, who said it reminded him of *Sanctuary*. So I read *Sanctuary*. I've never loved anything by Faulkner as much.

THE SHORT STORIES OF FRANZ KAFKA by Franz Kafka

I was traveling in Austria when I ran out of books. A Canadian woman I met while staying in a nunnery gave me Kafka's short stories,which she had just finished. I have reread some of them as many as fifteen times.

THE BOOK OF LAUGHTER AND FORGETTING by Milan Kundera

The landlord of our basement apartment in Toronto was a Serbian librarian who could check out books for unlimited amounts of time. One day she gave me *The Book of Laughter and Forgetting*. I loved it. She eventually brought me everything Kundera had written. I read those books in the cold dark of the basement while waiting to see my husband's shoes and trouser cuffs moving through the leaves outside the window.

NATASHA: AND OTHER STORIES by David Bezmozgis

My friend Lindsay gave it to me. She said, "You'll love this." I did. I have since bought the book at least seven times to give as a gift. I even bought a copy for my husband, David, as I loaned my copy to someone who never gave it back.

CRUDDY, AN ILLUSTRATED NOVEL by Lynda Barry

My friend Tracy gave me this because we both love these single-page Lynda Barry stories, which Tracy first found in some magazine years ago. The book is funny. And weird, in the greatest sense of the word. It has sentences like, "In the garbage ▶

> " The landlord of our basement apartment in Toronto was a Serbian librarian who could check out books for unlimited amounts of time. One day she gave me *The Book of Laughter and Forgetting*. "

ravine there is a nude man who crouches among the trash piles and his name is Old Red and he has very yellow skin like freezer-burned chicken and his thing in life is to suddenly run out and do a two-second display of his dinger and then run back in."

MADAME BOVARY by Gustave Flaubert

My high school–aged daughter, Maddie, often finishes a book every day or two. Last summer she handed me *Madame Bovary* and said, "You should really read this, Mom." She was correct—what kind of writer/Francophile was I, never having read *Madame Bovary*?! I could quote Flaubert effortlessly, *"Madame Bovary, c'est moi."* Yet I had no idea who this Bovary lady was. The book was spectacular.

Don't miss the next book by your favorite author. Sign up now for AuthorTracker by visiting www.AuthorTracker.com.